As a brilliant, dedicated doctor, Jan Petrie had cared for Jeff Weston when she found him in the wards of a vast mental hospital.

As a beautiful, vulnerable woman, Jan Petrie had fallen in love with Jeff Weston as he emerged from his strange cocoon to reveal his extraordinary powers.

But now as Jan stood by Jeff's bed and saw him reaching out to her, she felt only fear . . . of what was being done to him . . . and to her. . . .

Reckoning

The most terrifying medical thriller since **Coma!**

RECKONING

S. D. NORRIS

C
CHARTER BOOKS, NEW YORK

RECKONING

A Charter Book / published by arrangement with
the author

PRINTING HISTORY
Charter Original / February 1985

ISBN: 0-441-71084-0

Charter Books are published by The Berkley Publishing Group,
200 Madison Avenue, New York, New York 10016.
PRINTED IN THE UNITED STATES OF AMERICA

prologue

BACKGROUND STATIC FILLED the Wilson Observatory with a steady, hissing sound. The mammoth radio telescope was mounted atop the building that housed its controls like a student's globe on its pedestal. The bowl of the telescope, two hundred fifty feet in diameter, rotated slowly on its ball bearings, collecting and focusing radio waves from the outer reaches of the galaxy. At a work table in the control room, Dr. Nathan Stockwell, chief radio astronomer, looked up from the papers spread out before him. He ran his slender fingers through his curly brown hair. "It's overwhelming sometimes, isn't it?" he asked his colleague Dimitri Kilko, a spectrophysicist. "Do you think we'll ever make a dent in this?"

"Chin up," Kilko responded from his table across the room. "It's late. Maybe we should call it a night before this paperwork depresses both of us."

Nathan Stockwell and Dimitri Kilko were one year into a seven-year project, privately funded by a coalition of universities and big business interests, to map the Cygnus II area of the galaxy. Stockwell analyzed radio waves; Kilko followed spectral emissions. They had been selected from the most respected scientists in the country for this challenging and groundbreaking task. Stockwell had been recruited from the Rand Corporation; Kilko from Princeton. No expense had been spared to set them up with the most sophisticated equipment and the finest staff available.

"I'm good for another forty-five minutes, but why don't you leave if you're beat? Harry's downstairs to keep me company."

Before Kilko could respond, a throbbing, low-pitched sound emanated from the telescope's speakers. "What was that?" Kilko asked, pushing aside the spectral emissions charts he had been studying.

"Just some low-level bursts from neutron stars." Stockwell walked to one of the consoles and examined a printout that charted the rise and fall of the stellar wave chatter in smooth undulations on the graph paper.

Kilko stood up and stretched. "I'll stay a little bit, but I'll need some coffee. Can I get you some, Nate?"

A burst of electronic blips filled the room. Both men stared at each other.

"Forget the coffee." Stockwell took a seat at the main console and scanned the radiograph. The waves were irregular. The peaks and valleys on the graph paper were jagged. "I'm getting a strange pattern here. We don't have it on previous reception."

Kilko ran to the far end of the room to another console. "I'll get a spectrum analysis of this transmission." Twisting dials and flicking switches, he turned the spectrogalactoscope to the same coordinates as the radio telescope.

"Come look at this." Stockwell frowned as he watched the printout. "This pattern doesn't follow any of the traditional wave patterns in this area of the universe. I've never seen one like this before."

"Well, if you haven't, I don't know who has." Kilko joined him at the telescope printout and studied the erratic pattern. "What could it be?"

"I don't know." Stockwell rubbed his forehead. "I'll see if there are any references to this in the literature."

He shoved his chair back and propelled himself to the end of the console. He flicked the Slexis machine, an information retrieval system with an up-to-the-minute index of thousands of publications in astronomy. The screen read:

STATE PROBLEM: AREA

Fingers poised over the keyboard, he hesitated for a moment, then typed:

RADIO WAVES—SOURCES

The machine instructed:

PROBLEM TOO BROAD—DEFINE BY ELIMINATION.

Stockwell thought carefully before responding. If he narrowed the area too quickly, he might lose valuable source information. On the other hand, if he left things wide open, he would receive a massive printout of mostly useless information which would take far too long to analyze and review.

The blips continued to fill the air, repeating in ten-second bursts. "The signal's coming stronger," Kilko said as he headed for the Slexis screen.

Stockwell nodded and typed:

NOT: QUASAR, PULSAR, BURSTER STAR, NEUTRON STAR, COSMIC BACKGROUND RADIATION, GAMMA WAVE RADIATION, X-RAY RADIATION, ELECTROMAGNETIC RADIATION.

Kilko, now standing behind his colleague, whistled softly. "You've just eliminated every source of radio wave radiation known to man." Kilko's eyes glistened behind his owlish glasses. "Maybe our 'ears' need a cleaning."

Stockwell smiled at Kilko's reference to the radio telescope. "I doubt it. We just cleaned it last week. There's no malfunction there."

Both waited impatiently for the Slexis machine to respond. The screen lit up with green letters which read:

PROCESSING REQUEST:

BASED ON INFORMATION FURNISHED—NO PREVIOUS REFERENCES

ENERGY SOURCE UNKNOWN

"What does that mean?"

"Well." Stockwell drew in his breath, staring at the screen. "It means that no one has ever picked up those signals before."

"Obviously," Kilko said. "That's not what I'm asking."

"What I mean is . . ." Stockwell shook his head in disbelief and turned to Kilko. "What it means, my friend, is that we've discovered a new source of energy in the universe."

"That's not possible." Kilko's face reddened with excitement.

"I know." Stockwell gnawed on a thumbnail, then said forcefully, "I'm telling you, either we're picking up signals from another universe—a billion light years away—or from an unknown object within our own."

Kilko rolled his eyes. "How could it be?"

Stockwell shrugged, too immersed in his own thoughts to talk.

"We'd better call Brandon," Kilko advised nervously.

"He'll think we've flipped. I'd like to put a call into Arecibo first. Let's see if they've picked up anything there."

"I hate to be such a stickler, but Brandon will be

furious if we don't notify him immediately. Call him first, then the Cornell guys in Puerto Rico. This whole project could go up in smoke if we alienate Brandon and his committee."

"I'm supposed to call Brandon to tell him the two great geniuses his committee's funding think they've discovered that an entirely new source of energy has suddenly appeared in our universe, right?"

"Right. I'll monitor the signals. You make the call."

"Thanks a lot, pal. Think I'll get some air before I do." Stockwell left the control room of the radio telescope. Outside the skies were dark and threatening. The air was electric, the prestorm stillness heavy. Listening to the grumbling of the distant thunder, Stockwell prepared himself to make the call with the most astonishing news of his career.

chapter 1

A JAGGED FINGER of lightning ignited the sky, and the whiplike crack of the thunder's retort announced the start of a sudden, violent storm. The rain came crashing down against the windshield of Jan Petrie's car. She squinted, looking for the tree stump that marked the blind turn off the coast road.

"Late again, damn it," she muttered to herself. She swerved her car onto the winding, one-lane road that led to Fairchild State Hospital. She pressed down on the accelerator and her Rabbit picked up speed in the driving rain.

Jan usually loved the flash storms that exploded along the Pacific Coast in the fall. She loved the screaming winds, the wildly swaying eucalyptus trees; the awesome violence of nature never failed to astonish her. But on this particular Monday morning, the storm filled her with a sense of foreboding. Things hadn't been going well at work and she knew that she would have a tough day with her supervisor.

From their first meeting, Jan realized that Dorothy Campbel would make life difficult. Six months later she could recall that initial encounter vividly . . .

When that scarecrow of a woman had interviewed her, she'd sat behind an institutional gray metal desk.

Her dyed blond hair was lacquered in a flawless bouffant hairdo, fashionable, no doubt, in her heyday. Her skin was tanned, but leathery from overexposure to the sun.

Jan watched the Director of Special Services expectantly. She was eager to make a good first impression.

"I see you're an honor student," Dorothy remarked without looking up from the résumé she held in her hands. "What brings you *here*, Dr. Petrie?"

"The back wards of a state mental institution are a challenge to me. I think I'd like to work with people who have been written off by society. All through school I've wanted to help lifelong mental patients." Remembering the naiveté of her response still made Jan cringe.

Dorothy Campbel drew her lips into a straight line. She could barely contain her contempt. "So you think we could benefit from your dedication and expertise?"

"I believe so. I have energy and I do want to help these patients."

Dorothy began to tap her pencil on her blotter.

"We'll see about that." Dorothy tossed Jan's résumé into the outbox. "Dr. Deutch tells me you're starting next week."

Though Jan could not imagine it at the time, that first meeting was the high point of her working relationship with Dorothy. Her first months on the job as the Assistant Director of Special Services had been a painful awakening. Jan had thrown herself into her work with the enthusiasm and determination that had made her a success at her previous endeavors. But Fairchild State and the bureaucracy that ran it were unlike anything she had ever confronted.

Fairchild, a fifty-year-old, three-hundred acre facility, housed over 4,000 mentally ill patients of every age with every imaginable affliction, ranging from severe behavioral problems to catatonia, from brain damage to paranoid schizophrenia. Jan had been drawn to a large institution because of the great need for dedicated professionals, because she felt she might be able to make a difference for the hundreds of patients who spent their entire lives warehoused there.

In the course of her orientation, she had quietly observed several biweekly staff meetings, which were chaired by Dr. Paul Deutch, the head of the hospital. Jan was very fond of Dr. Deutch. They had met through Jan's advisor at Stanford when she was writing her dissertation. She had been bowled over by his keen intellect and his no-nonsense ability to solve problems. Paul Deutch had obviously been impressed by her, too. He had recruited her for a high-level job at Fairchild as soon as she got her degree. Jan had all intentions of making him her mentor.

Though she realized that to keep a place like Fairchild running smoothly was no easy task, she was appalled by the routine, lackluster meetings at which the various department heads complained about everyday problems. She watched and waited for her chance to make a significant contribution.

One morning, carefully dressed in a beige raw silk suit and a black-and-gold foulard-print blouse, her auburn hair tied neatly at the back of her head and her tanned cheekbones accented by only a grace of blush, Jan fidgeted in her seat as the twenty key administrators took their customary places at the rosewood conference table. She had worked out a program which she wanted to present to the group. Finally, the distinguished Dr.

Deutch rushed in holding a leather folder that contained the agenda, which he distributed. When Dorothy, who sat at Dr. Deutch's right, saw Jan's entry, she grimaced, pushed the paper from her, and clasped her arms around her chest.

She's not exactly receptive, Jan thought.

Dr. Deutch, a kind-faced, slightly overweight man of about sixty, pulled his half-reading glasses from his pocket and set them low on his sloping nose. "Ah—our new colleague in Special Services has a presentation for us," he said by way of introduction.

At least she was on first. When Jan cleared her throat, she realized how dry her mouth was. She wished she had poured herself some ice water.

"Yes, Dr. Deutch. I would like to organize a series of activities for adolescents that would parallel social events they would experience outside the institution—things like dances, picnics, hayrides on the grounds, maybe even some outings." Jan paused and noticed the psychiatrist sitting across from her was doodling on a legal pad. Thrown by his inattention, she forced herself to go on. "Dr. Rabinowitz has been so articulate about the problems he's having with that age group. I thought this might be a way to deflect some of that energy by channeling it into more normal outlets." Jan looked to the piles of notes before her. "I have a . . ."

Dr. Rabinowitz, a hefty, athletic man in his mid-forties, nodded in bored acknowledgment of her suggestion and interrupted her. "Yes, we tried that in '69, when we had more funds available to us—with disastrous results." He looked around the table with amusement, "as I'm sure a number of you remember."

There were groans and snickers. Jan flushed and could actually hear her heart thudding.

"Why don't you share the joke with Dr. Petrie?"

Paul Deutch gently rebuked the senior staff member.

"To make a long story short—the kids went wild in a local bowling alley and frightened the proprietor half to death. It was as traumatic for our patients as it was for the townspeople. It took us days to calm them down. Quite frankly, life here is hard enough without the added excitement you propose."

"But it doesn't have to be that way." Jan refused to allow herself to fold so easily. "My program allows for gradual exposure . . ."

"Excuse me, Jan." Dorothy's voice was sharp. "I suggest you write up your program and let me review it. We really shouldn't waste time arguing the merits of a program no one has studied. We'll discuss procedure later."

Jan felt as if she'd been slapped. She lifted her chin, not willing to give in to the stinging humiliation she felt. "All right," she managed to stammer.

"Dr. Petrie, let me have a look at that program, too." Paul Deutch came to her rescue. "It might just be time to try what you suggest again."

Jan smiled gratefully. "Thank you, Dr. Deutch. I'll make certain you get a copy."

Dorothy and Dr. Rabinowitz exchanged a sardonic look that no one at the table missed, including Jan. She felt deflated as she heard Paul Deutch say, "Let's see, next on the agenda is Paula Fox and the attendant problem."

Jan glazed over as the meeting droned on. For the first time in her life, she felt impotent. She sensed there was no way to penetrate the indifference of her colleagues. They seemed so jaded, so willing to do what was easiest, most expedient. Jan felt like a fool for wanting it any other way.

She had been so involved in her indignation, it was

only when her colleagues began to collect their papers that she realized the meeting had concluded. She slapped her untouched notes into a manila folder and shoved back her Danish modern chair, wishing she could disappear. She carefully avoided leaving the room with anyone.

As she approached the door, she heard Dr. Rabinowitz say to a handsome physical therapist as they left the conference room, "God, I wish we could give these novices a good dose of reality in orientation. Really! Sock hops are the last things I could deal with at this point."

Jan hung back to keep from confronting them. As the two walked down the hall she heard Stan Miller respond, "Well, at least it's a treat to look at her. She could have been ugly."

Jan reeled from the overheard conversation. Oh, it was going to be a battle at Fairchild all right. Dorothy Campbel then surfaced on her right and hissed, "I expect you in my office immediately. If you ever go over my head again . . ." She left her threat unfinished and hurried off.

Rarely had she heard such animosity in a voice. It was downright unnerving. Just then, Dr. Deutch passed with the Director of Food Services who had been badgering him for more help.

"Dr. Petrie, are you all right?" He disengaged himself from the discussion and turned his attention to her.

Embarrassed, Jan smiled and replied, "Oh, I'll survive."

"I'm sorry we seem less than receptive. I, for one, am glad you are here." His sincerity was unmistakable. "We could use a little shaking up. But you'll have to develop quite a thick skin." He pulled his etched gold pocketwatch from his vest and checked the face. "I must run to yet another meeting. Please come to talk to me if you have any more problems here. Maybe I can smooth the way for you a little."

"That's very kind of you, Dr. Deutch." Jan was touched by his concern and generosity. "I certainly will."

Paul Deutch had become her ally in time, but their mutual respect only provoked Dorothy Campbel. Jan was increasingly troubled by the tone of their conflicts. Soon after the board meeting fiasco, and Dorothy's ensuing tirade on her authority, Jan and she had had a monumental and revealing clash.

Dorothy had stopped into Jan's office to discuss the forthcoming Arts and Crafts show, the big event of the Special Services department. "You should check through these old programs for ideas about the approach you want to take." Dorothy looked for a place to drop the stack of papers on Jan's already crowded desk. "This is one of the most important P.R. events of the year. Lisa Morris from the publicity department will help you arrange . . ." She stopped mid-sentence when she saw a handwritten note attached to some Xeroxed journal articles in Jan's box. She dropped the programs she was holding on the edge of the desk, causing some papers to fly. "I see you and our leader are pen pals."

Though Jan wanted to respond, "What's it to you?" her answer was far more polite than her inclination. "Oh, yes, Dr. Deutch and I were discussing neurotransmitters, synthetic enzymes, and control of the emotions yesterday and he was good enough to send me some of the most recent studies."

Dorothy picked up the articles and skimmed them with a sour expression on her face. In an attempt to distance herself from the inevitable attack, Jan wondered where Dorothy shopped. Her glen plaid, polyester pant-suit hung stiffly from her very thin body.

"You academics with your heads in the clouds. An internship and you think . . ." she began her harangue. "I've lived and worked with these patients for twenty-five years. New treatments come and go. Common sense is all that matters." She dropped the sheaf of papers into Jan's in-box. "You'll forget about neurotrans-mitters soon enough."

"I respect your experience, Dorothy," Jan coun-tered, "but why do you have to be flip about scientific investigation? Couldn't you and I pool what we know to help these people?"

"Why do you expect things to be easy for you?" Dorothy glowered at Jan, her hand on her hip. "What do you think your degrees are worth to a schizophrenic woman who has been here for fifteen years? What do you think your ideas mean to a staff that has all it can do to maintain the four thousand patients here?"

Jan gripped her earthenware mug and stared into her now cold coffee. "So what you're saying is that no one can do anything. That the *status quo* is it. That half these patients have to be drugged into a stuporous state to keep them from being trouble."

"Dr. Petrie," Dorothy said with a superior smirk, "I started here as a nurse and worked my way . . ."

"And I respect you for achieving what you did, when you did." Jan interrupted her. "You're the head of one of the most important departments here. But what does that have to do with improving the way things are done now? Why do you reject all of my suggestions? Why can't we work together?"

Dorothy sniffed irritably. "For the moment, I'm the head of this department. As much as that might frustrate you, you'll just have to learn to live with it. Just remember—you're here because Paul Deutch wants you here. Your credentials don't impress me." She turned on her sensible heel and left Jan in a state approaching despair.

At this point, six months later, Jan could look at the situation in black and white terms. As much as she might try, there was no way she could reach Dorothy. Her boss was not going to help her in any way. In fact, Dorothy would do everything in her power to keep Jan in her place. Jan realized that the most she could hope for was to keep their daily exchanges civil.

As she drove through the rain, she felt the familiar tension gripping her shoulders and neck. Just thinking about Dorothy tied her in knots and the storm wasn't helping, either. Keeping her hands on the steering wheel, she rolled her shoulders to loosen them up.

Her thoughts turned to Jeffrey Weston. If it wasn't for him . . . her work with him was going to make her reputation at Fairchild. She would prove to all of them that she was right.

She braked for a turn. She consoled herself with the thought that she'd learned a lot since those early days at Fairchild State. She was more practical now. And she had a breakthrough under her belt.

Jan nearly missed the narrow turn she was anticipating. She jerked the wheel. The squealing tires caught the edge of a puddle, creating a graceful spraying arc of muddy water but her Rabbit held the road.

"Close call," Jan said aloud with relief. She told herself to keep her mind on the road, but even after the hairpin, fishtailing turn, her mind drifted.

chapter 2

IT WAS DURING the third week of her orientation that she had first seen Jeff. Dorothy Campbel had taken her to observe several mildly retarded patients in one of the dayrooms, but something drew her attention to a man sitting in the corner. Perhaps it was the way he held the trembling child on his knee.

His classically chiseled features were framed by honey-colored hair. Over six feet tall, his body was hard and strong and beautifully proportioned. But though he was quite handsome, it wasn't just his looks that attracted Jan to him. There was a vulnerability to his manner that appealed to her even more.

She watched him wordlessly soothe the boy. He stroked the child's hair and smiled down at him. She was amazed that such a large man could be so gentle, so soft. A very tender caring radiated from him. Jan could feel it from across the room.

Surprised by the power of the man's presence, Jan heard herself asking, "Who's that attendant with the boy over there?"

"That's not an attendant," Dorothy said. "It's Jeffrey Weston, a case of mild brain damage and neurological impairment. He's spent thirty of his thirty-three years at Fairchild."

Dorothy paused to smooth her already perfect hair. "We know nothing about his background. He's been a ward of the state since the death of his parents, and he hasn't spoken a word since he's been here. He's always been a favorite among the staff because he never causes trouble. In fact, he's often quite helpful—as you can see for yourself right now."

Jan found it difficult to tear her eyes from Jeffrey Weston. He looked up. Jan's quick intake of breath was audible. A warm, rushing sensation flooded her as his alarmingly blue eyes met hers. With a questioning lift of his eyebrows, the man indicated he knew he was the subject of their conversation.

"Are you there?" Dorothy snapped, "or daydreaming?"

"Just wondering." Jan blinked hard and turned to Dorothy. "There's nothing at all on his background?"

"Very little, as I recall." Dorothy guided Jan out of the room to continue their rounds. "He was found near the scene of a terrible car accident along the cliffs. Little was left of the car for identification. No missing persons reports were ever filed. No one ever came to claim him from the hospital. The police assumed that his parents had died in the crash, but he had been thrown clear of the wreck. His brain function never got better, so he ended up here. It was before my time."

Jan stopped in the doorway to glance back at the man, who was once again absorbed by the child. "How sad—and strange. He never had a chance, did he?" She felt enormous compassion for him—a man so striking, yet so damaged by physical and emotional trauma.

Dorothy shrugged. "He's one of the happy ones."

"Has he been tested recently?" Jan asked.

"Why do you want to know?"

Jan wasn't prepared for Dorothy's defensive response.

"I'm curious to know if his intelligence scores parallel a normal curve for a man his age," she answered honestly.

"No. He hasn't been tested recently," Dorothy snapped. "As you'll learn soon enough, we're too short staffed to do longitudinal studies on patients whose behavior doesn't change. It's a question of maintenance in these cases."

"Well, I intend to have him tested and if need be work with him."

"If you have the time, Dr. Petrie," Dorothy Campbel cut her short, "you can do whatever you'd like."

"Then I think I'll try nonverbal therapy first. Perhaps art."

Jan's schedule was tight. In a normal day, she would visit and observe various wards on the grounds—there were thirty in all. She wanted to get a sense of the different groups in the institution, from the most severely disturbed in the back wards who received practically no personal attention at all to the more socialized and accessible patients. She supervised classes in the Craft Center, a separate cottage on the grounds. She was also staggering under the burden of one of her victories. She was administrating a rudimentary testing program to update files. To help her staff with the mammoth job, she tested patients herself in her office, as well as reviewed the cases the staff had worked on.

But she made certain to find the time to see Jeffrey Weston. The same day she first saw him, after supervising the Ward B kids in arts and crafts, she asked an attendant to bring Jeff from the dayroom where he spent most of his time. Since he was cooperative, he had been given a fair amount of freedom in the institution. He was allowed to leave his ward and to enjoy Fairchild's parklike grounds.

Even though her stomach was rumbling from hunger, she wanted to start working with Jeff immediately. She would have to skip lunch.

She had been cleaning up paint splattered all over the main worktable, when she glanced up to find Jeff standing timidly before her. He seemed ready to bolt like a frightened deer. His bashfulness was oddly out of tune with his impressive stature. She motioned to the attendant to leave and then smiled at the young man.

"Hi, Jeff," she greeted him. "I'm Dr. Petrie. I noticed what a big help you were yesterday with little Jimmy. It was good of you to take care of him."

Jeff stared at his sneakers.

"Do you like to be with children?" Jeff looked up at her. A tentative smile spread across his face. The way his calm blue eyes fixed on her was startling. Wrenching her eyes from his, she pulled out a chair. "Why don't we sit down?"

Jeff clumsily took a seat across from her. He stared down at his hands, folded in front of him.

"I thought you might like to draw a picture, Jeff." Jan noticed that he clenched his hands more tightly at her suggestion. His knuckles were white from the added pressure.

"Have you worked much in the arts and crafts room?" she asked, trying to get him to respond.

Without raising his eyes, Jeff shook his head no.

Jan was disturbed by his defeated posture and his obvious reluctance. She reached for a large newsprint pad and a piece of charcoal which she offered to him. "Why

don't you draw me a picture of something you like?"
Jeff sat motionless.

Jan gently pushed the large pad toward him. "Come on, Jeff. It's fun."

He bit his lip and began wring his hands. Despite his anxiety, Jan continued to coax him in a warm and even tone. "Why don't you just give it a try?"

She took the charcoal and carelessly drew a happy face. "See—it doesn't matter what you do. I've never been very good myself."

Jan edged the pad closer to him. "Silly, isn't it?"

A tentative smile played on his lips. Jeff took hold of the pad and charcoal. Jan nearly whooped with joy, but restrained herself and said, "Very good, Jeff."

"Look at those pictures on the wall done by the kids. They had a great time doing them. I bet you will, too."

Jeff obediently turned to the wall. He studied the colorful pictures, then looked bewildered at the empty pad in his hands.

"I've got an idea. Why don't you draw me?" Jan wanted to avoid frustrating him so she took a more direct approach.

He dropped the pad to the wood table and stared at the piece of charcoal he rolled between his thumb and fingers.

"It's messy, isn't it? The charcoal's turning your fingers black." Jeff continued to rub the charcoal.

"Don't you want to draw me?"

Jeff made the slightest of nods, his eyes still cast downward.

"Well, then you better look at me."

He lifted his eyes to her and Jan experienced the strange surge of emotion inside her and had to look away to compose herself. She would not allow her own confusion to interfere with their session.

"So," she said, her voice breaking. "Ready to start?"

He nodded enthusiastically, relieved of the burden of choice. Propping the pad on his lap, he began to work with tight-lipped concentration. Jan smiled each time he looked up from the pad. For several minutes he worked in broad, sweeping strokes. By the time he finished, he was beaming.

"May I see what you've done, Jeff?" Jan asked. She was delighted by the way he threw himself into the task.

His enormous hands gripped the edges of the pad and he slumped in his chair.

"If you don't want to show it to me, Jeff, you don't have to." Jan shrugged.

Jeff looked at the pad, then up at Jan, then back down again to the drawing. He tore off the sheet and folded it in half.

Jan tensed as she waited to see what he would do. "Please, please," she begged him silently, "trust me, Jeff."

He shifted nervously in his seat, averted his face, and shoved the piece of paper across the table.

"Why, thank you," Jan said softly. She chose not to communicate the excitement that flooded her. Jeff sat rigid with tension.

In that moment she knew why she loved her work. And she knew that she did it well. Jeff's trust was what it was all about. She was so excited by her victory, by the risk he had taken, that the drawing itself seemed insignificant.

"Let's see what . . ." she started to say while she opened the folded sheet of paper.

When she glanced at Jeff's drawing, she was too stunned to go on. Jeff leaned forward in his seat, waiting for her response almost hungrily.

She saw herself smiling from the page. Jeff had drawn a remarkable portrait. He had captured the lines of her face with fluid, simple strokes. Every detail was exact, but more than that, there was a vividness, an intensity to the drawing that left Jan speechless.

"Jeff," she finally exclaimed, "this is wonderful . . . it's . . . it's beautiful!"

Jeff sighed from a place deep inside himself. His strained expression softened and his face was transformed with childlike pleasure.

From that moment, Jeff had become her cause. Jeffrey Weston was the case she needed to show the hospital administration what she could do—what all of them could do.

After hours that day, Jan had stopped by Paul Deutch's office on the odd chance that he might still be there. His secretary was already gone. She had switched off her brass desk lamp and covered her typewriter. Jan noticed one of the phone lines was in use. She walked through the anteroom and stuck her head into the hospital director's office.

Paul Deutch sat in a high-backed, tufted leather chair which was burnished with age, behind a massive, mahogany partner's desk. He twisted the phone wire as he spoke in efficient, clipped tones. "Right. We'll work up those figures. It might convince the Board." He smiled when he saw Jan in the doorway and gestured for her to come in.

Jan took a seat on one of the Sheraton chairs that flanked his desk. She studied the framed degrees and French prints that covered the walls, while Dr. Deutch finished his conversation.

As he hung up the phone, he swiveled in his chair to

face Jan and asked, "What are you doing here at this hour? Why aren't you out with one of your many beaux?"

"I have had such a wonderful day that I can't tear myself away," Jan teased, "and why are you always so gallant—even at this hour?"

"You know what they say about old gents." Dr. Deutch tilted back in his chair and hooked his thumbs into the pockets of his vest. "Tell me why your day brought a sparkle to your eyes and a blush to your cheek."

"I thought you'd never ask." Jan unfolded Jeffrey Weston's sketch and passed it to Dr. Deutch without a word.

"Very lovely." Deutch looked from the sketch to Jan's face. "Quite a fine portrait." In a therapist-like tone, he asked, "Care to tell me about it?"

"Seriously, Dr. Deutch—this was done by a patient."

"A patient?" Deutch studied the sheet appraisingly. "I'm impressed. Who did it?"

"Jeffrey Weston!" Jan searched the doctor's face for recognition.

"Weston . . . Weston." Deutch shut his eyes, obviously trying to place the name.

"You know, that remarkably handsome man from Ward D."

"Oh, yes—he's mute, somewhat withdrawn? Plays with the children?"

"Right." Jan was bursting to share her story. She told Dr. Deutch how she noticed Jeff with the child, how she had just sensed he was extraordinary, and how he had produced the picture.

"This is it! This is the case to shake everyone up! Jeffrey Weston has been in this hospital for thirty years. In all that time, not a single person went out of his way to reach out to him. No one made the time for him alone."

"Let's not get carried away, Jan."

"I checked his file—it's very thin, Dr. Deutch. He's been on a straight maintenance program since he was a child. Since he was no trouble, he's been ignored. In just one session," Jan pointed to the sketch, "look what he's produced. Who knows what he's capable of doing?"

"Intriguing." Paul Deutch took his glasses off and put the ends between his lips.

"First thing in the morning, I want to run a battery of tests . . ."

"I know how excited you are, Jan, but you've got . . ."

"Oh-oh—when I hear that tone . . ." Jan leaned against his desk, prepared for a lecture.

"But I'm afraid it's necessary in this case, it has the potential to be very challenging. Also very gratifying."

Jan nodded in agreement.

"It's going to take a good deal of discipline for you to keep a sense of proportion. Believe me, I've been through this." Deutch tossed and caught a malachite paperweight abstractedly as he paused. "You know the staff/patient ratio makes it next to impossible to sustain intensive, one-to-one therapy."

Jan was ready to reply, but Dr. Deutch went on, "No, Jan, let me finish. As it is, you're overworked. Just remember, your everyday duties have priority. Dorothy Campbel will watch every move you make. If she finds your work suffers, I won't be able to intercede."

Jan heaved a sigh. "Well, working with Jeffrey Weston might just be what I need to put Dorothy

Campbel in proper perspective."

"Keep me posted on what develops." He winked and took another look at the sketch. "Think you could persuade him to draw me?"

Jan remembered having arrived early the next morning. She had been so early, in fact, that Fairchild was just beginning to come alive. She had found the grounds so peaceful that she decided to make a habit of getting to work at that hour. If she could manage it discreetly, it might be the perfect way to work with Jeff unnoticed.

As soon as she reached her cubbyhole of an office in the new wing of the Administration Building, she tacked up Jeffrey Weston's portrait of her. She wanted him to know just how pleased she was with it. Without even stopping for a cup of coffee, she dove right into her testing texts and manuals to devise an appropriate battery for Weston. It would be difficult, since he would not speak and could not read as far as she knew, but at least she could start with Wechsler's Scales for Clinical Appraisal and talk him through the Minnesota Multiphasic Personality Inventory. She chewed a pencil as she skimmed the familiar material.

"Well, we're up bright and early."

Jan stifled a groan. She should have known Dorothy Campbel got in at the crack of dawn. She'd have to meet with Weston elsewhere. "Good morning, Dorothy."

Her boss's attention was distracted. "Jeffrey Weston! What are you doing here?"

Jan dropped her pencil. "That's all right, Dorothy. I'd like to speak with him."

Dorothy stepped aside to let Jeffrey enter. He was so tall and broad he seemed to fill the office. He clutched a forlorn bouquet of wildflowers in his hand, which he looked at bashfully.

"Why, Mr. Weston. Are those for me?"

He did not respond to Jan's question. Jan wished Dorothy had the good sense to leave instead of embarrassing him by gaping.

"I bet I've ruined your surprise, haven't I, Jeff? You wanted to leave those for me, didn't you?"

He saw the portrait hanging on the wall. He turned to Jan, tears of embarrassment welling in his eyes. Jan got up from her chair and started toward him. He thrust the bouquet at her and then turned and ran from her office. Jeff brushed past Dorothy, leaving her standing in the doorway, sputtering. As Jan raced to catch him, Dorothy's words had followed her, "Don't go after him, Jan. This behavior should not be encouraged."

From the front steps of the Administration Building, Jan had surveyed the sprawling grounds, her hands shielding her eyes from the morning sun. In the distance she saw Jeff moving toward a stately old willow.

"Wait, Jeff, wait for me," she called, disregarding the stares of the employees who were just arriving. She kicked off her shoes and set out after him across the lawns, her hair flying and silk shirt clinging. "Jeff, Jeff, I want to talk to you."

She saw him slow down near the willow. Panting, she approached his slouching figure. In her entire life, Jan would never forget the apprehensive look in Jeff's eyes when she had recovered sufficiently from her sprint to notice. Gulping, as much to swallow her emotions as to catch her breath, she reassured him, "Jeff, those were lovely flowers. I'm very touched. It would have been wonderful to begin the day with such a thoughtful surprise. How kind of you."

He gazed at her from under thick lashes with gratitude. She wondered at how expressive his eyes were. He didn't have to say a word to communicate what he was feeling. She touched his arm briefly, then pulled her hand away.

"Jeff, I hung the portrait because it's the most beautiful gift anyone has ever given me. I'm proud of it and I'm proud of you."

He smiled with pleasure. Awkwardly, he put out his hand to shake. Jan took it in both of hers and said, "Yes, Jeff, we're friends. We'll be spending a lot of time together."

He grinned and extricated his hand from hers.

She checked her watch. "I suppose I should be getting back to work, but I want to discuss something with you first."

She sat down with him under the willow and told him that she wanted to test him. She had explained that she would work with him, that he had nothing to be afraid of, that she believed he was special and that she wanted to help him be all he could be. As she carried on her monologue, she had known that she was breaking every clinical rule. But her instincts were very strong. She felt viscerally that he understood, that he was ready for this bond. And the months that followed proved her right.

She had worked with Jeff every day for six months, if only for twenty minutes on more hectic days. Her monthly tests demonstrated that his skills in every area were getting stronger. His intelligence quotient, though higher than she had expected to begin with, had increased in very large increments as his mental age advanced. Neither she nor Dr. Deutch had ever seen such an astonishing IQ improvement in an adult whose intelligence should have leveled off. His comprehension was quite high. And what he lacked in information and verbal capacity he made up for with his extraordinary spatial abilities. The MMPI had also revealed that his personality was becoming increasingly more integrated. He was far better adjusted, not so cut off from his surroundings. All the time she had spent with him was certainly paying off.

She kept a very detailed journal of their exchanges and his ever-growing trust in her. She was charmed by his playfulness, touched by his clumsy displays of devotion, and fierce in her determination to make a difference in his life, to bring him to a point at which he no longer had to stay at Fairchild. But what she failed to include in her journal entries was her growing attachment to him.

Working with him was more stimulating than anything she had ever done. Paul Deutch had warned her about that. It would be easy to burn herself out with all her responsibilities plus her work with Jeff. But, to make progress with a patient like Jeff *was* more gratifying than anything she could imagine.

She had not been aware of just how deep her feelings for him were, until a day she dubbed the day of "bad connections." She'd arrived one hazy summer morning with the breakfast of bagels and coffee they had made a habit of sharing under the willow tree, away from Dorothy Campbel's curious eyes. She was uneasy when he did not show up. Her bagel tasted like sawdust. It was an effort to chew. Her eyes kept scanning the grounds, but there was no sign of him. She waited until the last possible moment before rushing off to prepare for a meeting with parents of a patient she had been treating. She returned to her office feeling strangely dejected.

All through her meeting, she kept looking out to the corridor whenever she heard footsteps. None were his.

When she rushed off to a rehearsal of the glee club, she left a message for him with Dorothy's secretary, Joyce.

When she returned, she asked, "Any messages?"

"The usual." Joyce handed her a stack which she began to leaf through. "He hasn't been here or left a message."

An alarm bell rang in Jan's head. "Who hasn't been here?"

"Jeffrey Weston." Joyce's tone was insinuating. "Isn't that the message you're looking for?"

"No, actually I was wondering where I was having dinner tonight." Jan was furious with herself for being so defensive. She didn't owe Joyce explanations.

"Oh. Sorry if I was being presumptuous," Joyce said with a smug smile.

Though she wanted to run to his ward at lunch, Jan controlled herself. After all, they didn't have a set appointment for the day. Still, it was odd for him not to make an appearance.

Jan realized that the teacher/pupil relationship was as heady for the teacher as it was for the pupil. She was finding that the dependence went both ways—transference and counter-transference and all that. But she knew that more was involved in Jeff's case. Jeff had such a special quality. He calmed her. When she was working with him she lost all sense of time. His gentleness was embracing, his indomitable good spirits a comfort.

Later that afternoon, Dorothy Campbel materialized in her doorway. "I've been meaning to catch you all day. I'm sorry, I just haven't had a moment."

"What's up?"

"Your Jeffrey Weston was here early this morning. He looked quite ill—some sort of virus I expect. I sent him to the infirmary. Bed rest and plenty of fluids are all we can do for him."

Jan felt relieved and furious at the same time. "Thanks for telling me. I'm glad I'll have the chance to stop in to see how he is before I leave."

Dorothy eyed her coldly and said, "I'm sure he'd like that."

On her way home, Jan made a detour to the infirmary. She stood at the door of the sick room. There, lying on a cot that was too small for him, Jeff stared into space. He looked listless, miserable, and quite helpless.

"I hear you'll be up and around tomorrow." Jan called to him from the door. "So why do you look so wretched?"

At the sound of her voice, Jeff sat up, a delighted grin transforming his face."

"Now that's more like it." Jan walked down the row of empty narrow cots. She wondered how she could have doubted him, how she could have imagined for a moment that their time together was any less important to him than it was to her. When she reached his bed, she asked, "Did you think I had forgotten you?" She leaned toward him and tousled his fever-damp hair. "You know I'd never do that, Jeff—you never have to worry about that."

Jeff's eyes shone with an apology, an understanding of what had happened that day. It was clear to Jan that he knew how she had felt, that the source of his distress was the worry that he had hurt or angered her. Jan took in his unspoken message and said, "It's fine, Jeff. Everything's fine."

• • •

Jeff had continued to learn and grow at an amazing pace. She had not been able to keep her work with him a secret for long. His presence was becoming a dynamic force at Fairchild.

As Jan drove through the storm, she reflected on an event that had occurred the week before that still left her confused.

She had organized a patient/staff picnic, complete with an olympics of events like three-legged potato and sack races. The day was bright, the activities lively. Children and adult voices mixed in a medley of shrieks and laughter. The patients not able to participate sat on the sidelines enjoying the games, the sun, and the general air of festivity. Jan had her hands full—there were over 500 patients to keep track of and a staff of 25 aides.

"Sharon," Jan called to an aide, "would you organize a group for a relay? I've got to check on something."

"How much longer does this last?" Sharon complained. "I'm exhausted!"

"So am I, but look at how much fun they're having." Jan pointed to a group clumsily playing kickball. "This will be a day to remember for them."

"How many of these people do you think will remember this when they wake up tomorrow?" the aide asked in disgust as she shuffled away.

"Great attitude," Jan mumbled as she shook her head and wove her way through the crowd to the food table. In the distance she saw Jeff running a race with a fifteen-year-old palsied boy on his back. What a picture it was! The boy was haphazardly clinging to Jeff. He was so excited to be a part of the race, he was spastically pounding on Jeff's chest with one of his hands. Every now and then, he would grab Jeff around the face, blinding him. They staggered toward the finish line in the lead of the race. When Jeff tripped over the line, a cheer went up in the crowd. Jan raised her hands over her head and clapped. The boy hooted with joy and proudly received a first-place ribbon.

Jan turned her attention to the food. There was plenty of punch and chips, but the hot dogs on the steam table would never last.

"Take it easy on the handouts, Rosey. We're running very low on hot dogs and when they're done that's it."

"What am I supposed to do?" Rosie protested as she handed yet another frankfurter to one of the many hands extended to her. "It's first come, first serve."

"Well, maybe we should halve the dogs now—everyone has had at least one."

Jeff had appeared at her side breathing heavily and mopping his brow.

"Great race, Jeff." Jan slapped him on the back. "You made one young man very happy. I bet he never thought he could win a race!"

Jan's reveries were abruptly interrupted. An immense eucalyptus tree snapped in the howling winds. The broad trunk smashed into the road less than ten yards in front of her speeding car. She barely managed to screech around the tangle of branches.

She pulled the car over, shut off the ignition, and put her forehead against the cool steering wheel. Closing her eyes, she waited for the shock of adrenaline to pass. She took several deep, even breaths to calm herself. She had no idea how long she had sat there waiting for her heartbeat to return to normal. All she was aware of was the rain pounding on her car and the blood rushing in her ears.

Opening her eyes with a flutter, she rolled her head

full circle to loosen the tension in the back of her neck. She looked at her wristwatch, noting the time and feeling the demands of the day begin to press on her.

"Campbel will be on the warpath if I'm late—near fatal accident or not," she muttered to herself. Still shaken, Jan started the car and tore off down the road.

chapter 3

WHEN HER RABBIT approached the twelve-foot iron gate which was set into Fairchild's imposing wall of massive stone blocks, an old security guard in a yellow slicker stepped out of an ornate ironwork booth that matched the gate. Recognizing Jan, he smiled and waved her through. "Mornin', Dr. Petrie."

"Hi, Tom."

"Gonna be a hell of a blow. On and off for five, six days," he said as he looked up at the sky.

"That's what the radio said—really a dramatic storm. A eucalyptus nearly fell on me down the road a few miles back."

The guard whistled. "You're lucky you weren't hurt. I'll call the highway patrol so they can send a crew out. Have a good day, Dr. Petrie."

Jan rolled up her window and drove down the half-mile lane that led to the Administration Building, which was formerly the main house of the Stanford Fairchild Estate. The canopy formed by the mature chestnut oaks that lined the winding road into Fairchild seemed eerie and menacing in the gray-green light of the storm. The individual wards, old stone buildings with bars on the windows and slate roofs slick with rain, were a gloomy sight in the distance. At times like this, Jan could not dispel the awful snake pit image from her mind. She thought of dark, windowless wards filled with dirty, neglected patients. And she was reminded of the degree of human suffering right here at Fairchild. A shudder ran through her.

"Now I'm getting morbid," she thought. "I'd better snap out of it before I start the day."

Pulling into her spot, Jan hurriedly collected her things. She ran through the storm toward the entrance of the main building. At the reception desk, two young nurses spotted her.

"I'm glad you're here," said Annette, a pretty blonde.

"What's wrong?"

"Well, first of all, Carolyn Martin's mother is furious because Carolyn wasn't picked for the chorus."

"But she can't sing a note." Jan wished the problems of the day would all be that simple.

"Carolyn's mother thinks so."

"I'll talk to her. What else?"

The other nurse, who had just started working at Fairchild, said urgently, "Freddy's at it again. He refuses to take his medication unless *you* give it to him. I'm really sorry—I know it's my job but . . ."

"All right, I'll take care of it. Anything else to brighten up the first day of the week?"

"Well," Annette started reluctantly, "I think your boss is on the rampage again."

"What is it this time?" Jan braced herself.

"Same old thing. Jeffrey Weston."

"Doesn't that woman ever let up?" Jan let her irritation slip.

The two nurses exchanged glances. Annette went on, "Rumor has is that Deutch is hung over and . . . he's waiting for you in the lounge."

"Is he furious or brooding?"

"Furious."

"Thank God."

She rushed to the employee lounge. There she found Dr. Deutch sitting at a table with a cup of black coffee, looking as if he had seen better mornings. The pouches under his eyes were puffy, his face a dismal shade of gray. He seemed to be having trouble holding his bald head up.

"You look awful," Jan said with concern.

"Forget my ills," he responded, mustering all the dignity he could give in his tender condition. "I'm afraid you're in for it."

"Don't tell me. Let me guess. The warm, wonderful Dorothy Campbel made another complaint."

Dr. Deutch propped up his aching head with his hand.

"Worse. She filed a request for an official hearing."

"You're kidding."

"I wish I were."

"I knew Dorothy was gunning for me, but this is outrageous."

"Outrageous or not . . ." Deutch began.

"Wait a minute, Paul. Before you start lecturing me . . ."

"My dear, I'm hardly in any shape to lecture at the moment," he moaned. "Jan, let's be frank. You do spend an inordinate amount of time with Weston."

"Yes," Jan protested, "and it's paid off. You've seen his paintings. You also know how greatly improved he is. He's less withdrawn . . ."

"Results aside . . ."

"What do you mean, 'results aside'? Results are why

I'm here. Results used to be what motivated you. I've heard you were really something when you were my age."

Dr. Deutch smiled, and said with affection, "Leave it to you to bring that up."

He jiggled his wooden coffee stirrer on the formica tabletop for a moment, then snapped it in two.

"But I'm not in the right frame of mind for a walk down memory lane," he went on. "And I don't have the strength to dissertate on the political realities of working here."

"Paul, I know that speech by heart, anyway."

"Well, it doesn't show in your actions," Deutch said bluntly. "What I have to say to you is very simple. I don't need the Review Board coming down here."

"What do you mean?"

"I spent last night jollying Pete Hansen . . ."

"*The* Pete Hansen from the State Office?"

"The same. You know what he said? He said that if his people have to come down to Fairchild to review your competency . . ."

"Competency!" Jan objected. "Come on, Paul. You know this whole fiasco is an ax-job. Campbel wants me out."

"Regardless, Jan, they'll come here to nail you. I managed to dissuade Hansen from holding the hearing this time. But I can't protect you forever. They *will come* and Dorothy Campbel will have her way unless . . ."

"Unless I play the game and promise never to pay attention to Jeff again, right?"

"There you go again, Jan," Deutch replied, shaking his head. "Always the extremist. Of course, I support your work with Weston, but you're still responsible for over four hundred other cases . . ."

"And they get my attention, too. You're starting to sound like her."

"It's not just Dorothy Campbel, Jan. Everyone's talking about you and Jeff."

Jan's face flushed. "What do you mean?"

"He's a striking man. You're a beautiful woman."

"What?" She was almost shrieking.

Paul Deutch shrugged. "Where there's smoke there's fire."

"Really, Paul." Jan was flustered by his bluntness.

"You're a therapist, I think you should examine your feelings."

"My feelings have nothing to do with it. Jeff needs . . ."

"For God's sake, Jan," he interrupted her, "I know you're dedicated—I know what Jeff means to you professionally. But sometimes professionals get overinvolved. Don't deny your feelings—look at them, analyze them."

Dr. Deutch reached across the table and patted Jan's forearm. "If you're going to help Jeff, really help him, you have to be clear in your own mind—you can't muddy the process with physical attraction."

"They think . . ." Jan said faintly.

"Never mind what *they* think. It's what *you* feel that matters."

Jan bowed her head, and stared at the way the light played on the facets of the amethyst ring on her finger.

"I don't expect you to say anything, Jan. This isn't a therapy session." Deutch's voice was gentle. "I just want you to know that people make harsh judgments. And if people suspect there's anything going on between you and Jeff . . ."

"My motives and Jeff's potential have nothing to do with it?" Jan lashed out.

"You are single-minded." Deutch leaned back in his chair and studied her. "We can't afford to lose you. I hope you heard what I said."

"I did, Paul, I did. I do appreciate it. You've been straight with me. But, back to the problem at hand . . ."

"Ah, yes, the Review Board." Deutch sighed. "The fact is they don't care about Jeff's potential. Dorothy Campbel has been running the show for twenty years. They listen to her."

"I don't understand," Jan's voice was laced with frustration, "why she has to undermine everything I do."

"You have to work with her, Jan. You can't fight her head-on. The way things have been going, you're giving her fuel for the fire. I know that Jeff is different, talented. But he's still a patient here and . . ."

Jan cut in hotly, "Jeff is more than different. He's extraordinarily special. I can't see why that interfering old biddy should resent my work with him so much . . ."

Jan stopped short at Dr. Deutch's alarmed response. She followed his gaze to her left and saw Dorothy Campbel standing at the far end of the table. There was a strained silence.

"This interfering old biddy," Dorothy finally snarled, "wants her department to run smoothly. I see no need to cater to the whims of the latest hotshot Ph.D. who joins my staff. Especially since your behavior is, shall we say, less than professional."

"Not another word, Dorothy," Dr. Deutch ordered. "Both of you get to work and allow an old man to nurse a splitting head in peace."

Stung by her director's words, Jan headed for the dayroom.

She regretted the episode with Dorothy Campbel—it was a new low. But she was even more shaken by her conversation with Paul Deutch.

She hadn't allowed herself to think about her feelings for Jeff. She had definitely been avoiding it. She cared about him very deeply, there was no denying that. She wanted more than anything in the world to help him, to make him whole. But could she deny that her feelings for him exceeded the narrow boundaries her profession allowed?

He had a magnetic quality that struck something deep inside her. When she thought of him, she felt a sensitivity to him, a profundity of spirit. She didn't understand it, but the feeling had nothing to do with physical appetite and it went beyond her professional ambitions.

Yet, in the oddest sense, the feeling was almost impersonal. She couldn't define it. Indeed, the bond was powerful and absorbing. Thinking about it confused her. She wondered if in her confusion, she had feelings she just wasn't facing. She knew the attraction wasn't sexual, but if not, then what was it?

As Jan entered the dayroom, sunlight broke through the storm clouds and spilled into the room. She surveyed the bustling activity. A number of children were running randomly around the room. Some of the severe cases sat insulated in their own worlds, peering vaguely around them.

In a far corner, Jeff was sitting at an easel, looking out at the hospital grounds. His blond hair gleamed in the sun. His face in profile was strong and handsome. Jan felt drawn to him. She sensed that being with him would comfort her.

While she passed through the busy room, an attendant cried, "Watch out!" Jan stopped dead.

Before she knew what had happened, the wind was knocked out of her. The back of her head and her shoulders slapped against the cinder-block wall with astonishing force. Stunned and choking for breath, she felt searing pain in her wrists, which were clenched in a vise-like grip, and pinned against the wall. She could not focus her eyes. She was hazily aware of a horrible howling, but couldn't tell from where it came. She felt as if she had been shattered, torn to shreds. Something dark began to butt at her stomach in fierce bursts. She realized it was a child. A frenzied child, charged with strength which surpassed his size, had lunged at her and was banging against her with his forehead. Too startled and winded to scream, Jan looked wide-eyed around the room for help.

With surprising agility, Jeff was instantly at her side. He gently placed his hand on the boy's small shoulder. The child spun around to attack him. Their eyes met. Jeff spoke gently, comfortingly, and the boy's rage vanished as if a switch had been clicked. He stood, facing Jeff, docile and quiet.

Jan rubbed her bleeding wrists as she struggled to recover her breath. Her shoulders ached so much she could barely lift her arms. The back of her head throbbed. She could feel a bump swelling. She hugged her stomach, testing to see how badly injured she was. The blows had been quite severe. She was amazed that she had been caught so completely off guard.

Still reeling, she watched Jeff draw the astonished boy to him. She was foggily aware of comments swirling from all over the room.

"That was unreal."

"Did you see him stop that manic kid?"

"If I could learn that technique I'd save a lot of wear and tear on my poor body."

An attendant rushed to help her. "Are you all right?"

"A bit shaky," Jan answered, unable to take her eyes off Jeff, "more stunned than anything else, I think."

"We'd better bandage those wrists and have you examined," another attendant suggested. He took her arm to lead her away. Jan shook his hand off. "Just one second."

Jan moved toward Jeff, who had the boy wrapped in his powerful arms.

"Jeff, I want to thank you. That was a brave and wonderful thing you just did."

Jan extended her hand. Jeff hesitated, then reached out, still holding the boy with his other arm, to cover her hand with his. Jan's eyes filled with tears as he smiled with childish pride.

chapter 4

THOUGH IT WAS only a little past noon, the clatter of typewriters and the activity in the City Room of *The Chronicle* had reached a clamorous level. Reporters were drafting their copy for the Late City Edition, which closed at 6:00 P.M. Their copy was being run to the rewrite editors, then to Peter Richardson, the city editor, and finally to the typesetter. The activity would peak at 5:00 P.M., then everyone would gear up for the next day's work.

David Kennedy, sandy-haired and lanky, dropped his copy into a metal basket on the rewrite editor's desk and surveyed the enormous, bustling room. The constant ebb and flow of pressure in a newsroom is what had attracted David Kennedy to journalism. Whenever he walked into the City Room he was aware of it. No straight nine-to-five job could keep him engaged for long. He'd tried on Wall Street. It hadn't worked.

David Kennedy had great visions for himself. He had tossed off his Harvard M.B.A. and the world of finance without hesitating and enrolled in the Columbia School of Journalism. After a stint on the *Boston Phoenix*, he moved out West for his first job on a major newspaper.

The longer he worked, the more he realized his image of himself as a star reporter was a long time coming.

Kennedy made his way toward the cubbyhole that contained the coffee machine. Walking past the rows of desks, he greeted various reporters. "Say, Bob—great story yesterday on the mayor's real estate holdings!" If there was anyone on the paper he envied it was Bob Wiley. He was the best investigative journalist on staff—a maniac, but also a star.

David entered the closed-off area that contained files and a stained formica table that held the coffee machine. He poured himself a steaming mug and spooned in some powdered cream.

"Say, David," Judy Lloyd, her angular body tense, appeared at the coffee machine just as he was wincing from his first sip of coffee, "Richardson's sending me out on another fabulous assignment."

"Whew, this stuff is strong enough to raise the dead." David leaned against the table as she helped herself to a cup. "So, what's the assignment?"

"I've been covering engagements, weddings, you know. But today I'm really lucky, a fashion show." She shoved her shining, blunt-cut, black hair behind her ear. "And look at me . . ." Her voice was heavy with sarcasm as she gestured to her outfit of khaki trousers, a white cotton boatneck sweater, and red espadrilles, "I'll be laughed out of the restaurant by all those ladies in their Adolfo suits and silks."

"You look terrific," David grinned at her, "and you know it."

Judy brushed aside his compliment with a wave of her hand. "They never told me it would be this tedious when I was in school."

"Yeah, they did," David corrected her. "Only none

of us believed them." David didn't want to start a gripe session at the coffee machine. His morale had hit an all-time low.

"Well, chin up." Judy took the last gulp of her coffee. "Another day, another thrill. Gotta run."

"See you later," David called to her as she sprinted away. "Don't you ever walk?"

"Not when I'm on such a hot story," she yelled over her shoulder.

David sauntered to his desk, blowing into his cup to cool down the murky coffee.

His editor stuck his head out the door of his office at the far end of the City Room. "Hey, Kennedy."

"Yes, Chief." David approached the doorway of Pete Richardson's office. Whenever he was summoned for an assignment, he always harbored the hope that this story would be his big break.

"What's up, Chief?" David stood in the doorway of Richardson's office. Richardson's desk was spread with rough layouts for the front page.

Holding a sheet in his hand, Richardson said in his no-nonsense manner, "There's an Arts and Crafts Fair at Fairchild State. Why don't you drive out there and write us a nice, heartwarming story?"

"From obits to nitwits," David groaned.

"Somebody has to do it."

"All right, all right, I'll head out there. Have anything juicier when I finish that?"

"That's open for discussion when you get back with a story," Richardson answered. He smiled at David the way he always did when David was overly eager.

An hour later, David was driving through the main gate of Fairchild State. He was sarcastically running his article through his head:

CRAZIES CREATE
AT FAIRCHILD STATE

In a stunningly pathetic event at Fairchild State Hospital, the inmates had a gala showing of this year's creative output with a collection of awkwardly designed ashtrays, knotty potholders and muddy fingerpainting . . .

David pulled into a space reserved for doctors near the entrance of the Administration Building. He lowered his visor to display a sign that read: PRESS—*The Chronicle*.

The main building at Fairchild was castle-like in design, complete with turrets and imposing, hand-hewn doors. David remembered having read that Stanford Fairchild had donated his three-hundred-acre estate to the state of California in the 1920s, when his wife went mad, with the provision that it be turned into an institution for the insane.

David entered the lobby, fully expecting to see suits of armor and heraldic banners hung from swords. Instead, he confronted what could be almost any hospital lobby. Yet despite the banks of elevators, the guards, the gift and coffee shops, and the standard reception desk, traces of the building's former grandeur remained. The floors were made of pink and green marble, gargoyles and carved moldings graced the walls, and the chandeliers were massive and intricately worked wrought iron. David took in the contrasts as he made his way to the reception desk.

"Good morning, sir. May I help you?" a young aide greeted him.

"I hear there's an Arts and Crafts Fair today."

"Yes, it's in the Blakemore auditorium." She gestured to the swinging doors on the right. "Just down the hall. You can't miss it. Would you like to make a donation? The proceeds will go for buying supplies for the patients."

David leaned on the desk and drew his press card from the back pocket of his crumpled seersucker suit.

"I'm here for *The Chronicle*," he said, flashing the card. "My piece should attract people to the fair. That's more than I could contribute out of my pocket."

"Oh. Well, I hope you enjoy the fair. Write a good article about us."

David smiled as he left the desk. He still got a charge from the response his press card inevitably drew from people—even if it was only a pretty aide at Fairchild State.

David whistled softly when he entered the auditorium. The room was magnificent, about 300 hundred feet square with thirty-foot ceilings. The walls were paneled in walnut which glowed with the patina of age. The crossbeams on the ceiling were inlaid with delicate patterns of ivory. The huge expanse of parquet floor was breathtakingly crafted.

"What a waste!" David could not help thinking. The scene in Blakemore auditorium not only clashed with the surroundings, but also confirmed his worst suspicions about his assignment.

The opulent room was festively decorated with crepe-paper bunting. The cheerfulness of the various colors and random placement of the decorations gave the room a desperate look. Tables displaying the predictable crafts were scattered throughout the center of the room, and the walls were hung with primitive paintings in primary colors and lurid, not very accomplished weavings. About fifty people, to David's eye mostly

Junior League types and blue-haired matrons, circulated aimlessly. He watched one particularly well-groomed woman, a Dina Merrill-type, exclaim over a crudely fashioned vase.

A quick survey of the work on display from the doorway convinced David that his only hope for a story was to go the human interest route. There was only so much he could do to describe the event. If he could come up with something to expand the focus of his piece, he might have a chance of convincing Pete Richardson to give him more space—maybe even a byline.

"I'd better find the art therapist. She'll give me some copy," he thought.

Then he noticed a large group of people gathered around five or six paintings. He changed his course to get a closer look. As he approached the group, he observed the faces of the viewers. They were all transfixed by what was before them.

His first glimpse of the paintings made him draw in his breath sharply. The portrait was of a lovely, auburn-haired woman sitting before a window. In half-profile, she gazed out from the canvas, madonna-like in her serenity, yet intensely vital. Behind her, through the window, the artist had depicted lush tropical foliage of unearthly hues, greens and mauves which glowed vibrantly. Somehow, the interplay between the delicacy of her features and the intense eeriness of the background was astonishing.

The other five canvases were all portraits of the same woman. They varied slightly in the position of her head and hands. Each painting represented the apricot-skinned woman before a different setting, one more glorious than the next. Through that window, the viewer saw a magical world of shadow and light—a beach dark with storm; a distant jagged mountain range, all blues and purples; the stark, glaring clarity of a desertscape; the yellow-green softness of a hazy, summer morning by a lake. Across the bottom of each painting was the childlike scrawl of the artist's signature—Jeffrey Weston.

As David studied the paintings, he felt a wave of tranquility wash over him. He stared at the portrait with the beach scene framed by the window. He could hear the crashing of the waves and the howling of the wind. He could taste the salty air on his lips. To his astonishment, every time he shifted his focus, he experienced the mood of the background in a very physical way. David realized he was so enthralled by what he was feeling that he had joined the hushed crowd around him. By sheer force of will, David managed to tear himself away from the paintings.

"Well," David thought, "now this is a story." He was exhilarated. "It's not hard news . . . but if I play my cards right it's a byline feature. This guy can paint." He stood, slightly disoriented, scanning the room.

Then he did a doubletake. There—twenty feet away—was the woman. Her thick auburn hair was swept back, revealing the fluid lines and harmony of her delicate face. Her huge, wide-set green eyes dominated her face, yet her sensual, full mouth was in a class of its own. She moved with long-legged grace and engaging vitality.

David looked from her to the paintings and back to her. She's attractive—no doubt about that, he thought to himself, but the paintings transform her. They have a quality . . . they . . . he couldn't put it into words.

He watched her shaking hands with an elegantly attired middle-aged man. David assumed he was the masculine equivalent of the well-preserved matrons at the show. Only he guessed a man of such obvious wealth and taste, who made time to attend the Fairchild Arts and Crafts Fair, would be a philanthropist—or maybe a politician. David made his way in their direction and insinuated himself within hearing range of their conversation.

"Who's this Weston?" the philanthropist/politician asked her. "One of the staff?"

"No," David heard her respond. The voice was surprisingly rich for such a fragile-looking woman. "He's a patient. Very good, isn't he?"

"I should say so, Dr. Petrie. But surely he's not . . ." the man paused, arching his eyebrow, "like the others."

"Yes. He is." David noticed reluctance in her response.

"Incredible! Has he had any formal training?"

David wondered why she hesitated. "Absolutely not, Mr. Bates. In fact, he just started painting a few months ago—on his own." Unmistakable pride crept into her voice.

Mr. Bates eyed the paintings appraisingly from across the room. "Those canvases are powerfully evocative. The nuances of mood and tone are extraordinary."

"I've always thought so. They're magical for me. I'm thrilled to see that they affect others the same way."

"Weston's certainly picked an exceptional subject," Mr. Bates went on rather pompously, "and he has rendered you quite faithfully, I might add."

"Why, thank you."

David was touched by her freshness, by the blush that spread on her cheeks, and by the way she brushed off the compliment.

He was disappointed when he realized that the affected Mr. Bates wasn't finished.

"But the backgrounds . . . I've never seen anything like them. These are scenes from a primeval paradise, scenes that are an archetypal reminder of a lost past and of what could be."

The exquisite woman just stared at him, visibly moved by what he was saying.

"The vision," he continued with enthusiasm, "is so riveting, so essentially comforting, that the impact of the paintings is almost mystical."

"Do you really mean that?" she asked, unable to contain her excitement.

David was glad she cut him off. If she hadn't, he would have.

"Of course I do. These are the most exciting paintings I've seen in years."

"You describe the effect they have so well," she said with a sigh.

"Well, Dr. Petrie, I've had a lot of practice. I own the Bates Gallery in San Francisco."

David saw her lift her chin with surprise.

"I'd be curious to know if the brass at the hospital know what a genius they have within their walls."

She paused briefly, as if to frame her response carefully. She appeared somewhat deflated when she answered, "As I said before, he's only just started to paint. I'm afraid we're all in a state of shock about it."

David sensed something evasive in her answer. She began to look around the room.

"Please call me." Bates drew a business card from the inner jacket pocket of his custom-tailored suit and handed it to her. "I would be most interested in showing Weston's work. Let me know when it would be convenient for me to drive out to meet him."

"I knew Jeff was good." She shook her head in disbelief. "But I thought I was too close to his work. This is terrific. You'll certainly be hearing from me, Mr. Bates."

As they were shaking hands, David saw his opening. He stepped up to Jan's left and said, "I couldn't help overhearing your conversation." She turned to him, her face radiant. "That Jeffrey Weston must be very special. And you must be quite a therapist to inspire such talent."

"I can hardly take the credit, Mr. . . ."

"Kennedy, David Kennedy."

"I'm Jan Petrie," she said as she extended her hand. "I'm the Assistant Director of Special Projects here at Fairchild."

Her green eyes glowed as David shook her hand. "She's a knockout," he thought in that first moment of contact.

"What was I saying?" she went on. "Oh, yes, Jeff *is* very special."

"I have to say I never expected to see such work at this Arts and Crafts Fair," David wasn't ready to reveal his purpose in being there. He had to talk to Jan without self-conscious barriers. "You're not selling these, are you?"

"That's why they're here."

"I don't know how you could part with them."

"Well, there are plenty more where these came from."

"You mean you have more paintings like this?" David asked, marveling.

"Oh, yes," Jan said with a smile. "Quite a few."

"Amazing!" David involuntarily flicked his eyes to the paintings then back to Jan. "Tell me about the artist—this Jeffrey Weston."

Jan shrugged. "There's not much to tell. He's been here most of his life with mild brain damage. He's never said a word."

"Is it customary," David probed, "to lock someone up for life because of mild brain damage?"

Jan cut him short. "Mr. Kennedy, I'm afraid I really can't discuss Jeffrey Weston's case history with you."

"Well, tell me this, how long have you been working with him?"

"About six months."

"And he's produced these paintings in that time?" David remembered what she had told Bates. "What did he do before you started working here?"

"He was a model patient—very gentle, very quiet," she responded in a clipped tone.

"But he didn't start painting until he worked with you, right?" David noticed her discomfort.

"You flatter me." She looked at her sandaled feet. "Jeff was just ready to paint."

"No," David objected, "I'm not flattering you. Do you have any idea what's causing the changes?"

At that question, Jan's eyes started searching the room as if looking for an escape. David pressed on. "Before you came here, what sort of treatment did he receive?"

She blinked and clasped her left arm with her right hand.

"The same treatment that everyone else gets," Jan replied. He sensed intentional ambiguity in her answer.

"Do I detect some criticism in that statement?" he prodded.

"Criticism . . . no, not exactly." She seemed to be struggling with herself. "It's just that there are so many shortcomings in this system. We simply can't do enough for these people. If we had more funds, a larger staff . . ."

Jan avoided his eyes. He saw her fix on someone or something behind him.

"You're being diplomatic," he challenged her.

She was staring nervously past him. "Not diplomatic . . . it's the truth." She was clearly distracted.

David glanced over his shoulder. He saw a bright blonde woman in a frilly violet dress glaring at them. She seemed to be making Jan as nervous as his questions. He pointed over his shoulder with his thumb. "One of the patients?"

Jan covered her embarrassed giggle with her hand. "No, my boss—Dorothy Campbel." She composed herself. "I really should be circulating, Mr. Kennedy."

"Spare me one more minute, please," he asked with earnest charm. David was already mapping out his story. The theme and approach were falling into place. He also knew Jan had a lot to say about the hospital, but she wasn't about to complain to a stranger. And she was obviously afraid to criticize the hospital. He knew manipulations would not work, so he opted to try to convince her to cooperate with him.

"Jan, I'm a reporter for *The Chronicle*."

Her back went rigid but her face remained calm.

"I came here today expecting to do a puff piece on the show. Instead, I found those incredible paintings. I think your work with Jeff will make a wonderful feature. Readers will love it." He watched Jan shake her head emphatically. "I'd like to spend some time observing you."

"I'm afraid that would be impossible." Her voice was icy. "I don't want any publicity."

"But, Jan, the exposure could help."

"I don't want this turning into a freak show . . ."

"What did you expect?" David was low-key. "You showed the paintings, didn't you? How did you think people would respond to them?"

Jan ignored his questions. "The exposure you're talking about could interfere with Jeffrey's progress." Her tone was strictly professional. "I must ask you, Mr. Kennedy, not to write about Jeffrey Weston. You'll get no cooperation from me or any of the staff."

"But . . ." David began to protest.

"You do not have my permission to quote me." She spoke with irritation. "You reporters should identify yourselves before you interview people. I can't believe the way you tricked me into giving you information. I am shocked, really I am. Now, if you'll excuse me . . ."

She pushed past him before he could say any more. David regarded her lithe body as he crossed the room. He was puzzled by her agitation.

Then she was stopped by her boss. As the two talked, Jan cast nervous glances in his direction. He wondered what they were saying.

Realizing he could not accomplish anything more in the auditorium, David decided to see what he could dig up on Weston. "David Kennedy, ace investigative reporter, will get to the bottom of this," he thought to himself as he whistled his way out of the auditorium.

"Quite a turn out."

Jan turned blankly to her boss, barely hearing what she was saying. "Yes, it's great."

"I would expect you to be happier," Dorothy said with a sneer. "Your Jeffrey Weston is the star of the show."

"Oh, I am." Her heart sank, but she responded as sweetly as she could.

"Who was that nice-looking young man you were

talking with? The tall one who looked as if he just finished prep school.''

Jan was distressed that her conversation with Kennedy had been noticed. Dorothy couldn't wait to ask.

''Just a guest.'' Grateful for a diversion, Jan spotted a familiar face. ''There's Laurie's mother. She was asking for you before.''

All the way home Jan berated herself. I blew it, she agonized. I talked too much. I know it. Campbel will have my head if he writes the story. I should have found him, tracked him down, and talked him out of writing the story. But I let him get away. He's gone.

In her crusading days, she would have been eager to use the reporter to do an exposé about the institution. It was obvious that's what Kennedy wanted. But she could not afford that now—too much was at stake. Her position was too vulnerable. She couldn't risk jeopardizing her work with Jeff. He was far too important to her. And she was becoming increasingly aware of just how special he was.

chapter 5

JAN CANCELED HER dinner date that evening. John Coleman, the man she had been seeing recently, had invited her to try Le Plaisir, the nouvelle cuisine restaurant that had just opened in town. She had been looking forward to their dinner but she didn't feel up to it anymore and she knew she wouldn't be very good company.

Instead of eating well with a charming and attractive companion, she paced her apartment, fretting over how to persuade *The Chronicle* reporter not to do the piece. Staring at its convoluted, floral pattern, she walked back and forth across the wine and navy Persian carpet—her most prized possession which her Aunt Phoebe had given her from the collection that filled her Nob Hill mansion. After hours of worrying about the reporter, she gave up—it was his will against hers. She'd just have to wait and see and hope for the best.

But this common-sense attitude didn't help. She couldn't quiet the apprehensions that ate at her. If Kennedy wrote that article, Jeff would be in the limelight, and so would she. Dorothy Campbel would never tolerate that. Watching Jeff grow had become Jan's life.

Nothing mattered to her more. And now a pushy reporter was threatening all that—as if she didn't have enough problems already.

She ran a hot tub, billowing with scented bubbles, and sank into it with a glass of wine and a paperback book. The water had grown tepid by the time she turned the last page of the thriller. She was still feeling apprehensive.

"When a bath doesn't work, nothing will," she thought as she crawled into bed. It was a record-breaking restless night.

Jan arrived at work the next morning feeling drained and exhausted. She entered the lobby of the main building. Was it her imagination or did everything come to a halt around her as she walked to pick up her messages? Things seemed more quiet than usual. In the middle of a conversation, two nurses stopped to gape at her.

"Morning." They were staring at her as if she'd put her dress on backwards. "I had a rough night, but is it that obvious?"

They tittered without responding.

Puzzled, Jan rested her briefcase against the counter and greeted the aide on duty. "Tell me that it's going to be a quiet day."

"How can you expect a quiet day?" the aide asked. "This place is in an uproar! Deutch stormed in with a copy of the paper crumpled in his hand." Jan gripped the edge of the counter, unable to speak.

"And Dorothy Campbel has never been nicer, she's walking around smirking and humming to herself."

The aide took stock of Jan's stunned face, drained of all color.

"You mean you haven't seen the paper yet?"

Jan shook her head gravely.

"Well," the aide was enjoying the drama of the situation, "Dr. Deutch wants to see you in his office immediately." Then she added, "Good luck."

Jan gathered up her belongings and set out for Paul Deutch's office in the elegant, old wing of the building. She was operating on automatic pilot. She had no desire to read the article first. It had never occurred to her that Kennedy's story would appear so soon. She was too numb to feel anything—not anger, not dread, not fear.

She knocked on the door with the brass nameplate that read "Dr. Paul Deutch."

"Come in," he answered her knock gruffly.

She entered the familiar office, normally such a welcoming environment. His desk seemed very far away. She covered the space from the door to the Sheraton chair where she had so often sat to discuss hospital business.

His distinguished face was grim. "So it's you."

He buzzed his secretary and told her to hold all calls.

Jan stood mutely at the foot of the desk.

"Sit down, Jan," he commanded. "I have a few things to say to you."

His face was set in a scowl.

"May I read the article?"

"I'm sure you know what it says," he snapped. "You finally got your way, didn't you? The great crusader has really done it this time."

"Paul, I haven't seen the article. I hardly talked to the reporter. You've got to believe me."

He was not to be deterred. "Do you understand what this sort of press will do to us? Do you know what your lack of discretion will cost us?" He picked up the newspaper and waved it at her like a baton.

"Please, let me see it."

Exasperated, he tossed the paper across the desk to her. She could see the headline across the top of the second section: GAUGUIN OF THE BACK WARDS—PAINTING GENIUS DISCOVERED AT FAIRCHILD

She took the paper and began to read:

> At the annual Arts and Crafts Fair at Fairchild State Hospital yesterday, crowds were captivated by the paintings of Jeffrey Weston, 33, who has been an inmate of the mental institution for 30 years and who has never spoken during that time.
>
> Mr. Gary Bates, of the Bates Gallery in San Francisco, who was among the viewers, commented, "These are the most exciting paintings I've . . ."

Jan skimmed the following few paragraphs of praise and picked up again at the mention of her name.

> Dr. Jan Petrie, the dedicated publicity-shy Assistant Director of Special Services at the Hospital, has worked with Weston for the last six months. Her miraculous efforts have produced an art phenomenon—the Gauguin of the Back Wards. Before her arrival at Fairchild, Weston languished as a lifelong patient.
>
> The services at the hospital are inadequate to meet the needs of the patients. According to Dr. Petrie, "We need more funds, a larger staff . . . there are many shortcomings in this system."
>
> When asked about her success with Wes-

ton, she responded, "Jeff is special . . ."

Jan covered her eyes and groaned: There was no reason for her to read on. It was obvious where Kennedy was headed.

"A nice piece of work, Jan." Deutch's comment was like a slap. "I've been on the phone with the trustees since the paper hit the stands."

She was so defeated she had difficulty mustering the strength to defend herself.

"But, Paul . . . he entrapped me. I told him not to write the article or quote me. He's twisted my words. He's using me."

"You've gone too far," he continued. "I can't pull you out of this one."

"You do believe me, don't you?" She realized losing his trust and respect would be unbearable. "You don't actually think I'd be that stupid, do you?"

"Jan, it doesn't matter what I think . . ."

"It matters to me."

"Look, you're in big trouble. And this article is making big trouble for me." He lifted his glasses and rubbed his eyes. "I regret the day Weston dipped his brush in paint."

"How can you say that?" Jan filled with anger. "How can you back down?"

"What do you expect?" Deutch pounded his fist on the desk and then went on more calmly, "There is nothing I can do for you now—I wish I could. There's no easy way out of this."

"Thank God," she said with relief, "at least you believe me."

"Yes, I do. But, you have to face facts. No one else will believe you."

Jan knew he was right. She had let herself be set up,

now she had to face the consequences. She braced herself for what she knew was coming.

"You'll be brought up before a review board tomorrow. I'll do what I can, but I'm not optimistic."

Dr. Deutch got up and walked around his desk to her chair. He put his hand on her shoulder and said gently, "I'm sorry, Jan, I really am."

She reached up and covered his hand with her own. "Thanks, Paul."

"And, though I shouldn't have to tell you this, I will anyway. Stay away from Kennedy. He'll just dig you deeper into the hole."

Jan stumbled through what seemed like an endless day. She was determined to perform her duties efficiently. But she felt like an untouchable. Everyone was ill at ease when she entered a room. There were no joking conversations, no genial greetings. Even Dorothy Campbel stayed away.

In her initial shock, Jeff hadn't entered her thoughts. As the hours passed, though, she could think of nothing else. How would Jeff react if she was fired? Was he as dependent on her as she imagined? Sometimes she had the feeling that the reverse was true. His sure calmness was always a comfort to her.

She paused at the door of the dayroom. There, in the center of the room, Jeff sat with a large sketch pad in his hand. A group of problem children were gathered around his feet. Jan surveyed the faces of the children. She couldn't believe it. Some of those patients never sat still. Others among the group were so withdrawn they never responded to anything. Yet, they all sat on the floor, smiling, watching Jeff with rapt attention.

Jeff finished his sketch and tore the sheet from the

pad with a flourish. He held up his drawing. It was a whimsical, imaginary creature. Delighted peals of laughter were the reward for his magic. The children clapped and giggled, and called for more.

Jan's heart swelled with affection for him. He was remarkable, there was no question about that. All she had to do was to look at the faces of those troubled children to know how much he touched people. Jan knew that she wasn't alone in her strong feelings for him. She couldn't imagine not working with him, not seeing him, not being with him.

Jeff noticed her standing in the doorway. He waved cheerfully and made a move to get off his stool. The children moaned and pleaded with him to stay. Jan gestured to him to keep up the good work.

When she glanced at her watch, she was relieved to find that she had made it through the day. She returned to her office to pick up her briefcase and her purse. She had grown fond of her cubicle in the new wing, an addition of offices to the Fairchild mansion. As she tidied her desk, the thought occurred to her that it was the first real office she ever had. Her eyes rested on the original charcoal sketch Jeff had done—the drawing that had started it all.

She found it difficult to believe that she had only been at Fairchild for six months—she felt like an entirely different person now. Jeff had enriched her life so much. She had never felt so directed, so full of purpose. And now all that was in jeopardy. She stacked her unreturned phone messages, realizing it might be the last time she did.

She slipped out of the hospital quietly, trying to attract as little attention to herself as possible, anxious to get to her car without running into anyone she knew.

She stopped short when she saw the lanky frame of David Kennedy leaning against the driver's door of her Rabbit.

"How dare you show your face here!" she exploded. "Get out of my way."

"Jan, I've got to talk to you," he said urgently.

"No way. You've caused me enough grief."

"Look, I'm sorry if the article got you in trouble . . ."

"Trouble?" She gritted her teeth. "You might have thought about it before you wrote it. I asked you not to do it. And you had to go use my name."

"But . . ."

"Leave me alone. Go away. I have nothing to say to you."

"What happened?"

"I'm going to lose my job, that's all." She sneered. "I go before a review board tomorrow. I hope you're happy."

"They can't . . ."

"Oh, yes they can. And they will."

"Listen to me, Jan," David pleaded. "They can't afford to fire you. You can do more damage on the outside than you can if you're still working there."

"What do you mean?" she asked warily.

"If you're fired," he began, "what's to stop me from writing about it? And what's to stop you from cooperating with me?"

He lit a cigarette and went on persuasively. "I'm sure there's a lot you could tell me about Fairchild. An exposé could bring them to their knees."

Jan dropped her briefcase and relaxed with a thoughtful sigh. "I see what you're getting at."

"It makes perfect sense. You've got them where it

hurts. If they fire you, they're screwed."

"So what do you get out of it?" Jan was suspicious. After all, Kennedy had gotten her into this mess in the first place.

"I get what I wanted from the start—a soft piece on you and Weston. The hospital will be bonkers to get some good press."

"How do you reverse yourself after the first article?"

"No problem—just leave it to me. People love to read about miracles of modern therapy."

He was convincing. While Jan pondered his solution, Dorothy Campbel's gray Oldsmobile drew near them. Remembering Paul Deutch's parting words that morning, Jan panicked.

"Christ, there's my boss."

David smiled. "That's good. She *should* suspect something's up."

Dorothy slowed her car almost to a stop beside them. She craned her neck and peered. Then she took off.

"Subtle lady," David remarked. "She must be a joy to work for."

Jan sidestepped his comment and got back to the matter at hand. "What am I supposed to do, threaten the Board?"

"I don't think you'll have to. Once they've cooled off, they've got to see the risks. And you can help by dropping a hint or two."

"You make it sound so easy."

"It will work. You'll see."

Jan knew he was right. She had been so caught up in the general hysteria the article created, she hadn't analyzed the problem clearly.

"You have all the answers, don't you?" She still couldn't let go of the anger she felt for him. "Do you always manipulate other people?"

"I am really sorry for what you've been through. I never would have written the article if I actually thought you'd lose your job."

"Somehow I find that hard to believe."

Filled with a sudden rush of tenderness, a need to physically comfort her, David took her by the arm and pulled her to him.

"Let go of me," Jan cried. "Just because you're cleaning up the mess you made doesn't mean you've won me over."

"Okay, okay." He made an empty-handed gesture. "I thought you might like to have dinner tonight—I owe you."

"I'll pass on that," she said acidly.

"Well, in that case, I'll wait for you here tomorrow. I'm sure you'll want a drink after the Review Board has grilled you."

He stepped aside to let Jan into her car.

As she turned the key in the ignition, she relented and said, "Thanks, David. At least I'll be able to get some sleep tonight."

chapter 6

JAN SAT IN the parking lot the next morning, not yet ready to begin the day. She listened to the radio.

"This is KBIJ, your station for mellow sound. Our weatherman Don Scott has a report today that's not so mellow. But I'll leave it to Don to lay the bad news on you. Don . . ."

"This is Don Scott with word that this might turn out to be one of the ten worst days of the year. That's right, folks. Meteorologists report that the worst atmospheric disturbances in thirty-three years have been causing our spell of bad weather. These disturbances have grown more severe, and heavy rainfall is predicted, with up to three inches in the valleys. Because of gale force winds, small craft warnings have been issued . . ."

"How fitting," Jan thought as she switched off the radio.

Despite David's hard-nosed appraisal of the Board's options, Jan couldn't suppress the jitters. At eleven that morning, she would be on the firing line.

She went straight to the employees' lounge to sip a soothing cup of herbal tea. She spread a journal open on the table, but kept reading the same sentence over and over.

"Here she is, our very own celebrity." Dorothy

Campbel's strident voice cut into her.

Jan looked up from her journal and bit the inside of her cheek. "Just what I need," Jan thought.

"Today's the day." Dorothy baited her. "You seem pretty calm for someone who's going into a review board hearing in a couple of hours."

"Dorothy, I know how much my problems thrill you, I've never seen you so cheerful." A smug smile spread on Dorothy's thin lips. "But if I were you, I wouldn't be so certain of the outcome."

"Even you can't get out of this one." Dorothy arched a penciled eyebrow. "I saw you talking to that reporter yesterday. That wasn't very clever, Dr. Petrie."

"Wasn't it?" Jan asked, forcing herself to look amused.

"Of course, I had to tell the appropriate people."

"I bet you enjoyed that. I can always count on you." Jan said without a hint of sarcasm in her voice, "Thanks a lot, Dorothy. I really appreciate that."

She got up to leave the lounge and had to giggle at Dorothy's puzzled expression. David *was* right.

Jeff leaned against a high hurricane fence at the edge of the hospital grounds. Dark clouds billowed in the sky. The air was heavy and still. His fingers grasped the thick wire as he watched six young boys playing football in the adjacent field.

A stocky boy in a striped polo shirt yelled, "I'm gonna punt."

One of his friends tossed the ball to him. He fumbled it, and executed a clumsy dropkick. The ball sailed off the side of his foot, over the fence and landed near Jeff.

"Good work, fatso," a wiry boy taunted him.

Jeff smiled as all six walked toward the fence.

"Hey, mister," the boy in the striped shirt called, "throw it back, will you?"

Jeff's face lit up. Excited, he ran to the ball. With all his might, he imitated the punt he had just seen. The results were similar. The ball flew high into the air and landed in a tall tree on his side of the fence. The boys groaned in unison. A loud crash of thunder exploded.

"Come on, mister," one of the boys demanded. "You kicked it there. Go get it."

Jeff, still playful, ambled to the trunk of the tree. He looked up at the ball, wedged in a thin branch twenty-five feet up. Rain began to fall gently.

The boys followed him down the length of the fence. One called to him, "What are you waiting for? Climb up and get it. We're getting soaked."

Jeff turned to them confused, his blond hair slick against his forehead with rain.

"Hey, maybe he's one of the dummies," the wiry boy observed.

"Nah, he's too old," another responded.

"Come on, will you?" the boy in the striped shirt called impatiently.

Jeff surveyed the tree. He wrapped his arms around the thick trunk and started to shimmy up toward the branch.

"Look at him go!"

"What muscles—I'd hate to make *him* angry."

Jeff turned to grin proudly at his new friends.

"Don't stop now—we've gotta get out of here."

Jeff labored up the trunk to the branch where the ball was wedged. He eased himself onto it and carefully edged toward the ball eight feet away. As he worked himself along the narrowing branch, it dipped from his weight. Afraid to go farther, Jeff stretched out trying to grasp the ball. The storm suddenly broke with a flash of lightning and thunder. Rain pelted the tree and drenched the waiting boys.

"Let's split! This lightning's dangerous."

"What about my ball?"

"Get it later. Come on."

The boys ran toward their bicycles on the other side of the field. One called over his shoulder, "That cost fifteen bucks, mister. You better have it when we come back."

Jeff watched the boys sprint through the open field. Lightning slashed the dark sky. Peal after peal of thunder deafened him. Realizing he was alone, Jeff was paralyzed with fear.

The furious wind tossed the branch he clung to. Desperately, he tried to inch his way backward. The sound of cracking wood made him freeze, but not soon enough. The branch swayed, then plunged three feet.

Jeff clutched the branch with his arms and legs. When he looked behind him, terror spread across his face. He saw the raw wound where the limb had started to split from the trunk. He looked down at the ground over twenty feet below him. He filled his lungs with a quaking inhalation, and bellowed, "Dr. Petrie! Dr. Petrie!"

The branch dropped a few more inches. Wild-eyed and sobbing, Jeff hung on as the rain pelted him.

At the hospital, nurses and attendants were gathering the last of the stragglers from the playing fields. In Ward B, aides were helping children out of their wet clothing. Jan walked through the room with a nurse, toweling her wet hair.

"They predicted this storm today. I didn't expect it to be so sudden. Did you get all the equipment in?"

"Yes."

Jan looked at her watch. "Oh God."

"What is it?" the nurse asked, concerned.

"I'm going to be late for the hearing. And I look like a drowned rat."

"We're rooting for you, Dr. Petrie. Good luck."

"Thanks, I'll need it." Jan started for the door, and tossed her towel into a laundry cart filled with wet clothes. She stopped and turned to ask, "Did everyone get in?"

"Yes, according to my head count."

"Where's Jeff?"

"Probably in the crafts center. You know how he is."

"Do me a favor, will you?" Jan asked hurriedly. "Look in on him. He's probably still in his wet clothes."

"Sure, Dr. Petrie."

She rushed to the reception desk. "Are they ready yet?"

"For the past fifteen minutes."

"Oh, no."

"I'm keeping my fingers crossed." The aide held up her hands to demonstrate.

"Thanks."

Jan started down the corridor when she noticed an attendant, soaking wet and angry, running through the reception area toward her.

"Dr. Petrie," he called. "We've got a problem, Dr. Petrie."

"It'll have to wait, Greg. I'm late already."

"It's Jeff." He was having trouble catching his breath. "He's stuck up in a tree on the north end of the grounds."

"Well," Jan said impatiently, "get him down."

"We've tried. He's scared to death. Says he wants you."

Jan jerked around to face the attendant.

"He *what?*"

"He's asking for you."

Jan clapped her hand to her mouth.

"You mean he spoke?"

"I mean he's howling for you at the top of his lungs."

"My God . . ."

"I wouldn't bother you, but he's pretty high up and the wind's really shaking that tree."

Jan didn't even stop to consider the Review Board. "All right, come on."

Dr. Deutch stepped into the hallway, closing his office door behind him. Dorothy Campbel was waiting for him.

"They're ready inside, Doctor." She smiled sweetly. "Will Dr. Petrie be joining us?"

Paul Deutch wheeled around to face her. He grimaced, about to say something, but restrained himself with obvious effort. Instead, he shot her a look of contempt and entered the conference room.

Dorothy threw back her shoulders, straightened her dress and followed Dr. Deutch into the room.

Using flashlights to make their way through the black storm, Jan and the attendant arrived at the tree. Jan's white coat clung to her body. She shivered as she beamed her light up through the branches. She saw Jeff gripping the branch, crying.

"Jeff," she screamed over the furor of the storm, "I'm here. You can come down now."

Jeff squinted into the bright light. "I can't."

"Yes you can."

"No! I'll fall!"

"No you won't. I promise. Hurry up now."

Jeff slowly started to creep backward on the limb. It cracked again. Hearing the sound, Jan scanned the limb with her flashlight. She gasped when the light fell on the spot where the limb, now barely attached to the tree, was split.

"My God. Jeff, stop! Don't move!" she screamed. "Quick, Greg. Get a ladder. Hurry!" The attendant raced toward the main building.

Jeff looked down at her upturned face and moaned again and again, "Dr. Petrie, help me."

"Don't be afraid. You're going to be fine, Jeff." All Jan could do in those agonizing minutes was to reassure him. "Just stay where you are. Don't move. We'll get you down."

She felt his terror as her own. "Oh, hurry, Greg. Please make it in time." She wrapped her arms around herself. In the distance, she saw the outline of the attendant running, carrying a long ladder. She moved to meet him, but Jeff begged, "Don't leave me."

"All right, Jeff. I'm here."

The attendant arrived, panting. "Oh no," Jan shrieked when she saw what he was carrying. "Are you crazy? We can't use a metal ladder. There's enough lightning out here to light the city for a week!"

"It's all there was nearby." His lack of concern infuriated Jan.

"Well, find something else, this won't do." She tried to control her temper, knowing that the more upset she became the worse it would be for Jeff. "Go to the gardener's shed, near the laundry. There'll be some ladders we can use."

Jeff whimpered and rested his head on the branch, which swayed perilously.

"That branch will never hold," Greg cried, clutching the ladder.

"I guess you're right. We'll have to use it—go ahead."

Jan pushed him toward the tree. He quickly extended the metal ladder up to Jeff and wedged it behind him. Backing away from the tree, he shined his flashlight on the ladder.

"Use the ladder, Jeff!" Jan called to him.

"What?" Jeff turned his head. The branch dipped dangerously.

"Next to you. See it? Climb down the ladder!" she urged him. Her hands were bunched into white-knuckled fists. She had to scream to be heard over the storm.

Jeff felt the top of the ladder with his outstretched leg and cautiously slid down the limb. "Good, good, Jeff," Jan encouraged him. He managed to swing one leg off the branch onto the top rung.

"That's it, be careful."

He got his footing and hesitated a moment. Then he crawled down a few rungs. Suddenly a shaft of lightning exploded from the clouds.

It sliced through the darkness. Like a palsied hand, the lightning seemed to reach for the metal ladder. Quivering, crackling, it illuminated Jeff's terrified face for a split second, then struck the metal ladder with a harsh hiss.

Jan watched with horror as Jeff's body jerked into a stiff, arched spasm. He and the ladder shone with an unearthly, glowing energy that was palpable from where Jan stood.

"Jeff!" Jan shrieked as the limb broke from the tree. Frozen to the ladder, Jeff fell to the muddy ground. Jan flung herself at his motionless body. Automatically, she felt his pulse, then put her ear to his chest.

"Oh no . . . no . . . get an ambulance. Oh God!"

David Kennedy flicked his cigarette ashes out of his car window, which was open a crack. "I'm going to suffocate if this storm doesn't let up," he thought as he took another drag. He wished he could put an ear to the keyhole and listen to the hearing. Jan Petrie was a spunky lady. And he would like to see her challenge that Review Board.

The urgent wailing of a siren pierced through the sounds of the storm. An ambulance shot through the lot and passed his car. In the back window, David saw an unmistakable head of auburn hair bent over an inert body. It was Jan!

"What the hell is going on?" he muttered as he crushed out his cigarette.

He started the car, gunned the motor, and took off after the ambulance. When they arrived at the emergency entrance of Good Shepherd Hospital, David jumped from his car, oblivious of the pouring rain.

The rear doors of the ambulance swung open. Two attendants emerged and pulled out a gurney which held a large body wrapped in blankets. Jan, bedraggled and tearful, followed them as they rolled the gurney into the building.

chapter 7

THE ATTENDANTS PROPELLED Jeff's gurney down the white-tiled hall. Jan raced to catch up with them. A gray-haired woman wearing a white coat and a stethoscope draped around her neck ran to the moving cart.

She spoke in shorthand to Jan. "Dr. Deutch called, struck by lightning, right? Glad you brought him here—"

She pulled out a stethoscope and placed it on Jeff's chest. As the gurney disappeared through two swinging doors, the doctor called to Jan, "Wait here. I'll do my best."

Jan slumped against the wall and covered her face with her hands. How could this have happened? Poor Jeff—he had to make it. If he didn't she had no idea what she would do.

"Dr. Petrie?" A gentle voice pulled her back to her surroundings. "Why don't you go sit in the waiting area? I'll get you some tea or coffee if you'd like."

"Oh, thank you." Jan focused for a moment on the face of a young nurse. "I'll sit, but I'll skip the drink."

The nurse steered her into a yellow room, decorated with standard plastic hospital waiting room furniture. The room was stuffy with the stale smell of cigarette smoke, and the ashtrays needed to be emptied. The nurse gestured to a chair and said, "Make yourself comfortable. Dr. Frohm will be in as soon as she has news."

The sunniness of the room was a brash contrast to the gloom outside. It seemed like the middle of the night. All the lights in the room were on because it was so dark outside. As soon as the nurse left, Jan drew the drapes.

The clock on the wall said 11:45. She sat in a Naugahyde armchair, prepared to begin her lonely vigil.

"Who'd they just bring in?" David Kennedy asked the aide at the emergency room reception area.

"Are you a relative?"

"Would I ask if I was?" David brushed his wet hair back with his hand. "I saw the ambulance leave Fairchild State. I know Dr. Petrie who was with the patient. In fact, I had a lunch date with her."

"Oh . . . well she'll be tied up for awhile."

"What happened? One of her colleagues get ill?"

"No, no nothing like that. It was one of the patients, let's see." She looked at the admission papers on her clipboard. "Jeffrey Weston is his name."

"Weston!" David exclaimed.

"You know him?"

"I know of him. What's wrong?"

She glanced at the clipboard and shook her head. "He was struck by lightning."

"My God." Sympathy for Jan flashed through him. No wonder she looked near hysteria. "What are his chances?"

"He's on the critical list. I can't say with any authority, but it doesn't look good."

"Could I be with Dr. Petrie to wait for the news?"

"I'm afraid not—intensive care is restricted."

"But she must be terribly upset. Weston was her

favorite patient. Could I see her for a moment?"

"Sorry, it's impossible."

"How about getting a message to her?"

"I can't promise." David heard her softening. He assumed a hangdog expression. "It would mean so much to me and I'm sure it would help her deal with this awful . . ." He covered his eyes, pretending to be overcome.

"If you give me a note, maybe I can make a special trip during my break."

"Thanks so much. I really appreciate it." He tore a piece of paper from his notepad and scribbled a message. Handing it to the nurse, he said, "Whenever you get the chance. I'll stay here—if you hear anything, let me know."

At 3:05, Dr. Frohm stepped into the room, wiping her perspiring forehead with a handkerchief.

Jan leaned forward in her chair. She couldn't bring herself to ask the question.

"I'm sorry. I did everything I could."

Jan bowed her head and shook it, as if to deny what had happened.

Helen Frohm put an arm around her. "You need a drink . . . come on up to my office." She led Jan, whose face was streaked with tears, to the elevator.

A slightly stooped attendant pushed a sheet-covered body strapped to a gurney through the swinging doors marked "Morgue." He rolled his cargo in front of a desk where the man on duty continued to read *Club Magazine*, without looking up.

"Come on, Julio. Hurry up. I'm off in ten minutes."

Julio tore his eyes off the page. "Who's that?"

"What's it to you?" The attendant handed him the clipboard that had been hanging on the gurney. "Just sign it, will you?"

Julio started to sign the form, but stopped. He whistled softly, "Man, what a rotten way to go."

"Are you gonna sign that or not?"

"All right, relax, will you?"

Julio's pen scratched across the paper. "Put Weston in 27B."

The attendant rolled the gurney through another set of swinging doors, which led to the morgue. He hurried along the rows of stainless-steel pull-out drawers. He was eager to complete the final task of the day, but that wasn't the only reason he was rushing. The morgue always spooked him. The shining surfaces of the steel, the white tiles, the bright lights, the oppressive silence, and the loneliness of it, made him want to hold his breath until he left.

Finding #27B, he pulled the drawer open to its full length, dropped the sides and moved the gurney next to it. He always hated the next part. Even after fifteen years at the hospital, the corpses always got to him. He unstrapped the body and pulled the sheet down.

If he could have undressed the body with his eyes closed, he would have. He had to force himself to look at the large, lifeless form before him.

"Poor guy," he said out loud as he studied the handsome face of the corpse. "You're a regular Robert Redford." He had discovered some months before that talking to the bodies he was handling took the edge off the jitters.

"I bet you never knew what hit you, did you?" He bent down to remove the hospital gown. He tried to lift Jeff's body with his left arm and untie the back of the gown with his right. He grunted and said, "It would take a bolt of lightning to stop you. You're a solid one. I'll probably bust my gut trying to lift you."

"Who the hell are you talking to?" Julio called from the door. "You okay, man?"

"Yeah, doin' fine." He strained to get the body in position but didn't have the strength. He let the body fall with a thud to the pallet. The corpse's head rolled, facing him. The sudden movement made his heart lurch.

The attendant put his hand to his own chest and gulped to compose himself. He started for the entrance and then picked up his pace. There was something about turning his back on the morgue that always set his teeth on edge. He always had the gut-wrenching fear that some grim force would pull him back and keep him there.

He shoved his way through the swinging doors with more force than was necessary. When the door banged against the tiled wall, Julio was startled into dropping his magazine.

"Hey, Julio, give me a hand, will you? This guy weighs a ton."

"What'sa matter, old man? Getting jumpy?"

"Nah—this guy's a giant. I can't handle him alone."

The low, muffled sound of a siren bled into the morgue.

"Say," Julio taunted. "Maybe you should put in some extra hours. This could be another stiff for you."

"Give me a break."

The siren grew more piercing as the ambulance approached the hospital. The lull in the storm was shattered by a machine-gun rattle of thunder. The lights in the morgue flickered, then dimmed for several seconds, before coming back up to normal.

"It sounds like all hell's breaking loose." The attendant raised his voice to be heard over the blaring siren and the screaming winds. A crack of thunder shook the hospital.

"That was close," shouted Julio.

The lights went out. It was so black in the windowless morgue that the two men couldn't see each other.

"I'm getting out of here. My day's finished."

"Yeah," Julio retorted, "Well, I don't give diddley squat when you're supposed to get off. Find a goddamned flashlight!"

"Getting jumpy, Julio?" The attendant couldn't miss the chance to get back at him. "Don't want to be left alone?"

"All right, all right—you got me."

"Relax. They'll have the emergency power on in a second."

The lights began to flicker like a strobe without much power behind them. They cast an eerie, blue-gray glow over the darkened morgue. Embarrassed to be frightened, the two men avoided looking at each other in the wavering light.

"I wonder why the emergency power isn't working—that generator is a monster," the attendant said nervously.

"Do me a favor, get me some candles . . ."

Julio's request was interrupted by a crash from the morgue behind them. Both heads snapped up.

"What the hell was that?" Julio asked.

The attendant shrugged with forced nonchalance.

"Did you lean the clipboard on something?"

"No . . . no, it was hanging in place on the gurney."

"Maybe the building's shaking from the storm. Maybe . . ."

A loud thud made him stop. They stared wordlessly at each other, not even trying to hide the fear that stiffened their bodies. The on-off, on-off of the lights intensified their startled expressions.

"Better check it out," the attendant said.

"You were the last one in there," Julio responded lamely.

"Screw you. You're the one on duty here."

All too eager to prolong the argument, Julio put his hands on his hips and eyed the attendant coldly. As he was about to speak, a faint, tapping sound echoed from the morgue.

"That's just a loose shade or something. We'd better go . . ."

"What's this *we* stuff?" the attendant taunted Julio.

"As I recall, turkey, there's a stiff in there that has to go beddy-bye. Come on—I'll give you a . . ." He stopped short and turned toward the swinging doors, mouth agape. "Did you hear something?"

"Naw—just the wind." The attendant denied what his own ears had heard. "The storm's dying down. It's just the wind."

Julio gasped. He pointed to the swinging doors. Behind the translucent, milky glass, something was moving—something big.

Both men stood frozen, eyes glued to the doors as the shadow loomed closer. An ear-jarring blast of thunder jolted them. The two men grabbed onto each other in terror, their eyes fixed on the entrance to the morgue.

The body of Jeffrey Weston burst through the doors with such force that the door's hinges were ripped off, glass shattering.

"Holy shit!" Julio screamed. "Where did he come from?"

The attendant gawked in disbelief. Jeff stood in the debris, gulping air. He stared about wildly, his eyes glistening with an animal-like intensity.

"It's him! Weston! He's alive!" The attendant backed away. "Damn—that guy was dead!"

From the depths of his massive frame, Jeff's voice erupted into a primal groan. The groan increased in power and escalated to a chilling wail.

"Well, don't just stand there, stupid," Julio said, shaken. "Get a doctor down here."

"Right." The attendant gladly followed this order. Julio backed out of the room after the attendant. His eyes glued to Jeff, he felt for the door behind him. The lights suddenly came up to full power as he shoved through the doors.

Jeff covered his eyes with a reflexive gesture. Slowly, he dropped his hands from his face to stare, blinking, at his strange surroundings. He looked down at the white hospital robe. He took a few confused steps. His eyes darted around the sterile room.

"Dr. Petrie! Dr. Petrie!" he bellowed in terror. He began to stumble toward the door but collapsed on the floor. His eyes rolled back in his head, the lids only half-closed. His shallow breath deepened and assumed the low, regular rhythm of unconsciousness.

Jan took a sip from a water glass and closed her eyes as the warm brandy slid down her throat.

"There's nothing more you could have done, Jan." Dr. Frohm sat next to Jan on the sofa in her office. She tried to comfort Jan with words she had used so often; they seemed flat to her. "Stop torturing yourself."

She handed a folded piece of paper to Jan. "Someone is waiting for you downstairs—an aide left this note for you. Would you like me to send for him?"

Jan took the note and glanced at it absently. "No—no, I couldn't . . . I . . ." She crumpled the paper and shoved it into her purse. "Dr. Frohm, I should have known," she kept repeating the same litany. "I mean—there was lightning everywhere . . . and I had to hand him a metal ladder."

"Jan." Dr. Frohm reached for her hand. "You had no choice. It was Jeff's only chance. The branch would have given way. He couldn't have survived that fall. You did the best you could for him."

"I know in my head that what you're saying is right. But I'll always blame myself." Jan held back her tears. "It was so strange. The lightning that struck him—the shaft seemed to be seeking him. I just don't . . ."

A quick knock sounded on the door. A nurse, face flushed, rushed into the office before Dr. Frohm had a chance to respond.

"He's alive!"

"What are you talking about?" Dr. Frohm asked with a quick intake of breath.

"Weston. He's not dead!"

Jan's glass slipped from her hand and shattered on the tile floor. Frohm did not stop to marvel at the news. Her professional response was cool and practical.

"Let's go." Dr. Frohm pulled a stunned Jan to her feet.

chapter 8

DAVID TAPPED ON the window of the glass-enclosed nurse's station.

"Yes?" A nurse stuck her head out the information window. "What can I do for you?"

"Any word on the condition of Jeffrey Weston? He came into the emergency room a little over three hours ago."

"Weston? Let me check." She went to a rack of charts on clipboards and studied one. She walked slowly toward David, put her hands on the counter, and said, "I'm sorry. He's dead."

David frowned and made a clucking sound. "Thanks for telling me. That's a shame."

The nurse nodded sympathetically.

"Any way I could be with Dr. Petrie?"

"I'm afraid not. Now, if you'll excuse me . . ."

"Sure."

David wondered if there was any way he could reach Jan. She had his note. There was really nothing he could do. Maybe she would talk after she got over the initial shock of Weston's death. He decided to go back to work.

On his way out of the emergency ward, he nearly collided with Dr. Deutch, who rushed headlong through the reception area. Recognizing Deutch from his snooping at Fairchild, David put out his arm to stop him. "What's your hurry?" he asked bitterly. "Weston's dead. Not that the life of one patient matters much to you or Fairchild's administration."

Paul Deutch drew himself up to his full six feet. "Have we met?" he asked the young man before him icily.

"You know my work. The name's Kennedy."

"If you'll excuse me, Mr. Kennedy." Dr. Deutch started to edge around David.

David was puzzled by Dr. Deutch's obvious urgency.

"What's the rush? I'd like to talk to you."

"I have nothing to say to you," Deutch shot back with disdain.

"Will you give Jan Petrie a message for me?"

"Mr. Kennedy," Deutch ignored his request, "I'd appreciate it if you would let me pass. If you don't leave this hospital immediately, I'll arrange to have you forcibly removed. You've caused enough trouble already."

"I was leaving on my own steam, Doctor. But I have as much right to be here as you do."

David watched him walk away. Deutch's smoothness seemed faked. He clearly was restraining himself from breaking into a run.

A buzzing crowd of nurses and attendants surrounded the stretcher on which Jeff was lying. Dr. Frohm and Jan pushed their way through the crowd to the stretcher. Jan clutched at Jeff's hand, lying still by his side. Dr. Frohm placed the ends of her stethoscope in her ears, and leaned over Jeff's chest. She lifted Jeff's eyelids and checked his pupils.

Jan stared at Jeff, still unable to believe what had

happened. His mouth started to move.

"He's trying to talk!" Jan moved to listen more closely to the indecipherable words he was rapidly whispering.

Dr. Frohm held up her hand to restrain her. "Stay out of the way." She turned to an attendant, and said, "Take him to Intensive."

"Yes, ma'am."

"Julie, you go with them," she instructed a nurse.

Just as the attendant was about to wheel Jeff up to ICU, the morgue doors swung open. Paul Deutch flew across the room and looked from Jeff to Dr. Frohm.

"He's alive," she said. For the first time since receiving the news she allowed herself to show her amazement.

"I know. What are his vitals?"

"Haven't had time yet. His heartbeat and respiration seem normal."

Deutch grabbed her stethoscope and bent over Jeff. He stopped abruptly, confusion spreading on his face. He let the stethoscope hang from his neck and put his ear next to Jeff's mouth.

Jeff's voice was barely audible, his breathing labored. But words poured out of him, tumbling automatically without expression. Dr. Deutch was having difficulty making out what he was saying. It wasn't English, of that he was certain. Without lifting his head from Jeff's mouth, he shushed everyone observing. A hush fell over the room as he listened intently.

"Me praedatum penitus iuventutis flore . . . Mors invasit funditus . . . Renascendum denuo nescio quo amore."

He could only pick up a phrase here and there, but recognition was dawning. Stunned, Paul Deutch looked up at Dr. Frohm and Jan.

"What is it, Dr. Deutch?" Jan asked.

"He's . . ." Deutch stopped himself. He looked at the nurses and attendants who were tensely waiting for him to continue. "Everybody. Get back to work. Come on. Let's go."

"What's wrong, Paul?" Jan asked again.

Paul Deutch glared at the curious faces of the crowd. "You people deaf? Move, dammit."

When the group dispersed, Jan persisted. "May I listen?"

"Give me a moment, Jan." Deutch leaned over Jeff again. Now that he had bearings, he could pick up more of what Jeff was saying. Jeff was speaking an unbroken stream. Deutch listened to him murmur, *"Regnum Dei aliter nequeo intrare . . . Hinc ut nascar denuo me humiliare . . . Ad hoc mater propria regem animavit . . . Eiusque conceptui ses acceleravit . . ."*

"Dr. Deutch . . ." Jan tugged at his sleeve, her voice desperate.

He stood up and put his arm around her. "Take it easy, Jan. I need you to be calm now and so does Jeff."

"Yes, of course." Jan regained her composure. "I'm sorry, but this has been . . ."

"Don't apologize." Deutch reassured her. "I want you to do me a favor. Stay with Jeff. He's delirious. I want you to be there to help him as he becomes less disoriented."

"Okay." There were so many questions Jan wanted to ask, but she knew Paul Deutch. When he gave orders in that firm tone, you followed them.

He turned to the attendant standing at the foot of the gurney. "Get him up to Intensive Care."

"Yes, sir."

Jan took Jeff's hand and signaled to the attendant to leave.

Drs. Frohm and Deutch watched the swinging doors close behind the gurney before they started talking.

"Come on, Paul," Dr. Frohm said. "We've seen people come back to life before. Why are you so upset?"

"Who was his doctor?"

"I was, but . . ." Deutch's face hardened critically. "Now wait a *minute*. Don't start . . ."

"I'm not."

"I did everything I could for this sort of trauma. I used shock . . ."

"Did you establish brain death?"

"Of course!" She passed the charts to him with irritation. "See."

He looked bewildered as he examined the pages. He ran his fingers along the edge of the clipboard.

"But that's not what's bothering you. What is it, Paul?"

"You wouldn't believe me if I told you."

"Try me."

Deutch held the clipboard to his chest and tapped it distractedly.

"Are you going to say something, or are you going to just stand there tapping your fingers?"

"I've never . . ." he paused.

"Out with it, Paul."

"Latin."

"What are you talking about?"

"Latin. Weston was speaking Latin."

"Paul, seriously now." As he had predicted, she didn't believe him.

"I am serious, Helen. I may be a bit rusty in some of my college subjects, but that man was speaking fluent Latin."

Helen's eyes widened. "What does this mean?"

"I'm not sure. I've heard of cases where people speak in tongues, but never like this. Weston was delivering an oration like a Roman senator."

"This is incredible!"

"I know."

"What now?"

"The only thing I can think of doing is to put a recorder in his room. If he repeats what he just did, we'll at least have something to go on . . . *if* he lives."

The storm quieted late that afternoon. The sun broke through the black clouds for a short while, but dense fog, which rolled in from the ocean, soon masked its brightness. For hours, Jan sat vigilantly next to Jeff's bed. I.V. tubes and electrode wires ran from his arms. Across the room, a male nurse watched the screens that monitored Jeff's life signs.

"Dr. Petrie, he's sleeping quietly," the nurse said. "You look as if you could use some rest. I'll wake you if there's even the slightest change."

"Thanks, Bob. You're right. I am exhausted." Jan looked fondly at Jeff before curling up in the armchair. Within minutes, she drifted to sleep.

The melancholy moan of a distant foghorn broke the stillness in the room. Jeff twitched and moved fitfully. Suddenly, the room came alive with buzzes and bleeps. Jan woke with a start. The dozing nurse snapped his head up and stared at the monitors which were going wild. The lighted blips on the screen raced furiously.

"What is it? What's wrong?" Jan asked, rubbing her eyes.

"Look at these things! There must be a malfunction."

Jan checked Jeff's pulse and listened to his heart. "He's normal."

"Look at how this pulse rate reads," Bob said, pointing at one of the screens.

Jan turned from the bed. On the screen, a thin, white light modulated erratically and moved faster and faster. A loud click startled both of them. The reel-to-reel recorder, which they had been instructed to turn on if Jeff spoke, started to revolve on its own.

Jeff's hospital bed began to rattle. Coarse tremors were shaking his body. Jan stroked his hand and called softly to him, "Jeff, can you hear me?"

His body went stiff and his eyes popped open.

"My God—what's happening?" she cried to the nurse. "Push the emergency call button over there."

Staring hypnotically at the ceiling, Jeff began to speak. The voice that filled the room was deep and grumbling.

"Die Trägheitskraft eines Körpers muß zunehmen, wenn wägbare Massen in dessen Nähe angeheuft werden."

Though Jan had only heard Jeff speak once—those terrible moments during the storm—the sound coming from his mouth astonished her.

"What's he saying?" the nurse asked.

"It sounds like German—I can't understand him."

"His voice—it's much older sounding than he looks."

"It's not his—it's someone else's."

They both stared at Jeff as he rambled on.

Ein Körper muß eine Beschleunigungskraft erfahren, wenn die ihn umgebenden Massen beschleunigt werden, und diese Kraftist in der gleichen Richtung wie die Beschleunigung . . ."

David Kennedy was staking out the Good Shepherd Hospital. No matter what line he used, he couldn't get any information about Weston or Jan. The night before, he had hung around at the hospital gates, hoping to catch Jan as she left. He gave up at 1:00 A.M. Not taking any chances, he tried to reach her at home. He was fearful that she might have slipped out of the hospital without his noticing. She could have collapsed at home and unplugged her phone.

He had driven to the address listed in the phone book. It had taken him a long time to check the mailboxes at the townhouse complex, but he finally found Jan's door. After ringing her bell repeatedly, he had to conclude she was still at the hospital.

"What the hell is going on?" he wondered as he sat in the hospital parking lot, smoking cigarette after cigarette. One thing was certain—he wasn't budging until he got to the bottom of it.

Later that morning, Paul Deutch sat behind his imposing desk at Fairchild listening to the last few seconds of a tape.

"Es ist sicher unbefriedigend, solch eine weitreichende Begrenzung ohne irgendeine physische Grundlage dafür vorrauszusetzen."

"That was Jeff?" Helen Frohm asked. She stood at the window looking out at the fog-enshrouded grounds of Fairchild State.

"No." Dr. Deutch held up another tape. "*This* is Jeff." He rewound the reel, replaced it with the second tape, and switched on the recorder to play.

"Die Voraussetzung, daß das Weltall unendlich und in Unendlichkeit euklidianisch ist, ist von einem relativistischen Standpunkt eine komplizierte Voraussetung."

Listening to the German words, Frohm pulled on her earlobe.

"I don't understand. The tapes are identical." She

crossed the room to Deutch's desk. "I've lost most of my German, but this sounds familiar."

"It is . . . it is." Deutch turned off the recorder. "I was totally baffled this morning, so I took Jeff's tape to Dr. Heinze, the head of the German Department at Berkeley, and played it for him."

"And? You should have seen his face! He grabbed the tape and we ran down to the record library there. He scrounged around in the language files for about a half hour, then surfaced with an old wire recording and played it for me." He held the first tape he had played. "*This* is a copy of the wire recording." He looked at it and shook his head.

"Well, go on, don't leave me hanging!"

"Sorry . . ." he paused. "The wire recording was a 1934 dissertation made by Albert Einstein on his theory of relativity." He pointed to the tape on the machine. "Jeff's recording is an exact duplication. Same voice, same speech . . . verbatim. But that's not all of it."

"Hold on, hold on." Helen held up her hand to stop him. "Give me a chance to react to this."

Dr. Deutch held a chart in his hands and watched her as she paced to and fro.

"Okay, I don't know what to think. I can't believe it's happening."

"Wait 'til you see this." He handed her the chart.

"Jeff's blood is O positive . . . normally, that is."

"So?"

He pointed to the chart. "Look at this. When we made the recording early this morning, it had changed. Completely. His blood was B negative."

"This is bizarre." Helen Frohm looked up slowly from the chart. "I've never heard a single case of blood type change. It's phenomenal."

"I know."

"What could cause it? What could it mean?"

"You might want to sit down for this one." Deutch gestured to a chair.

"Thanks, I'll stand. Go on."

"Do you know what Einstein's blood type was?"

Helen looked at him in amazement. "You're kidding—you're telling me . . ."

"What I'm telling you is that yesterday Jeff delivered the dissertation on the theory of relativity in Einstein's voice. And that the same day his blood type changed to match Einstein's."

"I think I will sit down after all." She lowered herself into the antique chair. She furrowed her brow. Resting her chin on her hand, she tried to evaluate the news Deutch had just told her.

"Well?"

"I'm speechless. I don't know what to make of it." She paused. "Where do we go from here?"

"*We* don't, Helen."

"But, Paul, this case is extraordinary . . ."

"Exactly, Helen. We're simply not equipped or qualified to handle such a case. What's going on with Weston is beyond the scope of Fairchild and Good Shepherd."

"Well, I beg to differ with you, Doctor. And I'd imagine many members of your staff would, too."

"Helen, be reasonable. It's time to put self-interest aside."

"I don't see why we couldn't do the preliminary workup, at least. This is a once-in-a-lifetime chance."

"I have to ask you to keep what is happening strictly confidential." Dr. Deutch tapped his palm with a brass letter opener. "So I want to explain the situation to you fully. Jeffrey Weston has already been the source of some very bad publicity for Fairchild. The Board of

Directors is up in arms about an article that appeared in *The Chronicle*."

"Weston's the painter? I didn't make the connection."

"I've determined to turn Weston over to someone else for observation for two reasons. First, and foremost," he jabbed at his blotter with the letter opener for emphasis, "regardless of your evaluations, I do not think that we are sophisticated enough to deal with Weston."

Helen Frohm tried to protest, but Deutch went on. "As the head of Fairchild, I have the authority to judge our capabilities in this case. Your concern at Good Shepherd is strictly medical. I also have the responsibility to make certain a patient gets the best care available."

"Of course. I did not mean to question your authority," Dr. Frohm said, chastised.

"Secondly, the reporter who wrote that article has been snooping around the hospital. I want as few people to know about this as possible. We cannot afford to let this story get out until we are ready to. The press would have a field day. I want to avoid that sort of sensationalism at all cost . . ."

"What about the reporter? Isn't he going to know something's up?"

"He already does, I'm sure," Dr. Deutch sighed in frustration. "But Jeffrey Weston is my immediate concern. I'm most interested in getting to the bottom of this."

"So who's going to take over?"

Dr. Deutch leaned back in his chair and made a steeple with his fingers. "Richard Vale."

"You've got to be kidding!"

"No, actually, I'm quite serious."

"You'd entrust Weston to that kook who runs the supernatural research center?" she asked in disbelief.

"That's the Metaphysical Test and Research Center."

"Same difference."

"Your prejudices are showing." Deutch wagged his finger at her. "Dr. Vale happens to be the foremost expert on parapsychology in the country, if not the world. I taught him at Harvard Medical School. He was very young and very precocious. He was without question the most brilliant student I've ever encountered."

"He may have been brilliant. But from all I've heard he's flipped his wig."

"All that's hearsay, Helen. But even if he is crackers, his Center has surpassed Duke and Stanford. He is the man to work with Weston, I've no doubt about that. I'm going to turn the whole thing over to him."

chapter 9

THE METAPHYSICAL TEST AND RESEARCH CENTER, a twenty-acre modern complex located on a lush green hillside, overlooked sprawling Los Angeles below. Sitting alone against the mountainside, isolated from the other buildings, was the Medical Theater. Inside, Dr. Richard Vale was running an important test.

The thirty by fifty-foot glass screen in the theater flickered when the houselights were dimmed. Suddenly, the screen burst into a kaleidoscope of vivid reds, purples and greens. The intricate patterns shifted in a breathtaking whirl of colors. First, the red dominated, then the green. With the next shift, the colors began to recede, slowly at first. They whirled around a vortex with increasing speed. The visual effect was magnetic —like being pulled backward down a shaft of colored lights. The screen became a huge hypno-wheel. With a flash, the colors melted and the screen turned a dull gray. Then it went blank.

"All right, terminate," a weary voice called from the rear of the four-hundred seat theater.

The houselights came up to full. Several technicians were shutting down the rows of computers that banked the sides of the screen and were lined up below. The blinking lights went off in sections and the tape discs came to a halt. Dr. Richard Vale, a compact, gray-haired man in his late forties, walked down the aisle. He gazed at some notes in his hand.

When he came to the stage steps, he shoved the notes in the pocket of his white coat. Beneath the screen, a man was lying on a reclining chair, apparently asleep. He wore a metal cap which covered his forehead and the top half of his head. Wires spaced at different points on the helmet fed into one of the computers.

Dr. Vale sat down next to the reclining chair. He took off his black-rimmed glasses and rubbed his eyes. He leaned over the sleeping man and said softly, "All right, Bob. I'm going to count to five. When I reach the number five, you will wake up, feeling alive and alert. Better than you've ever felt in your life."

He massaged his own temples as he began to count. "One, two . . . you're waking up. Three, four . . . waking up . . . and five. Open your eyes."

At five, the man's eyes blinked open. He focused on the white-coated man at his side. One of the technicians approached and carefully removed the headpiece. The man rubbed his scalp, yawned. "How'd it go, Dr. Vale?"

"Same old thing." Vale's voice was disgusted. "Everything goes smoothly until you enter Alpha state. Then we lose it."

He called to another technician, "Sid, recheck the C bank feed-in tape, will you?"

"Right." The technician rewound one of the discs.

"How'd it go for you, Bob?" Vale asked.

"Tremendous. It was like I was falling away from all these beautiful colors. Really pretty."

"Yeah, we got that much on the screen. If we could

only go beyond that damned Alpha, though."

Bob sat up in the chair. "I hate to sound stupid, Doc." He pointed to the screen. "I still don't understand how this thing works."

Vale's quick, perceptive eyes lit up. There was nothing he loved to do more than to talk about his Laser Projector, the project that had consumed him for the past twenty years.

By the time he had reached his mid-twenties, Richard Vale had risen to the top of his field in neurophysiology. In fact, his research on enkaphalins and endorphins came close to winning him a Nobel Prize. He had been beaten out by a Belgian scientist who made the breakthrough before him and took the prize.

To his dismay, his colleagues in the medical establishment were made gleeful by his loss. He had been so absorbed by his work that he had been blind to the envy and competitiveness that smoldered in the scientific community. The realization made him set himself apart from his colleagues even more.

His research about how the brain works gave him an increasingly mystical sense of its capacity. No longer willing to be restricted by the formality and etiquette of the research community, he had single-handedly struggled to create the Metaphysical Test and Research Center. The core of his vision was the Laser Projector, but the Center was involved in countless experiments and projects to ensure government funding.

Fortunately for Richard Vale, when he was ready to launch into a new field, the government got wind of Russian advances in parapsychology. The threat of psychic warfare freed up Defense funds . . . figures that otherwise would never have been available for psychic research. Once again, Richard Vale found himself at the forefront of research, a pioneer in a newly important field. He was indifferent to the criticism of the medical establishment. The only thing that mattered to him was having the funds and the freedom to develop his Laser Projector.

He began to explain that project, his obsession, to Bob.

"Everything your mind experiences—consciously or unconsciously, can be monitored in neuroelectrical impulses."

"You've lost me already."

"Sorry." Vale leaned back in the chair and crossed his legs. "In the simplest terms, brain waves. The electrode cap you just wore during hypnosis transmitted your brain waves to the computer and ran them through a digital decoder, which converted them into two-dimensional images. Everything you just saw in your own mind was projected on that screen."

"Like a movie of my thoughts." Bob tried to bring the scientific jargon to the level of his own experience.

"In a sense, yes."

"Jesus." Bob laughed. "I'm glad I wasn't hooked up to that thing last night. My date would've been shocked."

Vale chuckled.

"I still don't understand *why* you're doing all this. I mean, isn't it kind of expensive just to . . ."

"Do you have any idea," Vale cut in hotly, "how much money the government spends on space research and exploration every year?" His eyes bored into Bob. "Billions. Everybody's so damned busy looking out *there* for answers, they've forgotten about answers that may lie hidden in the mind."

"You've got a point."

"Damned right I do." Vale stood and began to pace. "Did you know that we use only three to five percent of our brains?"

"Really?"

"Really! Three to five percent. What about the other ninety-five? What are we doing with it? Why is it there? Does it hold secrets, truths . . . or is it just dormant and purposeless? When we get the Laser Projector functioning, we'll finally know the answers to those questions."

Bob shifted uncomfortably in his seat as he watched Vale grow more and more excited about his obsession.

"To actually observe a person's thoughts, his dreams, his visions . . . his forgotten memories. To delve into the depths of a man's subconscious. And perhaps . . . even beyond. What will we find there? Is there a collective . . ." Vale didn't complete the sentence. One look at Bob made him aware that he was getting carried away, that he was touching on things that would only confuse a layman. "Anyway, *that's* the point of all this."

"Whew, sounds kind of frightening."

"Bob, it's not frightening. Discovering the key to our minds is the ultimate challenge. It's thrilling."

"Yes, I can see that." Bob smiled at Vale, clearly wanting to leave. "Need me anymore?"

"No. We'll wrap it up for today. See you next week."

"Till next week, then." Bob grabbed his jacket and left the theater.

Vale remained on the stage and looked up at the screen. Buried in thought, he rubbed the bridge of his nose. After a few minutes, he shrugged and sighed. On his way out of the theater, he called to the staff, "Nice work today. Shut everything down."

Shading his eyes from the brightness of the Los Angeles sun, he surveyed the Center from the door of the theater. From his vantage point, he could see the buildings of downtown L.A. thrust into the azure sky some twenty miles away. He set off along the white gravel path to the main building of the Center, a two-story, strikingly stark modern structure, surrounded by smaller buildings which housed various laboratories.

"Better check out today's testing," he muttered to himself, his feet crunching on the gravel.

Inside the main building, he moved down a corridor with windowed rooms on each side. He stopped to observe the activities in some of the rooms. In one, a very attractive woman in an elegant suit was lying on a reclining chair. Wires were attached to her hands and arms, which led to a machine that charted her responses on a graph. Two doctors sat across the room from her, watching her intently. A technician stood nearby filming the experiment with a fifteen-millimeter camera.

Vale quietly entered the room and stood behind the doctors.

"How are Mrs. Amburn's readings today?" he whispered, not wanting to disturb the subject.

"She's having trouble going into a deep enough trance. We've tested her at this level before." The doctor showed Vale the figures and charts. "It's difficult for her to reproduce the trances we've witnessed outside in an experimental situation."

"Well, keep on trying," Vale said, and tiptoed out of the room.

These experiments in parapsychology were rudimentary, but every breakthrough in E.S.P. research or whatever the specific field, created a climate for the acceptance of his Laser Projector. Their research explained and documented the psychic phenomena that had mystified and fascinated people for centuries. In true scientific spirit, the researchers at the Center were trying to get to the physical root of such phenomena.

Vale hesitated at the door of another room. He watched a young doctor hold different colored objects in his hand. Sitting across the table, which was divided by a metal screen, was a blindfolded man.

Vale entered the room.

"Good afternoon, Mr. Chase. Excuse the interruption."

"No bother. I could use the rest."

"Are you getting anything?" Vale asked the doctor.

The doctor turned nervously. "Mr. Chase is reading the shapes, but the colors are hit or miss. I read a monograph about Russian research—maybe we should try having him hold the objects for color."

"Interesting. It's been done a lot in the U.S., too—at Duke and Stanford, but I'd like to read the paper. Give me a copy, okay?"

"Will do." The young doctor was pleased with himself.

"Mr. Chase—we are grateful for your time."

"It's nothing. I enjoy coming here. I'd like to develop my sixth sense."

Vale laughed. "Well, we'll see what we can do for you."

Back in the corridor, he decided to shorten his rounds and return to his office. He wanted to tackle the problem with the C bank feed while he could still decipher his scribbled notes.

Not long after he had spread out sheets of figures and several thick computer manuals, his secretary stuck her head in the door. "Paul Deutch at Fairchild is on the phone. Do you want to speak to him?"

"Sure." As he looked once more at the papers spread

before him, Vale lifted the receiver and cradled it between his ear and his shoulder.

"Hi, Paul. It's been an age." He drew a circle around a set of figures on a computer printout. . . . "Not too good. I'm so close to getting this Laser Projector functioning—it's frustrating. How've you been?" Vale flipped through one of the manuals and studied a graph.

"Uh-huh." He grimaced and chewed on the end of his pencil.

"Wait a minute. Say that again. I mean—take it from the top." He dropped the pencil and grabbed the receiver with both hands.

"Incredible!" Leaning forward in his chair, he nodded his head. "I've never heard of anything like it."

"Would I? Are you kidding? That's like asking me if I'd accept the Nobel Peace Prize." A grin spread across his face.

"Is he in any condition to be moved?"

Vale frowned. "That's tough. It would be a crime if he died before we could test him. Under these circumstances, I'd recommend taking the risk. Get him down here as soon as you possibly can. We'll be ready for you . . . Uh-huh. Okay. Thanks, Paul. Keep me posted."

Dr. Vale hung up and whistled softly. He pounded his fist into his palm and called his secretary.

"Judy, call a meeting for senior staff members tomorrow morning. It's urgent."

At Fairchild State, Dr. Deutch had just hung up the phone. Dr. Frohm, who had been listening to Deutch's end of the conversation, looked at him expectantly. "What did Vale say?"

"He said he's never heard of a case like this before. And if he hasn't, nobody else has. He was very excited.

Wants Jeff down there as soon as possible."

"But Paul, he's in no condition to be moved. I had no idea that was your intention."

"It's a risk we have to take. What if he dies here before Vale can examine him?"

"Wait a minute. I thought I was responsible for his medical care. Moving Jeff now would be very risky. Can't Vale come here?"

"Vale has millions of dollars of sophisticated equipment—not to mention his staff—at the Center." Deutch was firm. "We'll have to get Jeff to L.A."

"I don't like it, but the research *is* important," Dr. Frohm said with resignation. "What about Jan? She's not going to sit still while Jeff is carted off to Los Angeles."

"As things stand right now, she'll be able to go with him."

"What about her job here?"

"Ex-job." Deutch handed Frohm a sheet of paper. "When she failed to show up for the Review Board . . ."

"But Paul," Helen protested, "that was an emergency."

"I know," he pointed at the paper, "but that's their final recommendation. I tried, Helen."

"Does she know yet?"

"No. I thought I'd wait for things to calm down a little before breaking the news."

"I'm glad I don't have to do it. Between moving Jeff and losing her job, you're going to have one furious lady on your hands."

"Yeah," Deutch held his head in his hands, "I know."

chapter 10

"NOW YOU UNDERSTAND why I pulled you away from Jeff," Paul Deutch said to Jan. "I had to explain."

"German? Einstein?" Jan's face showed the stress of the past day. There were dark circles under her eyes and she had pulled back her unruly hair with a rubber band. "I . . . it's . . ."

"I know." Deutch put his arm around her and patted her shoulder. "Dr. Frohm and I don't know what to make of it either. We've never seen anything like it. I don't know what the hell's going on here, Jan, but one thing is certain. That lightning changed Jeff—transformed him into someone or something else."

Jan turned to face him on the sofa. "The only thing that matters to me is that he lives. What are his chances?"

"All we can do is hope," Deutch said softly. He cleared his throat and tapped his foot nervously. "Jan, this case is so unusual that we've decided Jeff should be in the hands of a specialist."

"Of course, he should have the best there is."

"Do you know the work of Dr. Richard Vale?"

"Vale?" Jan's eyebrows shot up. "You mean the guy who does the ESP research?"

"Yes. We want him to study Jeff."

"But . . ." Jan looked at Deutch suspiciously. "But we need someone to keep Jeff alive."

"Vale has a complete staff of physicians at the Center. What's happening in this case has to be observed and documented." He saw Jan's green eyes spark in anger. "Nothing like this has ever happened before, Jan. For the sake of scientific . . ."

"Jeff is only a case to you—to all of you," Jan blurted out. "You'd sacrifice him for research, wouldn't you?"

"Jan, we've decided to move him to the Metaphysical Test and Research Center in L.A."

"He'll die." Jan clenched her fists. "He's too weak. He'll never make it."

Jan's accusations hit home. "We can't wait for him to regain strength." Paul Deutch struggled with his own doubts as he went on. "I've confided in you—I've told you everything that's going on because I want you to understand why we're taking the risk. I know how you feel about Jeff. But you have to step back—to distance yourself . . ."

"Step back and help you kill him, you mean."

"When I described the case to Dr. Vale . . ."

"Dr. Vale—the case—Paul, we're talking about a life, about Jeff's life, it was given back to him—please, please," Jan implored, "let him keep it."

Deutch stood up. The direction of the conversation made him uncomfortable. He was torn enough as it was without having to confront in Jan the arguments that raged within himself.

"Look, Jan, the decision is made. I want you to go with him. Jeff needs you."

"I won't." Jan stood to face him. "I refuse to watch

him tested like a guinea pig in his condition."

"You have to cooperate. He'll never make it without you."

"I can't go along with this." Jan was determined to resist helping in Jeff's destruction. "It's your decision—he's your responsibility."

Deutch propped himself against Helen Frohm's desk. "You make it so difficult—do you think this is easy for me?"

Jan studied her mentor. He, too, showed the signs of stress. His body seemed to sag under the weight of his decision. Added lines showed on his craggy face. Instead of the dignified and vital person she was accustomed to dealing with, he looked old and tired.

"Oh, Paul," she said, compassion softening her voice, "I know how you must feel . . ." She caught herself from slipping into feeling sorry for him. "But you've made a bad decision . . . we *can* wait. I'll go with him when he's stronger."

Deutch fingered a deep gouge on the edge of the old wood desk, and sighed. "I told you, we can't wait. And if you stay behind, you're out of work."

"What?" Jan looked at him, puzzled.

"The Review Board, remember?"

Jan gulped. She had completely forgotten about the hearing.

"When you didn't appear . . ."

"That's insane . . . surely . . ." Jan began to protest, but stopped. "At this point, I don't care."

"Maybe, maybe if you go with Jeff . . ."

"Don't try to bribe me, Paul. It's beneath you."

Deutch knew she was right. It was a cheap shot. He knew the only way to sway her was through Jeff's need.

"Jeff is going to L.A., whether you like it or not."

He hated being so tough with her; she had been through so many emotional upheavals in the past days. "If you aren't there, he'll be frantic. Can you do that to him, Jan? Can you stay away?"

Jan fell into the sofa's cushions. "I have no choice, do I?"

"Yes, Jan, you have a choice. It's not unlike the one I just faced."

"You know I'll go with him. But it's going to be the most painful thing I've ever done." Jan's voice wavered. "Paul, I'd like to talk to you about Jeff—I mean about our conversation the other day."

"You mean about your feelings for him?" Paul Deutch sat down next to her on the sofa.

"Yes, about our relationship." Jan tugged at a strand of hair that had escaped her elastic. She hesitated. If Dr. Deutch was capable of making a decision that could kill Jeff, should she confide in him? But given the circumstances, he was the only sympathetic listener available and she needed the release that this conversation would give her. "I've been thinking about it ever since we spoke. But when I thought Jeff was dead, I felt as if a part of me was gone. It crystalized everything. I felt empty, bereft."

"Naturally . . ." Deutch put his arm around her.

"The connection I have with him goes deeper than what a therapeutic relationship should be, Paul. I can recognize that, but I don't understand it."

Deutch didn't say anything. He waited for her to go on.

"There's nothing physical about it—at least, I don't think so. Though being with him has a physical effect on me."

"What sort of effect?"

"I feel excited, sort of charged, but not in a sexual way."

Deutch nodded.

"The best I can come up with is the notion that my maternal instinct is surfacing. That the attachment I feel with him has to do with protecting him. But I also know that I'm dependent on him." Jan massaged her temples. "I'm so tired and confused. I don't know what to think. I love him—fiercely. He can't die. I don't know what I'd do."

There was a knock at the door. Deutch stood and straightened his tie.

"Come in."

An attendant entered and handed Deutch a cassette.

"Dr. Frohm sent me up with this."

"What is it?"

"Jeff Weston's latest. Sounds like algebra. Just a bunch of letters and numbers, then a few seconds of," the attendant stopped, searching for the right word, "well, beeps. Kind of electronic sounding. They go real fast for about ten seconds, then repeat."

"Any changes in Weston?"

"No."

"How is he?" Jan asked.

"Sleeping like a baby." The attendant smiled at her.

"That'll be all, thank you." Deutch dismissed him.

"More Einstein?" Jan asked.

"Nothing would surprise me." Deutch held up the tape. "Just look at this, Jan. Who knows what it means? I know this is asking a lot of you, but can't you step back and look at what's going on here from a different perspective? If this were happening to anyone but Jeff, wouldn't you be in the front lines, pushing for research?"

"That question is academic. It's Jeff who's the guinea pig." Jan bit her lip. "I can't see it any other way. I'd also like to believe," she continued, unable to resist the barb, "that I'd never allow scientific inquiry to take precedence over a human life."

"Touché." Dr. Deutch sighed. "Why don't you go to Jeff?"

"Sorry," Jan squeezed Deutch's hand, "but it's how I feel. I'll go to L.A. because I have no choice. When do we leave?"

"Don't know yet. Why don't you make a list of what you need and I'll send someone to your house to pack. You should stay with Jeff."

"Will do," she agreed without enthusiasm.

Jan picked up her purse from the sofa and left the office. As she walked down the corridor, she searched through her bag to find a tube of chapstick. Her lips were dry and sore from the accumulated tension. While shuffling through the contents of her purse, she came across Kennedy's note. She took out the crumpled paper and read his message again. Forgetting about the chapstick, she headed for the pay phone at the end of the hall.

Though she wasn't at all certain she could trust David Kennedy, she had no idea whom she could trust anymore. Kennedy *had* given her the right tactic for the Review Board. And Dr. Deutch had betrayed her. An alarm had gone off inside her when he had warned that the trip was to be kept secret. She didn't like the sound of that at all. No amount of kindness toward her could ever compensate for his decision to move Jeff to Los Angeles before he gained strength. And wanting to cover it up—well, she would see about that.

• • •

Paul Deutch pushed the stop button on the tape recorder on Helen Frohm's desk. The room was oddly still after the intense electronic bleeps had ceased.

"What do you think?"

"Sounds like calculus—then, is it Morse code?" Frohm answered his question with another.

"Don't know. Understand any of the mathematics?"

"Are you kidding? After his first three equations he might as well have been speaking Chinese." Frohm perched, birdlike, on the arm of the couch.

"Well, I've jotted down a few of the early formulae —the ones at the end of the tape were far beyond my mathematical knowledge. Care to have a look?"

Dr. Frohm reached for the paper he extended and studied what was before her:

$$(\bar{E}_1/m) = \frac{1}{1 - \cos/_1 (1 + 2m/T)}$$

$$(\bar{E}_1/m)_{max} \approx (\bar{E}_1/m)_{min} \approx 1 \qquad \text{Small T}$$

The entire page was covered with similar formulae.

"What *is* this?" She dropped the paper back on her desk as if it were hot.

"I called over to Berkeley again. I spoke with someone in the math department who said the mumbo jumbo was physics—spacetime physics."

"Well—it fits in with Einstein."

"The beginning stuff does."

"So you called the physics department . . ."

"Right. I played the tape, since I certainly couldn't read one of the equations. Do you know what Weston did here?" He picked up the page.

"I can't begin to imagine."

"This is the test for positron-electron annihilation!"

"Sorry to say, it means nothing to me."

"Cheer up. Even after an explanation I still don't understand it."

"What about the end of the tape?"

"The physicist was fascinated. He had Jim Taylor, the head of the department, call me back. It turns out the later formulae are highly experimental and quite revolutionary. He declined to tell me more about the theory, but suggested I call Dr. Carl Heller of the National Science Foundation in Washington, D.C."

"National Science Foundation?" Dr. Frohm raised her eyebrows. "Sounds like we have one hot potato. Have you called?"

"Not yet."

"Do you think we should involve anyone else yet? Vale is bad enough. If the government gets wind of this . . ."

"Heller's all right."

"You know him?"

"Our paths crossed at Harvard, too. Years ago."

"Ah—the world of eminent men is a small one," Dr. Frohm teased. "Listening to you, I'd think everybody who's anybody went to or taught at Harvard."

"Well, haven't they?" Deutch chuckled, playing on her West Coast resentment of the Ivy League. "Heller and I both received fellowships and kept meeting at unendurable sherry parties. You can't believe the bonds you can form under fire!" He walked behind the desk. "Mind if I use your phone?"

"Go right ahead." Dr. Frohm rewound the tape as he punched out the number on her push-button phone.

Carl Heller was darkly handsome in a disheveled way.

The collar of his striped shirt was frayed, the sleeves rolled up. There wasn't a touch of gray in his shining black hair. He had a burly, bearlike quality. He sat at a desk piled high with scientific journals and reports.

He stubbed out a cigarette in an ashtray already overflowing with butts and gum wrappers, and flipped through the pages of a thick volume, then glanced up at a large blackboard covered with scientific notations. Still staring at the blackboard, he reached blindly into the bottom drawer of his desk and fished out a can of beer.

When he pulled the pop top, warm beer fizzed over the sides and dripped on the floor. Heller bent to suck at the foam and threw the pop top carelessly in the direction of the nearest ashtray. He took a long drink of beer. As he was wiping the floor with the front page of the *Post*, his intercom buzzed. He picked up the phone. "Yeah?"

"A Doctor Deutch is on line three."

"Deutch?"

"Yes, sir. Long distance from California."

Recognition lit his features. "Hell, yes. Put him on."

Excited, he picked up the phone. "That you, Paul?" Had any of those little sandwiches with the crusts cut off lately? How the hell are you? It's been years!"

"Fine, fine." Dr. Deutch laughed heartily. "Listen, Carl. I've got sort of a problem out here."

"You, too, eh? What is it?"

"It's hard to explain. We've had a strange thing happen here the last couple of days. I'd like you to listen to a tape. It may not mean anything, but . . ."

"Shoot." Heller drained his beer. He took a piece of gum from one of the packs strewn over the desk and popped it in his mouth. After a few moments of listening, he stopped chewing and sat upright in his chair. His bushy eyebrows came together in a worried look. He stood up and paced sternly in front of the blackboard.

"Well, Carl?" Deutch's voice came over the phone.

"Where'd you get that tape?" Heller demanded.

"I know this sounds ridiculous, but it's a recording of a retarded, thirty-three-year-old man."

"Come off it, Paul." Heller's voice was cold. "Who the hell are you trying to kid? What the hell's going on?"

"I'm serious, Carl. Why are you so upset? Does it mean anything?"

"Mean anything?" Heller was incredulous. "Christ, only three men in the world know what's on that tape. Me and my two associates. So tell me the truth."

"This *is* the truth, Carl," Deutch insisted. "He's in intensive care at Good Shepherd."

"Listen to me. Lock that tape in your safe . . . right now." Heller was emphatic. "Don't let anybody near it—anybody! Don't even mention this conversation to anyone. Do you understand?"

"Yes, but . . ."

"I'll fly out the first thing in the morning. Goodbye."

"Wait a minute, Carl. I'll do what you say, but why are you so upset? What does it mean?"

"Sorry, Paul. Look, I'll see you tomorrow."

"Hold on. Don't cut me off like this."

Heller rubbed his eyes. "I'm sorry for being so gruff. You'll just have to trust me. I can't talk about it now. I'll be out there in the morning. You said Good Shepherd, right?"

"Right."

Heller slammed the phone back on the receiver. He

picked up the empty beer can and crushed it in his powerful grip. He stared at the blackboard, then erased the bottom row of figures with his hand and he scribbled a new equation, studied it a moment and whispered, "Jesus."

He crossed to his desk and pushed the intercom button.

"Yes, sir?"

"Get me the President."

His secretary hesitated. "Of . . . the United States?"

"Yes, and hurry."

chapter 11

A LIMOUSINE PULLED up in front of the steps of Good Shepherd Hospital. Carl Heller, looking rumpled from his transcontinental flight, emerged from the back seat. Two men got out of the car after him, one with curly hair going to gray, the other with black slicked-back hair. As the three started up the steps, two men in dark suits approached them. Four more severely dressed men materialized behind the first two.

Heller observed the black-suited batallion and glowered. "What the hell's going on here?"

"I.D., please," one of the men demanded, his voice cold and indifferent.

"What?" Heller was annoyed.

"Have you been cleared?"

"Cleared? What are you talking about?" He turned to his colleagues. "Move it," Heller demanded and started to walk past the two men.

One grabbed his arm and said with a deadly calm, "Orders."

"Whose orders? Who the hell's in charge here?"

"Phil Kellog. I.D., please."

"Well, you listen to me, buster," Heller barked. "You tell your boss to get his fat butt out here right now."

Before the guard could answer, a tall, lean man with a blond crewcut stepped out of the building with three men at his side. He marched down the steps, ramrod straight. He clenched his teeth, and peered down at Heller and his colleagues. Finally he said, "Phil Kellog. What's the problem?"

"The problem is," Heller punched out his words, "I *specifically* requested a low profile on this operation. Just a couple of men for light security. Not the whole goddamned CIA."

Kellog ignored Heller's outburst. "Who are you?" he asked.

"Heller." Gesturing to the men beside him, he said, "These are my associates, Greenwald and Sinopoli."

Kellog pulled a black notebook from his pocket and flipped through it. "Oh, the physicists."

"Yeah, the physicists." His tone was sarcastic. "Now, get these goons out of here," Heller demanded.

Kellog handed him some papers. "Sorry, pal. As of 0400 hours, this baby is in our hands. Presidential orders."

Heller glanced at the passes and angrily thrust them at his colleagues.

"Where's Deutch?"

"Deutch?"

"Dr. Deutch!" he barked. "The head of Fairchild. The guy who's running this show."

"Follow me."

"Any messages, Debbie?" David Kennedy asked the girl in the city room.

"Yeah, one. Jan somebody called. I left a message on your typewriter. She sounded very upset."

"What'd she say?" David asked anxiously. He was

surprised to have heard from her. "Where is she?"

"She said she was going to L.A. with Jeff." She stopped when she saw David's bewildered expression. "Oh, I'm sorry . . . girlfriend problems?"

"*Debbie* . . ." he said with a threat in his voice.

"Said they were going to some metaphysical research center . . . didn't know when. That's all."

David raced to his desk, leaving Debbie staring after him. He grabbed the note and kept rereading it, half expecting an explanation to surface. The last time they had met she had been furious at him. It didn't take any great intelligence to realize there was trouble and that she must really be alone if she was turning to him.

He burst into Pete Richardson's office. "Pete . . ."

Richardson swiveled his chair around to face David. He held a phone in one hand and gestured to David with the other to hold off. "Okay, okay . . . we'll get right on it. Talk to you later." He clunked the receiver back on the phone and looked up irritably. "Ever heard of knocking?"

"Sorry, but," David waved the paper, "I can't believe it. Weston . . ."

"The retard from Fairchild? The one that died?"

"Right. I got this call from his therapist. It sounds as if he's alive."

"Come on, Kennedy. I think you've milked this story enough."

"All I know is I have this phone message that she's going to L.A. with him."

Richardson looked at him skeptically.

"Something's going on. Jan's still at the hospital. Deutch from Fairchild is practically living there. Everyone has hushed up about Weston." David paced back and forth in front of his boss's desk. "And now I hear they're going to some metaphysical research center in L.A."

David stopped his pacing. "I told you there was something freaky about Weston from the start—when I saw those paintings."

"So what do you propose?"

"I'd like to check things out at Good Shepherd and then go down to L.A."

"You don't think this is a wild-goose chase?"

"Who knows? But if Weston *is* alive . . ." David put both hands on the desk and leaned forward.

"Okay. Follow it up. Call in to let me know what's happening."

David beamed. "Thanks, Pete. You won't regret this."

Richardson rubbed the back of his neck and shook his head as David tore out of his office.

In the intensive care unit, Jeff tossed in his bed, thrashing against the straps that restrained him. When he woke, he looked around the unfamiliar room. He saw two men standing motionless on either side of the door, and whimpered in fright, "Dr. Petrie, Dr. Petrie."

Jeff sat up and peered into the dim light. "Dr. Petrie," he called.

"Hey, quiet down," one of the men said gruffly.

Jeff stared at him wide-eyed. "Dr. Petrie!" he screamed.

The door opened up and another man entered the room. "What's up?"

"He's asking for Dr. Petrie."

"I'll take care of it." The man shut the door behind him and crossed to the bed. He put a hand on Jeff's shoulder and tried to shove him back down.

"Hey, pal. It's three in the morning. Go back to sleep like a good boy."

Jeff clutched the man's forearm and threw the restraining hand off. "No. I want to see Dr. Petrie." His eyes bored into the square-jawed stranger in the black suit.

"You can't see her."

"Why not?" Jeff asked softly.

"Because she's not here."

A patient smile spread across Jeff's chiseled features. "I'll find her." Jeff swung his legs off the bed and started detaching himself from the equipment. A guard rushed from the door to try to hold him down. Towering over him, Jeff swept him aside.

The other man at the bedside called to the agent at the door, "Get the doctor down here, as soon as possible." As he hurried out of the room, the two men snatched Jeff's arms and tried to force him back on the bed.

"You listen to me, King Kong. You get your ass back on that bed, or I'll put it back."

Jeff was rock steady. The two men couldn't budge him. "No!"

"I mean it, dammit!" The men doubled their efforts, pushing at Jeff.

A doctor entered, accompanied by three more men. "All right . . . let him go."

The two agents stopped their shoving and moved away from Jeff. He let his arms drop to his sides as he warily watched the smiling doctor approach.

"What's wrong, Jeff?" he asked, as if talking to a child.

"I want to see Dr. Petrie."

"Tell you what. You get back in bed, and I'll have her come right down. How's that?"

Jeff was still suspicious. "When?"

"Just as soon as you're back under the covers."

"Okay." With a look of relief on his face, Jeff lay down on the bed. The doctor nodded to the two agents who positioned themselves on opposite sides of the bed. An orderly, carrying a tray, entered the room. "Dr. Petrie?" Jeff asked, straining to see if she had arrived.

The doctor took a hypodermic needle from the tray. "No. She'll be here in a minute, Jeff. Relax."

Seeing the hypodermic needle in the doctor's hand, Jeff frowned and started to sit up. The men on either side of the bed restrained him as the doctor brought the needle toward Jeff's arm.

"No!" Jeff exploded. He threw the men off him. His arm swung wildly and smashed the doctor's face. The force of the inadvertent blow hurled the doctor across the room. Jeff jumped off the bed and ran toward the door, pulling equipment down with a crash. The two burly agents pursued him. One man threw himself at Jeff's knees and tackled him.

Another agent ran into the room. "Holy shit. What's going on?"

"Shut up and help!" snapped the doctor, nursing a bloody nose.

"He is *not* violent!" Jan shouted.

Kellog sat at the desk in his temporary headquarters. "What the hell do you call that?" he asked, pointing to the men who had scuffled with Jeff.

Jan's lips formed a tight line as she looked at the men on the sofa. One agent had his head wrapped, another had a severely bruised face, and a third wore a cast on his arm. The doctor, scowling at Jan, had a broken nose.

"He only wanted to see me." Jan was too angry to apologize, even though she hated to see anyone injured for any reason. "Was that so much to ask? He was probably frightened and disoriented and you lied to him."

"Look, sweetheart . . ."

"Dr. Petrie to you, mister."

"All right, Dr. Petrie. The fact is . . ."

Jan wouldn't let Kellog complete a sentence. She turned to the doctor. "You can't keep him drugged like this forever."

"We don't intend to. Just until . . ."

"He's not an animal, for God's sake," she screamed.

"That's a matter of opinion," the doctor shot back.

"That's enough, Doctor!" Kellog intervened. "And you, Dr. Petrie, calm down."

"I won't calm down until you leave him alone."

"Look, we're not talking about a simple case of one retarded man." Kellog was unflappable. "We're dealing with a situation that concerns international security."

"He still has rights!"

"We determine what those rights are, Dr. Petrie."

"This is a nightmare!" Jan covered her eyes. "What's happening to everybody?"

"We've got orders," Kellog said flatly.

Jan was seething. "I'll go over your heads then." She knew full well that her threat was meaningless.

"Go where you will, Dr. Petrie," Kellog said wearily. "Until Weston's case is cleared, he's under our supervision."

"Well, *I'm* not under your supervision!"

"Everybody *here* is under our supervision, lady, so get off your Joan of Arc routine. This conversation is a waste of time." Kellog leaned back in his chair. "Look, let's make a deal."

"I don't make deals."

"Listen to me . . ." He slapped his hand on the desk. "I'll allow you to visit Jeff as often as you like—unlimited access. You can even travel by his side to L.A. How's that?"

Jan narrowed her eyes. "Why?"

"Obviously, you're the only person who can control him. We can't afford a repeat of what happened earlier. Just remember, if you're calm, he's calm. I don't want you throwing hysterics around him."

"Why would I want to upset him?"

"Maybe just to make my life difficult." His voice grew stern. "If for any reason whatsoever you interfere with procedures, that's it."

Jan glared at him.

"You'll never see that pretty-boy face or touch that well-developed body again." The injured agents snickered at Kellog's innuendo.

His words struck home in a way Jan didn't want to acknowledge. Her face flushed at his remarks. She wanted to strike him.

"You're despicable. I swear, if you do anything more to harm him . . . I'm not so helpless, you know. There's a certain . . ." She caught herself before exposing too much. The last thing she wanted Kellog to know was that she was the source of a leak, that a reporter knew what was going on. Her secret filled her with smug satisfaction.

"A certain what, Dr. Petrie?" Kellog said with a smirk. "Don't make threats."

Jan burned a look through him, turned on her heel, and headed for the door. Kellog picked up a fat cigar and bit off the end.

"I put that bitch in her place," he said, then dismissed the men with a nod.

He pushed the intercom button on the desk. A man's voice answered, "Yes, sir?"

"Put two men on Dr. Petrie. If she makes waves, lock her up."

"How many more times are you going to listen to that?" Paul Deutch restlessly paced the length of the conference room.

Heller and his two associates, Frank Greenwald and Jim Sinopoli, sat at the conference table. All three men were listening through earphones to a cassette tape recording. Heller pushed the stop button and took off his headset. Sinopoli and Greenwald did the same. They looked at each other in amazement. At the far end of the table, Kellog stomped out his cigar in a glass ash-tray. The guard at the door turned his head slightly to hear better.

"We're through for now, Paul." Heller and his colleagues got up from their chairs and started to leave.

"Wait a minute." Deutch was angry. "What's the reason for all this?" His eyes flicked in Kellog's direction but returned to Heller's downcast face. "I want some answers. This entire hospital has been disrupted. I have some explaining to do."

Heller didn't look up.

"Come on, Carl, tell me *something*."

Kellog cleared his throat to attract Heller's attention. He shot him a warning look, then nodded. Heller walked the length of the conference room to Deutch and put his arm around his shoulder.

"Paul," he nearly whispered, "that guy upstairs put together, in less than a minute, a nuclear device formula so complicated it took the three of us five years to work it out."

"That's it? All this melodrama for that?" Deutch was irritable. "That formula is Greek to all of us. Come on, Carl, stop treating me like some innocent child. Tell me the truth, dammit."

"That is the truth, Paul."

"All of it?" Deutch pressed.

"I'm sorry, Paul." Heller glanced at Kellog. "I can't give you that at this time."

"Well, give me something."

"Look, Paul." Heller paused. "I'm as sorry about this intrusion as you are. These agents are a pain in the ass. The only thing I can tell you right now is this. There's a ten-second portion on that tape that we don't understand. An electronic signal of some kind. It may be a code—we don't know yet. It might take us weeks to decipher . . . if we can decipher it."

"Carl, it might not mean anything at all."

"That's possible, Paul. But for national security reasons we can't take that chance."

"But . . ."

"Wait a minute, Paul. Let me finish. Weston has *already* equated a top-secret formula . . . how, why, from where we don't know." Kellog started to move toward them. "If that ten-second portion, those signals, do mean something, it's our responsibility to make sure that . . ."

"Look, Doctor," Kellog interrupted. "The simple fact is Weston knows too much. He's got to be watched. That's as simple as you can get."

"All right, play your games." Resignation sounded in Deutch's voice. "But I won't allow you to turn this hospital upside down."

"As of 0400," Kellog reminded with offensive authority, "it's under federal jurisdiction."

Paul Deutch looked at Kellog with distaste and headed for the door.

"Oh, and Doctor?" Kellog called after him.

"What?"

"Clear out the east wing—have everyone transferred. Our doctors will stay with Weston."

"But there aren't enough beds."

"That's an order, Doctor."

Deutch ignored the CIA man. He turned to Heller and said bitterly, "Thanks, Carl." He slammed the door as he left the conference room.

Heller stood immobile for a few moments, then resolutely pulled his attaché case from under the table. He worked the combination lock and removed several dog-eared folders, which he spread out on the table. Greenwald and Sinopoli followed suit. He looked over his shoulder at the agent by the door. "Get some food and a few gallons of coffee up here."

"Yes, sir."

Heller rewound the tape.

"What about the Research Center?" Kellog asked. "We still going to ship him down there?"

Heller nodded as he arranged papers in front of him.

"I'll arrange transportation."

"Oh." Heller looked up from his papers. "Tell Vale to keep it quiet, all right? No media coverage. Let's at least try to do something right."

Kellog squared his shoulders. "You're forgetting who's giving the orders around here."

"You're forgetting who understands the tape, pal. You better leave now. We have work to do."

"Can you find a quiet place at the Center for Heller and his boys to set up shop?" Kellog asked the agent who was the liaison with the skeletal force waiting for them in Los Angeles.

"The old radioactive materials lab," Davis replied.

"Isolated?"

"Yeah." The agent pointed to the location on a map spread out on Kellog's desk. "It's a separate building —at the far end of the center."

"Good." Kellog tapped the map. "When they get there, seal them off. That goes for everybody in the complex. Full security. Nobody leaves that place until those geniuses figure out that tape."

"Right. Who else is coming from here?"

"The fewer people the better. I've scratched Deutch. There's no reason for that old codger to go at all." Kellog darkened the line through Paul Deutch's name. "I wish to hell we could dump that Jan Petrie. She's trouble with a capital T."

"Why can't you?"

"Wonder Boy has already busted up a doctor and some of our boys. She's the only one who can get him to coöperate. She goes. But I know in my gut that she's up to something."

"Dumb broad wouldn't dare."

"If she gives us a hard time, we'll take care of her." Kellog circled her name. "I'll tell you one thing. I'll feel a lot better once we get him out of here. Things will be easier at the Research Center.

"See you in L.A." Kellog dismissed him. Davis, however, was reluctant to leave. "Well?" Kellog looked up from the papers he had begun to read.

"I was wondering, boss," Davis asked nervously, "what you think about all this?"

"I'm not paid to think about it. Our job is to keep this quiet—no leaks."

"But I don't get it—Weston doesn't seem dangerous. How could he have come up with that formula?"

"All that matters is that he did. He can't be allowed to blabber top-secret information."

"Something tells me that this is just the beginning."

Kellog arched one eyebrow. "Don't let it get to you, Davis."

chapter 12

RICHARD VALE KNELT in front of one of the computers for his Laser Projector. His prematurely gray head was bent over some exposed circuits. He squinted as he worked on the circuits with a tiny screwdriver. Behind him, Dr. Arnold Fortner, a skinny man with a sharp, pointed face, ruffled through a stack of papers in his hand.

Fortner pulled a paper out of the stack. "And what about this one, Richard?"

"Arnold," Vale said without turning around, "later. Can't you see I'm doing a delicate repair?"

"Five thousand dollars for one Coltran tape bank?" Fortner refused to be put off. "No wonder Washington wants to shut us down."

Vale continued his work. "Nobody's going to shut us down, Arnold."

"I could run my primate section for *two* months with five thousand dollars." Fortner's harping reached a higher pitch. "But no, every time *I* put in a requisition, it's the same. 'Sorry, Dr. Vale has priority.' Well, I'm sick of priorities."

Vale's eyes rolled at the familiar harangue. "Arnold, I'm busy."

Fortner surveyed the complex equipment. "And this . . . ridiculous, million-dollar toy of yours. Biotechnic research? Who are you trying to kid, Richard? We both know it'll never work. You know what I think?"

Vale's back stiffened at Fortner's condescending tone. "Frankly, Arnold, I don't care what you think." He rose from his squatting position and moved to another circuit.

"Wait a minute."

Vale turned to face Fortner. "No, you wait a minute, Doctor." Exasperation made his voice harsh. "You're my assistant . . ."

"You would have been *my* assistant if—"

"Let's not go through all of this again, Arnold." Vale looked at the little man fuming before him. "The fact is, you're not the director. And until you are, *if* you ever are . . ."

"Always the big man, aren't you, Richard? Well, let me tell you something. I'll be damned if you're going to get all the credit for that Weston boy."

Vale smiled knowingly. "So that's what this is about."

"I haven't seen such excitement here since we opened the Center. When the CIA arrived the place went nuts." Fortner was awed. "I've spent as many years as you have building this place. I deserve a piece of the action."

Vale shrugged. "We'll see."

"I demand to have an active role in the research . . ."

The static of the theater's intercom interrupted Fortner.

"Dr. Fortner, please report to Primate Test Block A immediately."

"Richard, please—" Fortner's voice took on a begging tone. "This case is big enough for the two of us."

"You're being paged."

"We're not finished with this." Fortner's ferretlike features were set in a determined expression. "You're not going to crowd me out of this one."

Vale returned to his work without a word.

"Jeff," Jan tried to keep her voice calm, "we're going to take a trip to see a new doctor."

She stood by the side of his bed, gazing fondly at him. His eyelids were heavy from drugs. Ever since Jeff's violent outburst, Kellog had seen to it that he was heavily sedated. He had not been conscious long enough for Jan to tell him where they were going. The line at the hospital was that the doctors wanted Jeff to get as much rest as possible to prepare him for the trip to Los Angeles. Jan knew differently. No one wanted any trouble. They all wanted the transfer to go without a hitch. And maybe they were a little afraid. But with Jeff knocked out, people did not have to think about him at all.

Her reflections were interrupted when Jeff mumbled thickly, "Not now . . . it's too soon."

Jan bit her lip to keep from crying. She knew it was too soon, yet she had to comfort him, to make the trip easy for him. "I know you're weak. But you're very important now. They want to take special care of you." She knew she was stretching the truth. During her training, she had seen the kinds of tests people like Dr. Vale performed. They probed and prodded their subjects with no regard for feelings or comfort, and it filled her with anguish to think of Jeff being put through that kind of torture at the Research Center.

Jeff's placid eyes swallowed her up. Locked in his stare, she felt as if she were swimming. Jan had expected him to be bewildered and upset. Instead, he lay there, calm and serene. It had to be the drugs.

"I know you tried." His voice was resigned. "This is the way it is to be."

Jan was confused by his fatalism. Jeff was different. It wasn't just the weird things he was doing, it was something more basic. Something Jan couldn't put her finger on. He was no longer the child-man she treated at Fairchild State.

Jan forced herself to be cheerful. "We're flying to Los Angeles to see Dr. Vale. So in about a half hour I'll come to get you." She gave Jeff's arm a squeeze and quickly left the room, not wanting him to know just how disturbed she was.

Paul Deutch was waiting for her outside the door. He caught her by the arm. "Jan, I've got to talk with you."

"What's there to say?"

"I want to apologize—not because of my decision to move Jeff, but because it's gotten out of hand."

"You know they'll kill him." Jan's eyes filled with tears.

Deutch took her in his arms and patted her back.

"Well, you take good care of him."

Jan pulled back. "Won't you be there?"

"No." Deutch shuffled uncomfortably. "You're on your own. Kellog decided I was expendable."

Jan sniffled and wiped her eyes with the back of her hand. "Oh, no . . ."

"Just do what they say. Don't cause trouble. As you said, they're ruthless."

"Paul, I can't do this alone. I can't be held captive and watch them destroy Jeff."

"Jeff is strong." Deutch comforted her. "He's improving every day. Vale is a good man."

"It's not Vale I'm worried about. It's Kellog."

"Watch out for yourself, Jan. You can trust Carl Heller."

"But he's responsible for this CIA takeover." Jan was alarmed.

"I felt the same way, but he filled me in." Deutch reassured her. "The President did this. Heller had no idea things would get so out of hand as they have. Jan, he's a scientist. All he cares about is his work. He's above politics. I've never known anyone with his powers of concentration. That man is a walking thought machine. He's utterly brilliant.

"So he's a mad scientist."

"Look, Jan, he hates Kellog and his zombies as much as we do. Trust him. He'll help."

"Okay, Paul. Thanks." She kissed him on the cheek and said, "Pray for us."

David Kennedy sat in his car observing from a distance the dark-suited men bustling in and out of Good Shepherd Hospital. The afternoon was dull and foggy, but something was obviously going on. In his rear-view mirror, he saw five dull-gray sedans entering the drive. The cars were moving slowly, evenly spaced, in a regimented motorcade. Their black-and-white license plates read GOV in the bottom corner. As they pulled up at the hospital entrance, he heard churning rotors of a helicopter. A dark shadow descended through the fog. A helicopter broke through the cloud cover and dropped out of sight on the roof of the hospital.

David got out of his car and nonchalantly walked to the main entrance. He peered into one of the gray cars. The driver stared at him coldly. David looked away and approached the front doors. A man with military bearing blocked his way.

"Sorry, no admittance."

"What are you talking about? I'm here to visit my sick aunt. Who are you?"

The man flashed a card at him. "State Health Department. Quarantine."

A look of wry disbelief crossed David's face. He was playing the scene to the hilt.

"Come on," he said confidentially, "just between you and me. What's really going on?"

"Shove off," the agent said none too politely.

"Just one more quick question. If this is a state operation, why do all your cars have federal plates on them?"

"You ask too many questions, Buster."

"Just observant." David smiled at the agent. "Bye."

The CIA man watched his departure suspiciously.

As David drove out of the lot in his banged-up old Volvo, he saw the agent on the steps with another in his rear-view mirror, both watching him.

David drove to a pay phone a block away from the hospital. He could see people loading into the cars from the booth. Turning back to the phone, he dropped a quarter in the slot and dialed Richardson's number.

"Pete, that you? You're not going to believe this. The place is swarming with federal agents. They're saying the hospital is quarantined, but there's a motorcade of five government cars here and a helicopter on the roof. Looks like big stuff." He kept his eyes glued on the entrance in hopes of seeing Jan. "Looks like the motorcade is going to be the advance guard. They'll probably fly Weston down later after they've set up security systems." Kennedy tapped his foot on the floor impatiently. He noticed a rented Toyota pull out of the lot and head in his direction.

"Oh-oh—I think I'm about to have a visit. Someone's on the way and you can bet it's not Florence Nightingale. Gotta run—I'll follow the motorcade down one way or another."

He strode to his car, trying not to look hurried. "Now you've done it. Had to be a smart-ass." He berated himself, then cleared his mind, hoping that a scheme would present itself.

He had no time to waste. As he headed to town, he did not even look in his rear-view mirror. He knew the Toyota was following him.

He drove to the town center and parked in front of Clyde's, an all-black jazz club where the music was hot and the drinks long. It was Clyde's day to try out groups —David often dropped in for a burger and free music. As he pushed through the etched-glass doors, he saw the Toyota double-park down the street.

"Say, man," Clyde greeted him as he took a stool at the bar. "How's my favorite honky?"

"In a jam, Clyde."

"This is one nigger that does not want to hear about it."

"Listen, Clyde. Could you do me a favor?"

"I said I didn't want to hear about it. But I'm going to anyway, right?"

"Could I borrow your car?"

"My car? Are you crazy, man?"

"No, just desperate. Is it out back?"

"Where it always is."

"Look, here are the keys to my Volvo." David pushed them across the bar.

"No way," Clyde said as he backed off.

"Look, my Volvo is worth more than that old heap."

"Old heap—you're talking about the jazzmobile. That Caddy and I go back a long way . . ."

"How about if I throw in five hundred dollars?"

Clyde whistled. "You must really be in trouble."

"Not trouble exactly. It's important, or I wouldn't ask."

"Okay, okay—forget the money. You'll owe me one, okay?"

"I'll owe you more than one."

Clyde pulled his keys from his pocket and took two off the Playboy insignia key chain. "Here you go, Bro. Happy trails. Here, take the registration, too."

David took the keys and gripped Clyde's hand. "I'll never forget this."

"Now don't go getting sentimental on me."

David ran out of the back exit and jumped into the '62 black Cadillac. "God, I hope this gas-eater makes it," he muttered as he pulled off.

The agent reached the door and swung it open just as David disappeared out the back. As he stepped inside, a hush fell over the room. A number of the patrons turned and stared at the intruder with open hostility. The agent quickly scanned the bar for David and, not seeing him, shrugged his shoulders in defeat and walked out.

The old Cadillac roared down the coast road to Los Angeles sounding like a motorboat. David thought of Clyde tooling around in his Caddy. "They sure don't make them like this anymore." David felt invulnerable, as if he were driving a tank.

Making his way through the L.A. traffic, David was sorry he had been delayed. Following the motorcade would have been easier than arriving an hour later, when security would be tighter. After finding the mountain road that led to the Center, he switched off his headlights. No reason to attract more attention than necessary.

He drove cautiously up the winding road, leaning forward in an attempt to improve his vision. He could only see two feet in front of him. Suddenly a spotlight blinded him.

"Oh shit!" he exclaimed as he rubbed his eyes.

A man in a dark suit and thin black tie appeared at his window. "What are you doing on this road without lights?"

"Am I glad to see you, Officer." David tried to make his voice as boyish as possible. "I went over a rock about a mile ago and the headlights went out. I only have a little farther to go, so I . . ." he started to explain.

"Oh, yeah? Well, I suggest you just turn around and head back into town."

David forced himself to be as easygoing as he could. "Now hold on a second, Officer, I'm looking for a big party. I met a gorgeous woman at a bar last night and she invited me to a big bash. She told me it was up this road."

The agent leaned closer. "No party here, Buster. Your lady friend was trying to dump you." The square-jawed agent smirked.

"You mean . . . now how do you like that?" He slapped the steering wheel. "Of all the luck."

"Now we're going to shine our spotlight." The agent waved to his partner and the area was flooded with light. "I want you to turn around here and go back down the road."

"Okay, Officer. Thanks a lot. While the light's on, I

think I'll jiggle some of these wires under the dashboard. Maybe I can get these darned lights to work.'' As the agent walked away, David turned on his headlights, executed a three-point turn, and headed back down the steep road.

At the foot of the mountain, he pulled off the road and found a spot where the bushes hid the car. The only thing he could do was to try it by foot. If he kept well hidden in the shrubs along the sloping side of the mountain, he knew he could slip by the agent outpost.

He half climbed, half crawled through the rocky brush on the moonless night, moving as quickly as he could, stumbling here and there. Terribly winded, he vowed to stop smoking once this was over. After about five miles, he calculated he was approaching the place where he had stopped. He took it much more slowly. Through the woodsy growth, he finally saw the two agents in their car. One was asleep, head thrown back on the seat; the other stared straight ahead. He hoped they were near the Center.

Though David wanted to bolt, he crept along by the side of the road, afraid even of rustling a branch. As he took a measured step, a loose rock rolled toward the road with a clatter. The agent jerked his head in David's direction. David flattened himself against a boulder and reflexively shut his eyes, acting in the magical belief that if you can't see them, they can't see you. Moments passed. The agent made no move to get out of the car. With knee-buckling relief, David picked his way out of hearing range, then jogged the last mile to the Center.

Quickly crossing the road, David darted behind the cover of the shrubs planted in front of the Center's fence. He cautiously parted the fragrant honeysuckle. Groups of agents were clustered around the cars. One man spoke into what looked like a radio. The agents scattered toward different buildings on the property.

David heard the unmistakable sound of a helicopter. "This *is* a smooth operation. Of course, they would wait until the dead of night," he thought as the helicopter touched down on the broad lawn in front of the main building.

The side door of the helicopter slid open. A lean man with a crewcut jumped out, followed by two more CIA men. Then David make out a shock of auburn hair in the doorway. Jan was wearing a teal knit dress. In the bluish light of the night, her normally bronzed skin looked like alabaster against it. An agent reached up to help her out of the helicopter. Three men carrying briefcases followed. Two attendants appeared. They hopped to the ground and waited as a gurney was lowered to them.

David's attention was riveted to the gurney. Strapped to it was a large man, his blond hair disheveled. He weakly reached out his hand to Jan. It was Weston! No doubt about that.

As the party headed for the entrance, the chopper accelerated and lifted off into the L.A. smog.

David stood clutching the fence. He had stumbled onto a major story. He couldn't believe his luck. If he played his cards right, this could even mean a Pulitzer.

He waited for things to calm down at the Center. Agents were scurrying all over the grounds, so he crept to the far end of the fence. His thoughts turned from his own ambitions to Jan and Jeff. If only he had been there when she'd called. Weston had been dead—now he's alive. But that alone wouldn't have called out half the CIA. David couldn't imagine what Weston had done to deserve such extreme security measures. And

Jan looked totally strung out. He wished he could get to her.

After the majority of the gathering had disappeared inside and only a few agents were left, posted as guards, David scaled the eight-foot hurricane fence at a spot obscured by a ginkgo tree. He paused, straddling the barbed wire at the top. He swung a leg over the top wire.

The sound of tearing cloth made him curse automatically. "Shit!" He froze, terrified that his voice may have carried in the still night. He watched the agents in the distance lift their heads like watchdogs sniffing the air. He saw one break away from the group and head in his direction.

Before he could get any closer, David jerked his pants leg free, got his other leg over the barbed wire, found a handhold, and silently lowered himself to the ground. A beam of light from the agent's flashlight swept over his head soon after he hit the soft earth. It passed again, then went out. David took several deep breaths, then crept to the shadows along the hillside at the far end of the Center. His eyes darted in the darkness as he checked out the area. In the distance, a light shone out of a window in a small lab building. David made his way quietly to the side of the building.

Jan's ears were still ringing from the helicopter ride. The glare of the industrial lighting in the lobby of the Metaphysical Test and Research Center stung her eyes. Kellog and his men were being guided to the special intensive care unit that had been set up for Jeff.

"Dr. Petrie." She saw an impeccably neat man in a white lab coat approach her with his hand extended. "Welcome. I'm Richard Vale."

"Hello, Dr. Vale." Jan shook his hand. "I wish we

were meeting under different circumstances."

"What could be more exciting circumstances, Dr. Petrie?" he asked, puzzled.

"Jeffrey Weston could be in better health before you start the tests."

"You don't beat around the bush, do you?"

"I'm sorry." Jan rubbed her eyes wearily. "It's been a tough few days. You must excuse my rudeness."

"You don't have to apologize. I admire that. I'm not one for the social graces myself." Richard Vale seemed relieved. "But first, let me explain the accommodations we have for you. There is a dormitory wing here for people working on time-lapse projects or those just burning the midnight oil. We have given you a room there. It's not elegant, but I hope you'll be comfortable. As for food . . ."

"I'm sure you're a wonderful host."

"Let me finish my welcome speech, please, Dr. Petrie." He smiled in a quick, nervous flash. "We have an adequate cafeteria, but if you don't find the food palatable, I'll be glad to have some delivered from town for you."

"Thank you, Dr. Vale. Anything will do, really. Food is the last thing on my mind."

He nodded. "Okay. Now, I must impose on you. I would like to speak with you in my office."

"Do you think it could wait until morning?"

"I'm afraid not. Every second is important."

"So you *are* aware of just how weak Jeffrey Weston is?"

He looked around the lobby which was crawling with agents. "This is not the place for discussion."

"Lead the way." Jan stifled a yawn.

• • •

David peered into the window and saw three men sitting at a large table in the center of the room. The table was scattered with papers, books and reports. There was a cassette player on the table. Some agents were assembling more sophisticated audio equipment in the corner.

The ruggedly handsome man facing the window was talking intensely. His shirt-sleeves were rolled up to reveal strong arms. He kept brushing his thick black hair from his eyes. Hoping to pick up snatches of conversation, David put his ear to the window. The sound of a door opening made him catch his breath. He dropped to his knees, too frightened to exhale.

Standing at the door was the agent he had confronted on the steps of Good Shepherd earlier that day. The agent closed the door, looked in both directions, and headed down the path toward David.

He flattened himself on the ground behind a low bush. His heart pounded wildly. As the sound of the CIA man's shoes crunching on the white gravel grew louder, David knew he was caught. He closed his eyes and waited for the inevitable.

The CIA man stopped directly in front of David. There was complete silence. "This is it," David thought, ready to give himself up. Suddenly he heard the sound of a zipper being opened.

The leaves of the shrub danced as urine cascaded on the bush. David lay helplessly in the ever-growing puddle beneath him. The CIA man zipped himself up, turned, and whistled his way down the path. David heaved a sigh of relief as he watched the figure disappear.

"If I made it through this," he thought as he lay on the damp earth, "I can do anything."

• • •

Jan wandered down the echoing halls of the main building at the Center. During the past forty-eight hours, she had only managed to catnap. The lack of sleep was getting to her. She was edgy and disoriented. If she planned to be any help to Jeff at all, she had to get some rest. It wouldn't do to expose him to her raw emotions, her frazzled state. And it certainly wouldn't help to be snapping at everyone in charge.

When she neared the door of the room that had been assigned to her, she noticed a small, nervous man with thinning colorless hair watching her approach.

"Dr. Petrie?" he greeted her anxiously.

"Yes?" Her response was flat.

"I'm Arnold Fortner, the Assistant Director here."

Jan shook the limp hand he extended. His blandness made her cringe.

"If you'll excuse me, I just had a meeting with Dr. Vale. I'm exhausted from the trip. I'd like to go to bed."

Fortner obviously had no intention of letting her go. "What do you think of our brilliant Director?"

Jan didn't like the wheedling tone of his voice. "At this point, I wouldn't know. I can't say I'm happy to be here."

"I've heard that you and Weston are very close. I'd like to talk to you about him."

"I've told Dr. Vale everything I know. Check with him. Right now, I'm too tired to say another word."

"But couldn't you spare me a minute? Dr. Vale is a busy man." He didn't bother to hide his resentment.

Jan was growing impatient. "Look, Dr. Fortner, I don't want to be here. I'll do what I have to for Jeff, but I don't plan to go out of my way for any of you."

Fortner's eyes narrowed.

"I certainly have no intention of repeating this story endlessly. It upsets me. If this place is so inefficient . . ." She stopped. "I don't want to get worked up again, okay? Talk to your boss."

Jan pushed past Fortner and closed her door. She threw herself on her bed and tried to calm her churning insides. The impulse to ask for a pill to help her sleep was strong. But Jeff might need her and she had to be alert. She took several deep, controlled breaths and prayed a silent prayer that Jeff would make it through the night.

chapter 13

DAVID PEEKED OUT from a door bearing the nameplate MAINTENANCE. He had spent what remained of the night huddled behind a cart of laundry in a workroom that was more like an oversized closet packed with supplies.

To his surprise and relief, security at the Center had been lax in the dead of night. Only a handful of guards were stationed around the grounds. Getting into the building had been the easiest part of the caper so far. He had simply stayed in the shadows along the hillside until he was as close to the rear of the main building as he could get. His senses were attuned to the movements and sounds of the guards, who only occasionally patrolled the back of the building. After mustering up his courage, he had zigzagged his way from shrub through open space to tree in a series of short sprints until he was home free.

Chest heaving, he had flattened himself against the building. There was no way of telling if guards had been posted at all exits or if there was an alarm system on the back doors. He had lurked in the bushes until the roving agents had passed. Then, keeping his head low, he had crept the length of the building, through thorny shrubs which tore at his clothes. He protected his face with his arms, but his clothing had taken a beating. He had no idea how he could maintain a cover if he looked like a beggar in tatters.

His lucky break was finding a window that was open. When he crawled through, he found himself in what appeared to be a janitor's office, filled with cleaning supplies, mops, tools and floor-buffers. Not only had he found a janitor's uniform, but he also came up with the prize—a stack of lab coats. David had to consider this cache a good omen. Knowing that the morning would bring him closer to his story, David felt the accumulated tension drain from him. He had curled up on a bed of laundry and fallen into a deep, untroubled sleep.

From the door of his not-too-luxurious accommodations, David spotted a CIA man posted at an exit. He stepped out and moved along the wall in the opposite direction as inconspicuously as he could. He wore a white technician's uniform and carried a clipboard.

At the corridor intersection, three more CIA men walked toward him. He nodded professionally and bustled past them. His eyes met the steely gaze of the agent he saw that afternoon in the government car.

David hurried down the hall and turned the corner. He expected to hear the agent's feet clattering after him or to hear him call out. His shoulders tensed with fear. He whistled softly when nothing happened at all.

He wanted to get to Vale in the Medical Theater. He'd find Jan later. On his way toward one of the exits, he saw two men were guarding the door of a windowed room.

When he passed by, he saw Weston lying in bed asleep. A confusion of lines, tubes and wires connected him to more equipment than David had ever seen in a hospital. A technician sat next to Jeff's bed watching the monitor screens and making occasional notes.

Without hesitating, David strode purposefully to the door. He spoke to the guards before they addressed him.

"Routine checkup—Vale's orders."

"Go ahead," one agent said.

David went straight to Jeff's bed. "Good morning. How's the patient?"

"Weak from the trip, but steady," the technician replied.

David picked up Jeff's chart. He could barely contain his astonishment. He pretended to rub his eyes to conceal his expression. He calmly returned the chart and said to the technician, "I'll check in later."

When he left the room it was all he could do to keep from breaking into a run. He found a pay phone on a deserted hall, shoved a quarter in the slot and dialed jerkily. He looked over his shoulder.

"Pete," he whispered. "It's David. Is the city edition run off yet?"

"David, what's happening?"

"I have a story that's gonna knock you on your ass!"

"What did you find out?"

"I can't talk."

"Why not?"

"I'm here at the Center. They're all over the place!"

"Calm down, David, just . . ."

"Look, trust me. Give me an hour and I'll call in a story . . ."

A hand shot out over David's shoulder and disconnected the call.

"You won't be calling in any story." The agent grabbed David's arm and spun him around. He dropped the receiver, which smashed against the wall from the violence of the action.

"Get your hands off me," David demanded as he faced the burly CIA man. "Who do you think you are, cutting me off?"

"Come along." The agent gave him a shove. "I know someone who wants to see you."

"Now hold on," David protested. "I'm a doctor with responsibilities here. You can't just . . ."

"Don't tell your troubles to me." The agent took the lapels of David's lab coat in his hands and drew him closer. "When I tell you to move, move," he snarled.

"All right, all right." The agent pushed him, stumbling, down the corridor. "Dr. Vale will hear about this, you can count on that. You can't treat one of his top people this way."

David kept up a steady stream of righteous indignation as the agent steered him through the hallway.

In the Medical Theater, Jeff was strapped to the reclining chair beneath the Laser Projector's screen. In addition to the metal helmet, he wore an elaborate set of earphones that were plugged into an oscilliscope next to the chair. He was inert, his face was so devoid of color, it appeared translucent. The robust, laughing man of a few days before had been replaced by a shadowy figure with dark circles under his eyes. Vale sat next to Jeff with a pad propped on his knee. Pencil flying, he took notes. When the technician turned the knobs on the oscilloscope, it emitted a high-pitched noise. Vale checked Jeff for a response.

"Nothing. Take it down."

The technician twisted the dials, creating a lower tone.

Vale leaned toward Jeff. "Still no response," he said, discouraged. He put down his pad and stood. Stretching, he said, "Two days and we still haven't found it. His response factor *has* to be somewhere in this range."

"Maybe it's the decibel count."

"No, we've already fooled with that."

Both men pondered the problem. The technician watched the continuous bead of light weaving up and down across the screen of the oscilloscope. His face lit up. "That's it!"

"What?" Vale asked dully.

"Modulation." He pointed to the screen. Maybe it isn't just one, steady sound frequency that projects him."

"Go on," Vale encouraged him.

"All right—yeah, it makes sense." The technician was excited. "The first time he projected at Fairchild—in the morgue —when he came back to life—a siren was blaring. That's what the detailed report said, right?"

"The second time—when he delivered Einstein's dissertation—there was a foghorn."

"Uh-huh."

"Both were *modulating* sound frequencies. Not steady."

"You're a genius, Ned."

The technician beamed.

"Let's take it to twelve hundred and start from scratch."

"Right."

Waiting for the test to resume, Vale took his seat next to Jeff and flipped through a spiral-bound notepad. He started to make notations with a brown felt-tip pen. As he wrote, he felt an unusual warmth building in his arm.

He made a tight fist around the pen and twisted his wrist joint. The hot sensation continued to intensify. His hand began to tremble slightly, then his entire right arm felt weightless, detached from his body.

Eyes wide, he watched as his hand started to write in minuscule, careful letters. Every time a line was finished, his hand slid across the page to start again. The writing was picking up speed on its own, the letters growing in size.

Richard Vale had witnessed automatic writing before. He was conscious enough to realize that's what was happening to him, but did not have an inkling of what he was writing. In all his years of parapsychological research, he had never had a paranormal experience himself. There was always a first time, he guessed. He sat back, and with a mystified detachment, watched his hand.

When a page was filled, the hand would flip to the next. As Vale observed, the writing became more urgent. The pen was slashing across the pages ferociously. The pages were flipping wildly on the spiral binding, sheet after sheet filled with savage script. No matter how he tried, Vale could not will his hand to stop. The fury of the writing crested. When the last page of the pad was turned, his entire arm waved in the air like a conductor's at a turbulent passage in a score. Then his arm fell limp.

Dr. Vale looked at the pad in his lap. He couldn't read the last pages because the writing had disintegrated to a violent scrawl. He began to flip pages back to a point at which the writing was legible. There, written over and over again—hundreds of times—were the words: NO TEST THURSDAY—TOO SOON.

He leafed through the pad in amazement, alarmed by

the increasing fury of the writing. His first impulse was self-protective. He wanted to make certain no one had seen him so out of control. Rumors could spread very quickly at the Center, given Jeffrey Weston's presence. It would be hard enough to stay in charge without those CIA thugs thinking he was possessed.

Vale turned to take stock of who was in the theater. Fortunately, his position afforded only a good view of his back to the technicians. As he swiveled in his chair, Jeffrey Weston's eyes sprang open. Unblinking, they bored into him. A glacial chill seized Dr. Vale's chest. An inexplicable terror welled up within him. The pad slid off his lap with a clatter.

"Here, let me get that for you, Dr. Vale." A technician rushed to his side. The doctor looked pale and shaken. "Are you all right? You seemed so involved I didn't want to interrupt."

Dr. Vale removed his glasses and rubbed his eyes. "Yes, I was." The technician had given him no indication of just how much he had seen, but Vale felt uneasy. "What do you have for me?"

"I've got it!" he beamed.

"What?" Vale was vague, distant.

"The reason we've never been able to get any of our subjects' images on the screen once they reach Alpha state."

Vale cocked his head and lifted his eyebrows. "Tell me."

"I was in the back just now, programming a C bank feed-in tape. I grabbed the wrong tape—an A instead. The readouts went crazy, rejected the program. The computer stopped."

"That's normal. So what?"

"That's what's been happening every time our subjects go into Alpha. Their pre-Alpha tape input is consistent with the computer's." Vale nodded. "But as soon as they hit Alpha, their biochemistry completely changes. They're no longer programmed to the computer. That's why all systems shut down."

"You've got something there." Vale reflected for a moment. A grin spread across his face. He slapped his knee. "So-o-o . . . we program the memory banks just up to Alpha, then cut off all tape input and let the computers play it by ear."

"That would do it."

"I'll be damned." Vale's eyes shone with excitement. "How long before your boys can make the change-over?"

"Two days at the earliest."

"That would make it . . ."

"Thursday," the technician volunteered.

A jolt went through Dr. Vale. He clutched his notepad, hands trembling. He could not take the obvious message of the automatic writing lightly. Whatever its source, the message had accurately predicted the day of the test, something he himself had not known.

"That means Weston will have to be our first test," he said to the technician.

"Couldn't we hold off and try someone else first? Weston is in very bad shape. He's running a temperature of 104."

"I don't know. How long do you think he can hang on?" Dr. Vale could not make himself look at Jeffrey Weston. He had already made his decision. He was not about to let this opportunity pass by. He had been late before, years of work went down the drain when that woman beat him for the Nobel Prize. He would not let that happen to him again. What he was about to do might be irresponsible. It certainly was cruel. If Weston died, he knew he would be in deep trouble with the government. But he would risk anything—everything for this chance.

"Weston will have to be our first test," he said in a firm voice. "As soon as we determine his projection frequency, we'll be able to run the test. Notify everyone. The tentative test date is Thursday."

"Right." The technician walked to the other side of the theater and gathered a group of men at the computer bank.

Vale turned to the technician who was preparing to work with Jeff on the oscilloscope. "I think we've finally got it. Do you realize the importance, the immensity of what we may witness on that screen Thursday?" His eyes blazed as he stared at the screen.

"It's amazing that it might finally work, but the thought that our first subject is Weston . . ." The technician shook his head.

Richard Vale noticed Jeffrey Weston's closed eyelids quiver with apprehension.

"Empty your pockets on the desk," Kellog ordered.

"I will not." David Kennedy knew he was caught, but continued to bluff. He was not going to make it easy for that CIA robot. "I insist on seeing Dr. Vale before I'm subjected to this indignity."

"If you don't stop stalling, I'll have one of the boys empty them for you." He glanced at the surly agents in the corner. "You wouldn't want that, would you?"

David shoved his hands in his pockets. "If you want something, you're going to have to take it from me."

"All right. You asked for it. These guys aren't gentle, you know." With a jerk of his head, Kellog called the agent by the door over.

David watched him coming toward him. The cold

gleam in the agent's eye convinced him to cooperate. No reason to be foolhardy.

"Okay, okay. You win." He dropped his wallet, keys and some change on the desk, leaving his plastic-coated press card loose in his rear pocket. He berated himself for not having gotten rid of it. Without that piece of identification he could have bought some time.

"Okay. Turn them out."

David did so.

"That everything?"

"Yes."

Kellog squinted and curled his lip. "Frisk him." He looked through David's wallet. David didn't bother to resist. The agent slapped him roughly up and down and felt the card in his pocket.

"Bingo!" He handed it to Kellog, who eyed the card.

"So, Mr. Kennedy," he sneered. "Want to tell me what you're doing here?"

A buxom woman wearing horn-rimmed glasses hurried up the aisle to Vale. She handed him a sheaf of reports.

"Lab reports of Weston's first blood tests."

"Thanks, Elaine. I'll look at them later."

"Richard, I think you'd better check them now."

Vale began to read, but Dr. Nichols had to describe the results. "Everything is normal except for his DNA analysis." She pointed to the section. "Look at his molecule count. Four, not three."

Vale looked up, stunned. "That's impossible."

"I know, but the fourth one is there."

"All right. Isolate the extra molecule and analyze it."

"Don't you think I've already tried that?"

"And?"

"It only exists when attached to the main group. Every time we separate it, it disappears."

Vale scratched his head. "Where the hell does that leave us?"

Before Dr. Nichols could answer, the radiologist appeared. He handed Vale more reports.

"What now? This Weston is getting to be more of a mystery every minute." Jeff, looking exhausted and gaunt, stirred in the chair. "What are these?"

"Brain scan pictures."

"Well?"

"Negative. Everything normal . . . except . . ." The radiologist leafed through a stack of X rays. "We ran all the pictures through the infrared photo analyzer." He chose two from the stack and clamped the X rays to a viewing screen. Turning on the back light, he stepped aside. Vale regarded the side and frontal views of Jeff's skull. The technician pointed with his pen to an area an inch above Jeff's forehead.

"In this area, here, we found something."

Vale got up from his chair and joined the radiologist at the viewing screen. He leaned forward to study the milk-white surface of the skull.

"I don't see anything."

"I know. It's microscopic. It's about five thousandths of an inch in diameter. Some foreign object —the size of a skin cell."

"Is Dr. Blum around with those fiber optics—you know, the microsurgery equipment he's been developing?"

"Yes."

"Well, let's get the damned thing out and look at it."

"Right."

• • •

Jan stood at the door of the auditorium, having talked the agent assigned to watch her into at least letting her wait there in case there was any news about Jeff. But her patience was wearing thin. Vale had been in there with Jeffrey for almost six hours, and Jan had no way of knowing what was going on.

Finally, she could stand it no longer. She had to do something to distract the agent's attention long enough to get into the auditorium. Jan looked over at the agent leaning against the opposite wall. He was reading a book and glancing up at her every few minutes to make sure she was behaving. She saw her chance. Jan took a deep breath and let out a piercing shriek. The agent turned and saw her pointing down the hall, her eyes wide with fear. He eyed her suspiciously, but her terror seemed so genuine that he trotted down the hall to see what had frightened her so. Without a moment's hesitation, Jan bolted toward the auditorium.

"Hey, where do you think you're going?" the agent said, trying to catch up to her as she disappeared through the double doors.

Vale was so involved in his latest disclosure that he didn't notice Jan burst into the room.

"Aren't you finished yet?" she asked.

He snapped his head up, startled. "Dr. Petrie, I told you that you were barred from these areas during testing."

"I tried to stop her," the agent broke in in his defense.

"You said four hours, Dr. Vale," Jan said, disregarding the agent's presence. "You've had him now for six. The red light above the door was off so I assumed you were finished."

"Obviously, we're not."

Jan bridled at his condescending tone, but one look at Jeff made her gasp. He had lost weight. The planes of his face were more angled and large, dark circles under his eyes dominated his startlingly pale features. Jan took his hand and gave it a gentle squeeze. Jeff slowly opened his eyes. They focused with difficulty. A faint line of pain creased his brow.

"Still drugged, I see. He's been like this for three days." Jan's voice was harsh. "You're going to kill him. You know that, don't you?"

"We're not going to kill anyone, Dr. Petrie."

"He needs rest."

"He'll get all the rest he needs . . ." Vale spoke tight-jawed, "after we finish our tests."

Jeff's mouth started to move weakly. He was trying to say something to Jan.

"Why are you doing this to him? Look at him—he's too weak to talk."

"To him?" Vale walked to the chair. "Let me tell you a few things about what we do here."

"Please do." Her tone was mocking.

"We've got a four-year-old who moves objects without touching them. He can stop a wall clock by simply looking at it. We've got an eighty-year-old Navajo Indian, a deaf mute since birth, who goes into trances and speaks fluent Russian. We've got people here who communicate telepathically with people on the other side of the world." He took off his glasses and put them in his lab coat pocket. "So let's stop talking about *him*. We're not dealing here with one retarded man. We're dealing with something that concerns all of mankind." He pointed to Jeff. "He's just one small part of it."

"You must be very proud, Doctor. Your scientific overview does save you from empathizing with pain and suffering." Jan was disgusted. "What impressive idealism—the blind pursuit of scientific knowledge."

"I don't think you have any idea of the risks I'm taking myself. If Weston doesn't survive, I'll lose the Center. The government would never give me another cent again, and without money . . . my research, my life . . ."

"I can't believe you are talking about money." Jan was livid.

"I am not talking about money, Dr. Petrie. I am talking about my life's work," Vale exploded. "Good night, Dr. Petrie. This is your last warning. Leave this theater or I'll have one of Kellog's men come and throw you out."

As Jan walked up the aisle, Jeff clenched his fists. His eyes fluttered and his jaw tightened.

Kellog intercepted her on her way back to the main building. "That was a nice stunt you pulled, Petrie. You can be sure my men won't let it happen again." He leered at her and said, "We also seem to have run into a friend of yours who is asking for you."

"I have no friends here."

"You'd be better off without this one."

"Get to the point, Mr. Kellog."

"We found a young man named David Kennedy posing as a doctor." She could tell he was playing with her, so she didn't say a word.

"When we went through his stuff, we found that he was a reporter for *The Chronicle*." Jan met his accusing look levelly. "How do you think he knew to come here?"

"How would I know." Jan shrugged. "If you'll excuse me, I'd like to go back to my room."

"As I understand it, you got into trouble for talking to this reporter once before," Kellog badgered her.

"Let's just say I've learned from my mistakes."

"Dr. Petrie, what was that man doing here?"

"Kennedy wanted to do a story on Jeff. He's an investigative reporter. They're aggressive—remember *All the President's Men?* It's his job to find things out. Ask him, don't ask me."

As soon as the words were out, Jan panicked. What if David already told them about her phone call? If he hadn't yet, would he? There was no way to tell what sort of pressure Kellog might put on him, or to know how important the source of the leak was to Kellog.

"We will, Dr. Petrie," Kellog said, smirking, "we certainly will talk with your friend."

"As long as you have him, I don't see what you're worried about. I'm sure under your watchful eye he won't have a chance to cause any trouble."

"You're a cool one, you really are. If you're involved with this . . ."

"Excuse me, Mr. Kellog." Jan didn't want to hear the consequences. "I really must get back to my room." He stepped aside on the gravel path to let Jan pass and executed a mock courtly bow.

chapter 14

A FROWN SPREAD on Jeff's face. Vale and the technician, busily occupied by the modulating frequency breakthrough, failed to see it.

"All right. Start at twelve hundred, drop to six, and swing it back at five-second intervals," Vale instructed the technician.

"You got it." The technician turned a knob on the oscilloscope.

A high-pitched tone pierced the stillness of the theater. The staff who had gathered to watch covered their ears with their hands at the unexpected sharpness of the sound.

"What the . . ." The technician twisted the dial, but the piercing sound persisted. The banks of lights for the Laser Projector came to life and blinked erratically.

A spasmodic, crackling sound made Vale cry, "My God, it's shorting. What the hell is wrong?"

"I don't know. We didn't activate that system."

Everyone in the theater stared at the face of the computer. The tapes were whipping around at high speed, the lights flashed. Suddenly, ice-blue flames burst from the computer.

"Get the extinguishers!" Vale's order energized the

gaping technicians. The fire spread quickly across the face of the computer.

"Hurry! We're going to lose Weston's entire memory input!" Vale watched white-hot sparks shower to the floor. Dazed by the fire, Vale felt a compulsion—a sort of energy field pulling him to the reclining chair in which Jeff lay. His eyes were drawn to Jeff. He lay there passively, a hint of a smile playing on his lips.

"It can't be . . ." Vale muttered. "Get him out of here."

Two attendants hastily unhooked Jeff from the machines and placed him on a gurney. As they wheeled him away, his gentle eyes never left Vale's face.

Unnerved by Jeff's unspoken message, Vale turned to see two technicians trying to put out the fire with small extinguishers. He raced to the computer and pushed the men aside. He agonized for an instant, then began to reach into the flames.

"What are you doing? You'll get burned!" a technician shouted when he realized what Vale intended to do.

Two men seized Vale and tried to pull him away from the flames. He struggled with them.

"Twenty years I've worked for this! I've got to save that tape!"

"We'll make another one." A technician tried to coax him from an act of madness.

"Weston may not live long enough. This was two days' work."

Vale threw the men aside. He reached for the reel. The flames licked his hands. He winced with pain. Sweat poured down his face.

"Stop him, you idiots!" a woman technician screamed.

Vale pulled off a singed reel of tape. When he backed

away from the computer, the technicians aimed extinguishers at the fire. Vale dropped the tape on the table. He held the wrist of his black, charred hand with his good hand. His face was twisted with agony.

"I saved it!" he croaked, then collapsed on the floor.

"I've already told you," David Kennedy said in annoyance. "I followed you down here. A motorcade of gray government cars was definitely a clue. The number of agents swarming all over Good Shepherd was another. How many times do I have to go through this story?"

"Until you tell us the truth," Kellog barked.

"I *am* telling you the truth. I was waiting to see Jan Petrie—to find out what happened to Weston." David shifted uncomfortably on the straightback wooden chair. "I couldn't reach her. You'd have to be an idiot not to know something was going on."

Kellog puffed on his cigar. The small office was filled with the choking scent of it. Kennedy coughed.

"Why did you follow us?"

"I'm a reporter, remember? I'm paid to snoop."

"What does your paper know about this?"

"Nothing—nothing, it was my day off. My editor thought the story was dead."

"But you knew differently."

"I have eyes."

"And you didn't tell anyone?"

David shook his head. "I didn't have time."

"Somehow I find that hard to believe," Kellog said churlishly.

"A call to the paper could mean big trouble for you. If they know . . ."

"Can you risk a call?" David laughed. "That would

be a green light for my editor. He'd send half the staff down here."

"We have our ways of finding these things out, Kennedy."

David knew Pete Richardson would never talk to the CIA. His news sense was too strong. He wouldn't jeopardize this scoop under any circumstances. At least, David hoped so.

"Okay, Kennedy. Back to the holding room. I'll be by later—and I won't be so friendly."

Kellog nodded to two security men, who started to lift David from his chair.

"I can walk by myself, thank you very much," David snarled, as they led him away.

"You're lucky you didn't lose that hand, Richard," Dr. Johnson said. He was painstakingly wrapping Vale's burned hand. "I'm going to have you taken over to St. John's."

"Sorry, Doc. I've got too much work to do."

"The shot I gave you is numbing the pain, but you've got third-degree burns all over that hand. Your body's going through a trauma." Distracted, Vale looked over Johnson's shoulder. "Listen to me, Richard. This is serious. You may need skin grafts. I want you to rest."

"I'll rest after the test."

"You're in no shape to work." Johnson leaned on the examination table. "I don't get it, Richard. You're such a bright man. Why'd you do such a stupid thing?"

"Not stupid, Doc, logical. I made a trade. Twenty years of research . . ." He held up his bandaged hand. ". . . . for one bad hand. Weston's tape is still good, the computers are all repaired, and the test will go off on schedule. If that's stupid, so be it."

"Okay, it's not stupid, it's deranged." Both men laughed. "I want to keep changing that dressing. After the test, you're going to St. John's if we have to drag you there."

Just as Vale hopped off the table, Dr. Blum, the microsurgeon, entered carrying a ream of papers.

"Excuse me. I hoped I'd find you here. How's the hand?"

"I'll live. What've you got?"

"You're not going to believe this one," Dr. Blum said with excitement.

"Why does everyone keep saying that to me?"

Dr. Blum held out a paper to Vale.

"The particle we took out of his forehead?"

Blum nodded. "It's a distant cousin of *Balanites aegyptica*. A porous wood fiber . . . a member of the thicket genus. The species is indigenous only to the Middle East."

"You said *distant* cousin. How distant?"

Blum paused. "It's been extinct for over six hundred years."

"You're sure?"

"Absolutely."

"Damn." Vale looked down at the reports. "Let's give it a carbon fourteen, find out just how old it is."

"Will do."

He returned the papers to Blum, who left the room. With a furrowed brow, Vale started to follow him.

"Richard, I can't force you, but I'm serious about that hand." Johnson broke his train of thought. "Immobilize it, or you might lose it."

"You heard Blum, Doc. How can you expect me to walk away from this?"

"Is it more important to you than your right hand?"

"I'll think about it, Doc."

"Something tells me that you've already made up your mind." Dr. Johnson couldn't refrain from adding, "This goes beyond a dedication to science, you know."

Vale ignored the comment and left the room.

Arnold Fortner was lurking in the hallway. He sprang on Vale. "I'm so sorry to hear about your injury. I guess you'll have to take it easy."

"Thanks for your concern, but don't get your hopes up."

"How can you say that?" Fortner blinked. "Why are you always so hostile to me? I'm worried about you."

"Sorry, Arnold. I've got a lot on my mind."

"Well, let me give you a hand." Fortner looked at him craftily. "Pardon the pun."

"You really are gleeful, aren't you?" Out of habit, Vale went to lift his hand to adjust his glasses. He grimaced as shocks of pain ran up his arm.

"You should get to a hospital to have that taken care of," Fortner suggested.

"And leave you in charge, right?"

"Well, Richard, you have to agree that I should be better informed about what's going on."

"I can't say that I do agree with you."

"Be reasonable, you happen to be incapacitated at the moment."

"Do you really think so, Arnold?" Vale held up his loosely bandaged hand and shook it at the Assistant Director without any indication of pain. "Do you think this injury will keep me from accomplishing what I've worked for twenty years to achieve? You know me better than that."

"Yes, I know you all too well," Fortner said bitterly.

A smirk spread across his face. "What you fail to realize is that you're not in charge here."

"What in hell are you talking about?"

"I just had a meeting with Phil Kellog. He's upset by your irrational behavior . . ."

"I bet," Vale interrupted hotly, "you really went to work on him. I can just see it."

"You're wrong." Fortner looked offended. "I did no such thing. Kellog is a perceptive man."

"The two of you deserve each other," Vale said in disgust.

"Richard, I'm not taking your job . . . if that's what you think." He paused to arouse Vale's curiosity, but the Director regarded him impassively. "Kellog has Presidential orders . . ."

"He reminds everyone of that every thirty seconds," Vale said dryly.

"So he's really in charge of the team."

"The *team*! Spare me."

"Whether you want to admit it or not, Richard, you're not the only person involved with Weston."

"I don't give a damn about national security."

"Your megalomania is showing—you and that Laser Projector."

Perspiration beaded on Vale's upper lip. "Look, Arnold, get to the point. I've got things to do."

"Getting a little shaky? You look palc. Sure you don't want to lie down?"

"I'm fine," Vale snapped. "Just tell me what you and Kellog have worked out."

"We will be having briefing sessions every evening. Each researcher will present all—and we mean *all*—the data to a panel including Kellog, Heller and myself. Of course, you're welcome to join us if you're up to it."

"*If* I'm up to it." Vale had to restrain himself from taking a swing at the arrogant little man. "Listen to me, Fortner, there is no reason why Kellog should know everything that's going on. He's here for security. Heller and I work together. We don't have to waste our time at meetings. Your pathetic attempt to worm your way into this case just won't work."

"We'll see about that."

"Yes, we certainly will. That overbearing West Point cadet is going to get a change of orders. As for you . . ."

"Richard, I was only doing what I thought was right under the circumstances." Fortner backed down.

"Well, you thought wrong, buddy." Before Fortner could go on, Vale turned his back and was gone.

Jan filled the hours when Jeff was being tested by reading and by walking the well-kept grounds of the Center. She was even growing accustomed to the laconic agent who followed her everywhere. She spent as much time as possible at Jeff's side, doing anything she could think of to make him more comfortable.

She walked through the days in a fog. No one told her anything. And she hungered for human contact—a kind word would have gone a long way. She felt cut off and impotent. If only Paul Deutch were there. At least she'd have an idea of what was going on.

She drank the last of her iced tea and checked her wristwatch. Jeff should have been finished with the testing by now. She set out for his room, her guard following her.

In the corridor, Richard Vale, looking sallow and moving with only a portion of his usual energy, walked toward her.

"I'd like to speak with you, Dr. Petrie."

"What happened to your hand?"

"An accident." Vale brushed her question aside. "I don't ever want you to interrupt my work again. Ever."

The harshness of his command made Jan bristle. "And I don't want you to exhaust Jeff," she retorted. "You're pushing him too hard, Dr. Vale."

"I'm the one who determines that, Dr. Petrie," Vale said curtly. "I'd appreciate it if you didn't upset Weston while I'm working with him."

Jan glowered at him. "I'm not the one who's upsetting him. He's always calm with me."

Frustration boiled in Jan. Vale, Kellog—all of them needed her. But she was a captive collaborator. There was no way she could hold out. Doing so would only deprive her of being with Jeff. It was a no-win situation.

"Then why don't you use some of your calming influence now," Vale snapped.

"It might help if I knew why you're so upset. I'm working blind."

"No need for that. Just handle him."

"That's easy to say." Jan put her hands on her slender hips.

Vale looked right through her. "You'll manage."

She wanted to shake him until he talked. She wanted to break through his secrecy. Instead, Jan watched him disappear down the hall.

Jeff lifted his head when she entered his room. "Dr. Petrie."

"Lie down, Jeff. Don't strain yourself." She took her position at his side and studied him. He appeared even thinner and weaker than he was when she had visited him earlier. Even his normally curly blond hair looked limp and lifeless. And his eyes bore a troubled look and his brows were drawn together, creasing his forehead.

"What's wrong?" Jan softly ran her fingers over his wrinkled brow, trying to get him to relax. "What happened today in the theater?"

Jeff closed his eyes.

"Dr. Vale was very upset."

Jeff nodded, his eyes still closed.

"No one will tell me anything. Not even you." Jan could not conceal the self-pity she was feeling.

Jeff reached for her hand. She stiffened.

"Don't pull away from me," he said. His eyes sent her reeling, spinning. "It will be all right, really it will."

Jan swallowed and tried to stop the whirling sensation. "Jeff, if you cause trouble, they'll make it worse for you. I couldn't bear it—it hurts too much."

"You're alone now, Dr. Petrie, but it will change."

Jan believed him. She accepted anything he said with a wholeheartedness that baffled her.

chapter 15

"YOU'RE LUCKY, KID. Your story checks out."

David had to fight back a sigh of relief. "So when do I get out of here?" His eyes swept the windowless cubicle which contained two beds, a night table and a single lamp, with a bathroom off to the side.

"When we decide to let you go." Kellog started to leave.

"Wait a second, why are you holding me?"

"Officially, I've arrested you for trespassing."

"What about my rights?"

"They've been waived for the time being." There was something menacing in Kellog's tone. Obviously, David knew too much. He wondered if they could possibly set him up in some way to get him out of the picture.

"I don't get a phone call?"

"Are you kidding?"

"Whatever Weston is doing must be major."

"It's none of your concern." Kellog puffed up with self-importance. "The less you know the better."

"You can't be more specific about how long I'll be here?"

"Consider yourself lucky that we haven't thrown away the key."

"Can I see Jan Petrie?"

"You don't give up, do you?"

David executed a mock salute. "Yes, sir." He threw himself on one of the beds and watched Kellog parade from the room.

"You've got to do something about Kellog, he's out of control," Vale said angrily.

"I'd say that he has entirely too much control. He's formidable." Heller did not like the way Vale looked. The fluorescent lighting in the cafeteria did not help. He held himself tensely, his eyes were haunted.

"Don't his intrusions get to you? He's such a pompous bully."

"That he is," Heller agreed. "I guess I'm used to it—working on top-secret projects all the time. The government always keeps a wary eye on nuclear physicists. Afraid we'll defect."

Vale lifted a Styrofoam cup filled with coffee. His left hand shook so much that the hot liquid splashed on the canteen's formica table and his wrist. "Damn. I wish I was ambidextrous." He tried to wipe up the mess with his injured hand, but gave up.

"Richard, put out your left hand."

Vale defensively drew it in. "Why?"

"I want to see something."

"Forget it . . . I'm tired." Vale was embarrassed. "I've got a case of the shakes."

"Thought so. You look terrible." Heller, who was capable of great excesses himself, had never seen anyone so driven.

"I just have to hang on till Thursday. That's why I'm so pissed off about Kellog. It's taking everything I've got to keep going. Sitting at meetings with that ass

Kellog and Fortner, the worm, could push me over the edge—I mean it."

"I don't relish the thought either. Tell you what I'll do, I'll put in a call to the President. The White House is the only authority that automation responds to."

"If you can get an outside line . . ."

Heller laughed.

"I'm not kidding!"

"Don't worry, I'll take care of it." Heller paused for a moment and then asked awkwardly, "What do you think about Weston?"

Vale slid his cup back and forth in the puddle on the table. "I don't know."

"I mean, my focus on the case is so limited. We can't seem to break that code. We've been working twelve hours a day." Heller propped his head up with his hand. "You've been good about keeping me informed about your discoveries. I just don't get it."

"I know, I can't put it together either." Vale started breaking pieces off the cup and floating them in the coffee. "I'm certain he started that fire yesterday. He told me he did without saying a word. If he has that sort of power, who knows what he could do if he set his mind to it."

"Do you think you should postpone Thursday's test?"

"No way!" Vale's expression was fierce. "That test will reveal everything. It's the key to this."

"I can't help feeling sorry for the poor guy. He's a pawn in everyone's game. Maybe if we allow him to get stronger . . ."

"It's out of the question."

"Why? Why is it out of the question?"

"He's not going to last."

"I think we're talking about a self-fulfilling prophecy," Heller argued. "He sure isn't going to make it the way he's being treated."

"Heller, I like you. My advice is to stay out of this. Work on the tape. Let me do my job."

"Okay, okay," Heller conceded. "I won't add to your problems. But just remember I am worried."

"Tell you what I'll do. I'll have a talk with Weston. Maybe that will calm him down." Vale looked at his watch. "I've got to run. Don't worry. Let's just stomp on Kellog."

Heller waved as Vale took off for the Kirlian Photo Lab.

A doctor and a technician sat at a long control panel in the Kirlian Photo Lab. A television console on a nearby table was wired to a computer.

Across the room, Jeff's entire body was encased by the Kirlian Body Frame, a transparent shell that looked like a bulky sarcophagus. It was propped up at a 45-degree angle. The frame was covered with thousands of tiny metal electrodes spaced at quarter-inch intervals. The contact points of the electrodes touched Jeff's skin. The body frame looked like a giant pin cushion. The twenty thousand wires leading from the electrodes converged at one thick power cable on Jeff's side, near his waist, that ran across the floor to the console. A thick tube, just below Jeff's chin, supplied air to the frame from a tank.

Inside the shell, Jeff looked terrified. His eyes were moist and pleading. The staff on duty were too busy with preparations to notice.

Richard Vale entered the room with a flurry. "All set to go? Morning, Dr. Miller, Jerry."

"Good morning, Dr. Vale, we didn't expect you here for this test."

"I'd like to look in. You run the test. I won't interfere."

A dull, muffled wail emanated from the shell.

"He's been doing that a lot. We didn't know how to handle it."

"Let me talk with him." Vale went to the frame. Jeff tried to move, but couldn't.

Vale shouted, "Don't be afraid, Jeff. It's a simple test. It'll be over in a snap."

Jeff stared back at Vale, uncomprehending. A single tear trickled down his cheek as Vale returned to the console.

"All contacts operational," the technician reported.

"Activate photo plates."

The technician threw a switch. "Photo plates activated."

The T.V. screen glowed with a dim, gray light.

"Lab lights down."

The technician pushed a button. The room went black, except for the viewing screen.

Dr. Miller ordered the start of the test. "All right. Let's take a shot of his right hand for a reading."

The technician flipped a series of switches. The dark silhouette of Jeff's hand filled the screen.

"On power."

"Power on."

The screen burst into a spectacular panorama of swirling colors, almost blinding in their brightness. Every color of the rainbow reached ever outward from the hand. The entire screen swam in a concert of reds, greens and deep violet. The colors twinkled, flared and sparked against a background of steel-blue, then burned up into a smoky spiral. Explosions of white gleaming sparks and starlike flashes erupted from the spiral.

The faces of the three observers were lit by the brilliance of the screen. They exchanged awed looks.

"My God!" Dr. Miller was astounded. "I've never seen images this intense . . . this varied before."

"Incredible!" Vale whistled.

"All right. Let's do the body shot."

The technician flipped switches and pushed buttons. The outline of Jeff's hand disappeared from the screen and was replaced by the silhouette of his entire body.

"We're going to need a lot more power for this one. Let's start with sixty cycles."

The technician reached for a dial below a small power meter. He twisted the dial to sixty, which registered dead center on the meter's range.

"Ready."

"Activate."

The technician threw the switches. They waited. Jeff's body remained a dark shadow on the screen.

"That's odd." Miller tapped a pencil. "Take it up ten points."

The technician turned the dial. The needle of the meter pointed to seventy.

"Activate."

As the power hit the electrodes, Jeff's body, trapped inside his plastic prison, arched with pain. The muffled sound of Jeff's sobbing filled the room. There was still no change on the screen.

"Damn." Dr. Miller was growing nervous as Vale watched. "Uh, take it to eighty."

"That's a lot of power. Maybe we . . ."

"Do it!" Dr. Miller ordered.

The technician hesitated, about to speak, then

reached for the dial. The needle on the meter climbed up ten points.

"Activate."

Jeff's body was blasted against the top of the frame by the electricity ripping through him. He screamed in pain.

"There! We got a reading." Miller pointed excitedly to the screen. The vague passing of dim light disappeared instantly. "It's not strong enough. It'll never come out on the prints."

"We can't keep giving him repeated charges."

Dr. Miller was in a bind. She didn't want to appear weak in front of Vale. Yet, she certainly didn't want to harm Weston. She knew about Vale's obsession when it came to work. She made a snap decision.

"Take it to Critical, give him a ten-second burst, then close all systems down."

"But, Dr. Miller," the technician gasped, "nobody can take that much. We might kill him."

Dr. Miller knew she couldn't waver at this point.

"We are here to get a body reading. And that's what I intend to do. So . . . activate."

Dr. Vale, who had remained silent, nodded his approval. The technician put his hand on the dial. He bowed his head and shook it.

"That's an order!"

The technician threw a helpless, disgusted look at the doctor and sighed angrily. He turned to the console and cranked the dial up to max. The needle on the meter swung into the red zone at 120 Critical Output.

He pushed the special safety button necessary to unleash that much power. "Activated."

Across the room, the frame rocked violently. Jeff's electrified body was battered about inside. His head pounded back and forth against the sharp points of the electrodes. A thick, crimson color filled the head section of the shell. Jeff screamed with terror. The technician buried his head in his arms on the console in front of him.

On the viewing screen, a momentary flash of light covered the area around Jeff's chest. Then the area glowed with green phosphorescence. The eerie shining instantly snapped into focus. A strange pattern of symbols flashed on the screen briefly, then disappeared.

Jeff's quaking body shook the massive frame. Like a falling mountain, the shell tore loose from its clamps. It shattered in a furious mechanical crash on the floor.

The technician sobbed with remorse. Dr. Miller stood paralyzed. Dr. Vale raced to the demolished body frame and said under his breath, "He's *got* to be okay."

In the Radioactive Materials Lab, the collection of papers, bound reports and stacks of opened books had grown. Coffee cups and ashtrays littered the table. Heller, Sinopoli and Greenwald listened to the last few electronic blips on the tape. They made notations and referred to reports spread out in front of them.

Sinopoli threw his pencil down on the table with an aggressive pop when the tape ended. Unaware of Sinopoli's restlessness, Heller and Greenwald continued to work.

"I've had it, Carl." Sinopoli rubbed his eyes. "I've spent enough time in this cramped room for today."

"I know what you mean." Heller pulled back his shoulders and stretched. "Let's all take a break."

Greenwald lit his pipe. "Thank God." He exhaled slowly. "If I have to listen to that thing one more time tonight, I'm going to start hearing things that aren't there."

Heller went to the coat rack, grabbed his jacket and picked up a fifth of vodka. He waved the bottle at his colleagues. "Care to join me?"

"I'll pass," Sinopoli said. "A drink right now would put me out of commission."

"No thanks. I need a walk under the stars."

As Heller started out the door, the CIA man, who was sitting in the corner reading a magazine, followed.

"I don't really need a babysitter."

"You know the setup."

"Terrific." Heller rolled his eyes. "Coming, Mother?"

chapter 16

JAN'S GREETING CAUGHT in her throat when she saw Jeff's condition. His silky hair was matted and caked with blood. Every inch of exposed skin was covered with pinpoint inflammations, except for his face which was ghostly pale.

Jan froze. "My God, what have they done to him?" she asked the attendant.

He shrugged indifferently.

"You *could* check the charts."

The attendant sauntered to the hook where the charts hung and checked the top sheet. "They took some Kirlian shots—had to use high voltage."

Jan glared at the attendant. "Why hasn't he been cleaned up? Look at him, he's not an animal."

"A nurse should be by soon, I don't do that sort of thing."

"Well, I do," Jan snapped. "Get me some alcohol and towels."

"I . . ."

"I know—you don't do that sort of thing." Jan's voice was cutting. "I said get me some alcohol and towels now."

"Okay, okay, lady, take it easy." The attendant shuffled out of the room.

Jeff moaned when he tried to shift his weight. Jan took his long-fingered hand in hers, afraid that her touch would be painful. "Oh, Jeff, what have they done to you?" she whispered.

His eyelids fluttered. With effort, he opened his eyes, and a look of terror flashed through them.

"It's all right, Jeff, I'm here. I'll take care of you."

He drew her hand to his face and gently rubbed it against his hollow cheek. She traced the ridge of his fine, aquiline nose, then her fingers grazed his full, soft lips. The warmth of his labored breath on her fingertips made her ache to bend over him, to draw in his breath. She wanted to pull all the pain out of him, to consume it, to swallow it up whole and to hold it inside herself. She trembled as she hovered over him, her lips open, her heart pounding. She leaned toward him, unable to resist the need to press her mouth against his.

"Excuse me." The voice of the attendant made her jerk away from Jeff. "I hate to break this up, but I've got the stuff you asked for."

"Well, bring it here—to the nightstand." Jan took a deep breath and tried to compose herself. She turned to find the attendant smirking at her.

She knew that an overblown account would quickly spread through the gossip network at the Center—like partyline, the game she remembered playing as a child. Resentment boiled in her. Even the purest of emotions got distorted and cheapened. They would reduce the tenderness she felt for Jeff to something kinky, something smutty. She wanted to explain, but she knew it would be futile. Saying anything would only make it worse.

"Help me undress him."

The attendant leered at her, but held his tongue. They quickly removed Jeff's hospital gown.

"This might sting a little at first, Jeff." She prepared a cloth to sponge him down. She pressed the cloth on his instep. He winced with pain.

With infinite gentleness, she worked over every inch of his bruised body. She dabbed at his feet, his well-shaped calves, his long thighs, his narrow hips and firm buttocks. His ribs were now visible, his stomach concave, but his back and arms were still rippled with muscles. He could have been sculpted in marble. The balance and grace of his body made tears well up in Jan's eyes—they were tears for his suffering, but they were also tears for herself and her longing.

She rinsed the blood from his golden hair and tenderly ran a comb through the tangles. Jeff's eyes were dulled by drugs, his mouth slack. She propped his head up with a pillow and whispered, "We're so helpless. I'm sorry, Jeff, for all you're going through. Sleep now."

He stirred and tried to speak. Jan placed two fingers on his lips to still him. "Don't talk, there's no need to."

Jeff struggled to speak anyway. Jan leaned to him and made out the words: "I'm not helpless . . ."

Outside Jeff's room, Jan was overwhelmed by a heavy, bone-aching weariness. She leaned against the wall and shut her eyes.

An agent appeared at her side. "You've been busy."

Jan looked at him disdainfully from the corner of her eye.

"Where to now?" he asked.

"I think I can make it back to my room without you."

"Orders."

Jan was too tired to spar with him. She shook her head and set off for her room, trying to ignore her guard.

Walking past the employees' lounge, she saw Carl Heller sitting alone at a table. He was lifting a half-full glass and toasting the agent sitting across the room.

Paul Deutch said she could trust him. She doubted it, but it was worth a try.

Jan turned to her escort. "I'll be right back." Before he could protest, she said, "Don't worry. He's part of your team."

He saw one of his colleagues inside watching Heller and decided Jan would be safe under his careful scrutiny. "I'll wait for you out here."

Jan walked into the lounge and stopped opposite Heller.

"Do you drink like this frequently?" she asked, looking from Heller to the vodka bottle.

"As often as possible, these days, Dr. Petrie."

"Why?"

"It beats the hell out of any other way of coping." He gestured expansively. "What'll you have? There's vodka, and if you don't like that there's always vodka."

"Nothing, thank you."

"Do you intend to stand there all night? Sit down, you make me nervous."

Jan pulled out a chair and sank into it. She studied the pattern of the formica tabletop. Heller regarded her with admiration.

"Well," he finally broke the silence, "you're obviously not here for socializing or sexual maneuvering. What's on your mind?"

Jan's face hardened.

"I just wanted to see what kind of man would allow a helpless person to be treated like an animal."

Heller took a swig of his drink. "Do you think I have anything to do with this? I'm half bonkers from listening to a tape recording."

"Don't any of you give a damn about him? I just came from his room." Jan's voice broke. "All you people care about is that idiotic machine and your stupid tapes."

"Look, I know how you must feel . . ."

"How could you possibly know anything about feelings? You're the one who started this whole thing."

"Wait a minute!" Heller banged his glass on the table. "I simply asked for light security measures, and for damned good reasons. This military parade is the President's idea, not mine."

Jan watched the anger rise in his strong, craggy face.

"You think I want all this? Hell, no." He downed the remainder of his vodka with a gulp and poured himself another. "Sure you won't join me?"

Jan shook her head no. "Why are you so bitter?"

"What do you want from me, lady?"

"I want you to help him. I want *someone* to stop this." Jan wrung her hands. "I want *somebody* to feel compassion."

"Listen. I've been in the lab for four straight days, knocking my brains out, trying to decipher ten lousy seconds of tape." He brushed his thick black hair back with both hands. "I'm exhausted. I came down here to get blind, stinking drunk. Not to think, not to feel. And, Dr. Petrie, compassion falls into one of those categories. So, if you'll excuse me." He lifted his glass and toasted her.

"You're a cold son of a bitch, aren't you?"

"No, Dr. Petrie." He looked into his glass. "I feel. I have needs. And believe it or not, when I get sufficiently drunk, I even cry sometimes. So get off your damn pedestal. There's nothing I can do for Weston."

Jan shoved her chair back, hurt and fury blending on her face.

"Don't go. Please." Heller reached out and took her hand. "I'm not really this much of a bastard. I honestly feel sorry for Weston."

Jan looked at the virile hand that held hers. The veins were gnarled and there was a patch of black hair below each knuckle. She remembered the sight of Jeff's wasted body, the weakness of his grasp. A reflex shot through her. Pulling her hand away from Heller's, she tucked a strand of hair behind her ear. He didn't seem to notice.

"I mean hell," he went on, "I wouldn't wish that on anybody. If I'd known this was going to happen, I'd have been more careful at the start of all this. But I was scared. Those formulae were top secret. If I had known . . ."

"Thanks," Jan said softly. "It's a comfort to know that someone is on our side." Jan felt Heller appraising her.

"Why is he so important to you?"

Jan's insides contracted. She wondered if he had the same suspicions Kellog had so crudely voiced. After what had just happened in Jeff's room, she was even more perplexed about her involvement with him than she had been. Maybe they were right—maybe sex was at the root of her feelings.

"Because I'm all he's got." She answered him from the most superficial level of her feelings for Jeff. "The only person he trusts. Nobody else gives a damn about him . . . if he lives or dies. He's just a freak to be tested, studied, used." Her eyes filled with tears. "I can't stand to see him this way anymore. He's innocent and gentle." She buried her head in her hands. "He's dying like a maltreated animal."

Heller touched her arm. "Don't cry." He handed her

a napkin and she wiped her eyes. "From what Vale tells me, Weston's powers *are* growing."

"How? He's so weak he can't even sit up."

Heller whispered to her about Vale's injury and his suspicion about Jeff. Once he started, he couldn't stop. All the recent findings at the Center spilled out of him.

Jan listened with a pounding heart, but managed to mask her astonishment from the probing eyes of the agent at the far side of the room.

"Thank you for telling me all that," Jan said breathlessly. "It really does help to know."

"You—of all people—deserve to know."

"I don't know what to think of all this . . ."

"Now's not the time to speculate." Heller shot a look at the agent who was walking toward them. "I can't tell you how sorry I am."

He spoke hurriedly, one eye on the agent. "Something evil's going on. Weston has polarized everyone. Raw ambition is surfacing everywhere. I wish I could stop it. I've tried, but I'm as helpless as you are. The only thing I have any say about is that damned tape." As the agent neared them, Vale said heartily, "Come on, have a drink."

"Don't mind if I do."

For the sake of the agent, he repeated his joke. "What'll you have? I hope it's vodka because that's all I've got."

"A double. Straight up. I might as well get where you are fast." Jan forced herself to smile. "I feel about the same."

Judging his charges' conversation to be aboveboard, the agent walked away.

"How's that? I mean—how do you feel?"

"Helpless. Tired."

"I was hoping you might say something else."

Jan gazed into his eyes, not quite understanding what he was talking about. The look that met hers was unmistakable.

"Are you married?"

"No, I've been too busy finishing my degree."

"Are you—uh—involved with anyone?" Heller swirled the vodka in his glass.

"Not really." Jan felt awkward. "Fairchild has taken all my energy. I see a few men—nothing major."

"And Weston?"

It was Jan's turn to look into her glass. "What about him?"

"Do you include him on your list?"

"He's a patient . . ." Jan avoided his eyes.

"I don't mean to embarrass you. It's just that I'd like to know. I . . ." Heller stammered.

Jan seized the opportunity to change the subject. "What about you? Are you married?"

"Was."

"What happened?"

"My wife thought I was too tied up in my work. She probably was right." He shrugged. "I'm also walking chaos. I leave debris wherever I go."

Jan laughed as he mugged. Heller grew serious.

"Listen. I didn't mean to offend you by asking about Weston. It wasn't idle curiosity." A wide smile spread across Heller's face. "Listen to me, I'm acting like a schoolboy."

Jan warmed to his good-natured self-deprecation.

"I might as well get to the point." Heller wrapped both his hands around the glass. "Maybe . . . after this damned thing is over . . . we can get together."

"Oh, I see," Jan teased. "You're asking me for a date."

"I guess you could say that."

Jan liked this man. There was always something touching about a man who was strong enough to be foolish for a woman. And, when he asked her about Jeff, there was no judgment attached.

Jan took in his dark, weathered face—the sort of face that grew more handsome with age. His elbows were on the table, his shirt-sleeves rolled up. His arms didn't look as if they belonged to a cerebral type. Instead, they were as well-developed as a professional tennis player's.

Jan was surprised that she felt no ambivalence about her attraction to Heller. Her love for Jeff didn't tug at her or make her feel guilty. She knew she could trust this man, that Heller would understand. He had the maturity and sensitivity to help her define her own feelings. For the first time in months, she didn't feel alone.

"I think I'd like that, Dr. Heller." She looked at him warmly through the curtain of her thick lashes.

"Carl to you." He grinned.

"Okay, Carl." She smiled with a faltering shyness. "But I'll need your help to get through this nightmare."

"At your service." He reached across the table. "Anytime you need me just call the radio lab."

The phone rang in the background.

"I'm going to stop them, you know."

"Be careful, Jan. These people play for keeps."

"Let them play. I'm going to stop it before they kill Jeff."

"Don't do anything crazy . . ."

"Pack it up, Heller," the agent called from the other side of the room. "You're wanted back at the lab."

"Why? I'm having a nice time here for a change." He winked at Jan.

"Greenwald thinks he may have an answer."

"For what?"

"The tape. Come on. Let's go."

Heller stood.

"So long, Jan. Be careful."

On their way out of the building, Heller and the CIA man passed a windowed room. Heller absently looked over his shoulder as he rushed by. He stopped in his tracks. There in the room was Jeff lying unconscious in bed. A quagmire of lines and tubes covered most of his body. When Heller looked at his face, which was barely visible, Jeff suddenly opened his eyes. Heller had the disturbing sensation that Jeff knew he was watching him.

He turned his head slowly on the pillow to face Heller. Jeff's arresting blue eyes sent a shock through him. Heller couldn't move.

"Come on," the CIA man said impatiently. "They're waiting for you."

Heller couldn't respond. Jeff's eyes flashed a soundless scream for help. Heller felt the plea in every cell of his own body.

The agent waved his hand in front of Heller's face. "You in a trance or something?"

The voice seemed to be coming from far away. The agent's hand did not break the magnetic force of Jeff's hold on him.

Suddenly, Heller felt as if his innermost emotions, his private world, were being viewed, exposed. It was as if Jeff was absorbing his entire being. There was nothing he could do to resist it. He felt light-headed, floating. He never wanted the sensation to end.

Jeff's eyes were warm and loving, but the pain returned, and with it, the plea for help. Heller committed himself. Weston could not die at the hands of Vale and

Kellog's army of thugs. He was filled with a certainty he'd never experienced before. Then the link was broken.

Heller blinked his eyes.

"You better lay off that vodka."

"Poor guy." Heller watched Jeff lie there peacefully, eyes closed.

"Come on. Let's get the hell out of here. That guy gives me the creeps." The agent tugged on Heller's sleeve and led him away.

Richard Vale dozed at his desk. His head, resting on a stack of reports, was lit by a tensor lamp.

"Burning the midnight oil, Doc?" Kellog's taunting voice pulled him back to consciousness.

"Hmmm?" Vale sat up and turned his head. His neck was stiff from sleeping in that position. "What time is it?" He tried to focus his eyes on his visitor. Aside from the tensor, the office was dark. He reached for his glasses.

"Close to one."

"I didn't mean to sleep that long. Turn on the light, will you?"

He blinked when Kellog flipped the switch.

"To what do I owe this late night visit?"

"It's a warning."

"A warning?" Vale was still groggy.

"Don't try to undercut me again," Kellog said through clenched teeth.

"What are you talking about?"

"I had a call from Central Office—a reprimand. I don't like being called on the carpet."

"Then don't overstep your authority."

"You and Heller hassle me, I'll do the same."

"Meaning?"

"You got your way—there'll be no briefings. And no guards on Weston. But from now on, all calls will be monitored." Kellog smiled smugly. "I can make things tough for you."

"Kellog, I have no doubts about that. You and your gestapo are a royal pain in the ass."

"There are reasons why we're here."

"Well, I wish Heller would figure out what's on that tape so you'll all pack up and go home."

"It's not that simple, Dr. Vale." Kellog looked serious. "The White House is very interested in Weston. A guy with a mind like that . . . who knows what he could do. He could be the biggest weapon since the H-bomb."

"I should have known," Vale moaned.

"On the other side of the coin, Weston could be very dangerous if his political leanings . . . let's say, if he isn't patriotic. You get my drift?"

"So you're in this for the long haul?"

"For as long as he lives."

"Hallelujah!"

chapter 17

"I DON'T FOLLOW you." Heller put his arm on the back of the sofa. Sinopoli sat next to him. He was so engrossed by what he was reading in *Science* magazine that he was unaware of the conversation going on.

"Those holes in the tape. The empty portions between the signals." Greenwald stopped pacing. "Maybe they *aren't* empty. Maybe they're just outside our hearing range."

Heller's head snapped up. "Ultrasonic?"

"Yes!"

"Damn." Heller walked to the recording equipment. "Frank, where's the nearest audiograph specialist?"

"He's already on his way."

"Christ!" Sinopoli looked up from the magazine, excited and bewildered. "Look at this." He passed the magazine to Heller.

"What is it?" Greenwald asked as Heller skimmed the article.

"Two months ago, Wilson observatory was picking up *unknown* signals. The article is by Stockwell and Kilko—they picked up the transmission. They said it sounded like Morse code."

The room was silent. Heller lifted his eyes from the

magazine and focused on Sinopoli with an unspoken question. Sinopoli let out a confused breath and nodded.

"Yep. Ten-second bursts. All the same, repetitive pattern."

"Call the observatory right away. Get one of their people down here in the morning. And tell them to bring those tapes."

Richard Vale stood next to Jeff's bed, his body taut with worry. He checked the monitors. The faintness of Jeff's signs made him gnaw on a fingernail. He looked down at Jeff, who was totally spent. Blue veins were visible under the pallor of his skin. His eyes were sunken and his high cheekbones jutted out of his gaunt face. A multitude of fine red marks, burned into his skin by the Kirlian electrodes, covered his forehead and most of his body in a burning rash of pinpoints.

"I wish there was something we could do to reassure him—it might make him respond positively," Vale said to the nurse by his side.

He tore off the paper from an EEG chart and folded it awkwardly with his left hand. He handed it to the nurse. "Get the comparatives on this and bring them to my office. And hurry." He looked at his watch. "We need those results before we take him to the Stress Lab. You've got thirty minutes."

"I'll get right on it."

Vale walked to the foot of the bed and checked Jeff's medication chart. He scratched out a figure on the chart, then went to the suspended I.V. bottle to increase the flow. He reached up with his left hand to turn the control valve on the I.V. line. While Vale's attention was on the I.V. control, Jeff thrust out his hand and grabbed Vale's injured right hand.

Blinding pain seared through him. A muffled scream tore from his throat. Vale tried to pull his hand away, but Jeff's viselike grip held fast. The pain throbbed through his body in ever-broadening waves. Vale's face was contorted in agony.

From the window, Arnold Fortner watched the grotesque tableau. His first impulse was to run to Vale's rescue. He took a step toward the door, hand poised to reach for the knob. Then a malicious smile spread on his face. He folded his arms in front of him and observed the scene from a concealed position.

Vale stared at Jeff's massive fist. His eyes bulged with panic. He lifted his gaze, prepared to see Jeff triumphant in his rage and hatred. Instead of wrath, Vale saw a look of gentle compassion. The barest of smiles touched Jeff's slightly parted lips. His azure eyes were fluid and tranquil.

Vale stopped fighting, relaxed, and gave himself to the pain. His body went limp and his panic was stilled. He felt as if he was moving through the pain, past it. A bittersweet feeling, a luscious aching, surged through him. The rapture was almost unbearable.

Fortner was dumbfounded by Vale's transformation. His colleague's face glowed with a sensual joy. Vale and Weston seemed to be in deep communion—a double trance. He saw Jeff loosen his hold on the bandaged hand.

Vale backed away from the bed. He felt weightless and elated. He looked down at his injured hand and flexed his fingers. The pain was gone. He glanced up at Jeff, whose eyes were closed. He wrinkled his brow in confused disbelief.

He began to unwrap the bandages with his left hand. When the last bandage was undone, his mouth dropped open. His hand was completely healed. There was no trace of the disfiguring burns. The flesh was perfect—as if nothing had ever happened.

Vale stared back at his hand, flexing and unflexing it. He couldn't accept that his hand was healed. He'd heard of healings before in his studies, but nothing this dramatic.

Jeff's power seemed to grow stronger as his body weakened. It was becoming more and more evident to Vale that he was onto something bigger than he'd ever dreamed. The Laser Projector test on Thursday was going to be the pinnacle of his career.

He quickly rewrapped his hand. No one needed to know about this latest development. Still thunderstruck, he headed for the door and turned out the lights.

Fortner scurried furtively away.

Jan sat on the lawn about twenty yards from the Radioactive Materials Lab. She had hiked her skirt up above her knees, stretching her long legs out in front of her while the sun melted the tension from her body. After the harrowing experiences of the past days, it felt wonderful to bask mindlessly in the southern California heat, even though an agent loitered nearby under a tree.

Carl Heller appeared in the doorway outside of the lab. He waved, loped down the stairs, and trotted to her side.

"Sorry to keep you waiting," he said as he sat down next to her.

"Don't be." Jan turned her face up to the sun. "I haven't felt this good in days."

"Neither have I." Heller stared admiringly at her supple calves. "We're finally getting somewhere on the tapes."

"Yes?" Jan said lazily.

Heller told her about the leads Sinopoli and Greenwald had stumbled upon.

"Great! Your job's almost done then." Jan was less than enthusiastic. She sat up, drawing her legs to her chest and wrapping her arms around them. "Does that mean you'll head back to D.C.?"

"That's what I wanted to talk to you about."

Jan turned to him expectantly.

"It's about Jeff." Heller plucked a blade of grass and twisted it in his fingers. "The strangest thing happened last night."

Jan lifted her delicately arched eyebrows. "What?"

"After I left you, I looked in on him. I don't know how to describe it, but he did something to me. It was as if he blasted my mind apart then put it back together. I feel different—changed."

"Did he talk to you?"

"No, I was standing outside the window. But he didn't have to talk—he seemed to be able to see right into me, into my thoughts."

"I know what you mean." Jan nodded.

"I thought you would. The whole experience was so passionate, so sensual. I've never felt anything like it."

"It was?" Jan's tone was guarded.

"I felt ravished—wide open." Heller shook his head. "I just don't have the words to describe it."

Jan's knuckles were white from clenching her hands together.

Turning his attention to her, Heller asked, "What's

wrong?'' He gently took her hand and held it.

Jan watched a cloud drift by, then she rested her cheek on her knees.

''Have I upset you?''

''No—no, I'm just thinking.''

''Well?''

''It's just that . . .'' Jan sat up and brushed a bee away. ''All along I've thought that something is really wrong with me. I felt ashamed—perverse.''

''You mean about Jeff?''

''Yes. I can't tell you how relieved I am to hear that someone else—that you—have . . .'' Jan groped for a way to finish the thought.

''I understand. If I couldn't talk to you about it, I wouldn't know what to think. And you've had to deal with the dirty-minded suspicions of everyone around you.''

Jan sighed. ''But what I feel . . . it is a kind of love, though. Just not the kind they think.''

''Without question,'' Heller agreed. ''I felt so strongly that I'm tied to him. I can't begin to understand it, but somehow I don't even want to try.'' Heller lay back on the grass and put his arms under his head. Turning on her side, Jan propped her head up with her hand. Her shining auburn hair blew in the breeze.

''So you'll help me?'' she asked.

''I can't stand by and let him die. We'll work something out, don't worry. We have until Thursday.''

Sinopoli stuck his head out the door of the lab. ''Carl, break's over. We've got a tape to work on, remember?''

''How could I forget?'' Heller responded. He sat up and circled Jan's calf with his hand. ''I'll see you later. Stay out of trouble.''

Jan watched him amble back to the lab, then shut her eyes and basked in the sun for a moment. Then she stood up and went inside to see Jeff.

Vale and Kellog supervised four attendants who were transferring Jeff from his bed to a gurney.

"Keep the glucose I.V. attached—he's very weak," Vale ordered.

"Then why are you moving him?" Jan asked from the doorway.

"I told you not to get in my way," Kellog snarled.

"Dr. Petrie," Jeff called feebly. He tried to lift his head to see her.

"Please, give me five minutes with him."

"I'm running a test at the Stress Lab—we're ready to go."

"Look, Jeff is in no condition to be tested, but since you're so adamant about subjecting him to your experiments, at least give me a few minutes with him. I think I can calm him."

Vale thought it over. The way things were going, he decided he couldn't afford not to give Jeff what he wanted. Why anger him before a test? "Okay, I'll give you five minutes with him."

Jan made her way to Jeff's side and took his hand. No one made a move to leave. She turned to Vale. "You're going to have him all day, Doctor. Could my few minutes with him be alone?"

Vale and Kellog exchanged looks. "All right, Dr. Petrie," Vale conceded. "Let's give this lady five minutes, gentlemen." Kellog waved the attendants out of the room.

Jan leaned toward Jeff and spoke softly. "I'm here, Jeff. Are you all right?"

There was no response. Jeff's eyes remained closed.

"Jeff? Can you hear me? Jeff?" Jan's voice was filled with concern. She rubbed his hand with both of hers.

Jeff opened his eyes slowly. He gazed numbly around the room. When he focused on Jan's strained face, he smiled weakly. Attempting to speak, he moved his lips and made a dry, coughing sound.

"You're parched. Let me get you some water." Jan went to the night table and brought back a glass of water with a bent straw so Jeff could drink lying down.

"Here, Jeff, sip slowly. You'll feel better."

Jeff drew on the straw indifferently. He gestured that he'd had enough.

"What were you trying to say to me?"

Sorrow washed over his face. "What have I done wrong, Dr. Petrie?" he managed to whisper hoarsely.

"Oh, Jeff." Jan had to fight off tears. "*You've* done nothing wrong."

"Why do they want to hurt me?"

Jan bowed her head. How could she explain this nightmare to him? "It's not that they're out to hurt you, Jeff. You're only a means to an end."

Jeff looked at her blankly.

"Do you understand what I'm saying, Jeff?"

He nodded his head mutely. "But my end is more important than theirs. Do I have to lose to win?"

"What are you saying, Jeff?" Jan couldn't tell if he was talking about his goals, if he had them, or his own death. His comment was inscrutable to her. He sounded so wise.

He smiled at her with an unnerving intensity. "You've always been so good to me."

Jan bent down to hug him, tears streaming down her cheeks.

"Oh, Jeff—you're the one who's good."

"Dr. Petrie, you have to help me." His plea was muffled against her shoulder. "I need more time."

"I will, Jeff, I'll help you." Determination swelled angrily within her. She brushed Jeff's hair from his eyes. She wouldn't let him die. She had to get him away before Vale's test.

As she watched him, she was gripped by the desire to talk to Jeff about his strange powers. She wanted to know if he was conscious of what he could do, if he could will things to be different.

"Jeff," she said tentatively, "I know you're tired, but I have to ask you something."

He gazed at her with affection.

"I spoke with Dr. Heller. He said you . . . the other night you . . ."

Jeff touched her forearm. A tingling shock went through her. "He's a good man."

The simplicity of his answer disarmed her. She could never tell how much Jeff understood. He always honed everything down to what was essential. Before she could press him, he closed his eyes. She leaned over him and whispered, "I'll help you, even if you won't help yourself."

"How can you help me?" He gazed at Jan.

"I'll get you out of here. I'll take you away."

"I would like that," he said softly.

"Jeff, I'm going to ask you this directly." She looked straight into his eyes, probing for any spark of response. "Do you have special powers? Can you do things, strange things?"

He did not have to say a word. His affirmation of her suspicions embraced and overwhelmed her.

"But why won't you help yourself?" she pleaded with him.

He turned his head away from her.

"Will you help me? Will you help me get you out of here?"

"Will has everything to do with it."

More gibberish . . . or was it? Jan could not tell anymore.

"Oh, Jeff," she sighed, "I'll do everything in *my* power."

"Okay, break it up," Kellog bellowed from the doorway.

In the Radioactive Materials Lab, two tape decks were turning. Synchronized electronic signals, ten seconds in duration, repeated again and again.

"So the tapes are identical." Nathan Stockwell from the Wilson Observatory turned off both machines. "You still haven't told me where the hell you got your copy."

"You wouldn't believe us if we told you," Sinopoli said.

"Try me."

The phone rang and the audiograph specialist arrived simultaneously. While Heller greeted Vince Marco, the CIA man answered the phone.

"Yeah? Who? Just a minute." He covered the receiver with his hand. "Heller, it's your playmate."

"Who?"

"Jan Petrie."

Heller excused himself to take the call. The CIA man went to get a cup of coffee from the counter on the far end of the room. He kept an eye on Heller, who turned his back to speak.

"Jan?"

"Can you talk?"

Heller glanced to the side at the CIA man. "Not really. What's wrong?"

"I need your help. Jeff's dying and you're the only one I could turn to. I don't care what they do to me. I've got to help him." Her words tumbled out in a panicky voice.

Heller spoke in a hushed voice. "Wait a minute. Calm down now."

"I can't. I don't have time. I just left him. He's fading fast. Please, Carl, believe me. One more day of this and he'll . . ." she sobbed. "I'm taking him out of here tonight."

"Don't be foolish. There's no possible way you can get him past all those people."

"Yes I can! Just before the late night shift change."

"Jan, listen to me. Don't do anything. I'll be off soon and we can talk."

"I'm going to do it, Carl. With or without your help."

"Don't be an idiot, Jan. If you get caught, Jeff doesn't stand a chance. Don't do anything until we talk."

The agent was interested in Heller's conversation. He put down his coffee cup and began to move closer.

"Listen. I gotta go. Just sit tight and I'll call you later." He heard a click at the other end of the line.

chapter 18

HELLER WATCHED AS the audioman placed a reel-to-reel tape on a recorder, next to the cassette. He ran the tape from one reel through the recording hands and wound it around the receiving wheel.

"Why the transfer?"

"Can't work off the cassette. This way I've got some control. I can play with it more—slow it down, speed it up, run it in reverse."

Marco plugged the tape deck input into the cassette. He started the cassette and pushed the record button on the larger machine. On the right, he had already set up a line recorder, which he also turned on. A band of paper moved under the marking arm. When the electronic blips began, the marker on the line recorder jumped to life. It moved in erratic, jerky strokes as it marked the sounds on the chart paper.

"Wow!" Marco's eyes opened wide. He made a quick check of his equipment. "Nothing wrong." He turned back to the line recorder. "Jesus!"

"Getting something?" Heller asked.

"Christ! I'll say. Look at these things."

Heller, Sinopoli, Greenwald and Stockwell rushed to the line recorder. The marker arm raced insanely across the paper. The continuous stream of high-peaked lines slashed back and forth. At times, the marker arm stretched clear off the paper, scraping across the metal frame border. The sound of the line recorder's motor wound up to a high-pitched whine.

"Better turn that off." Sinopoli backed away from the machine.

"Let's just watch it for a few seconds." Marco made a slight adjustment.

The marker arm strained to keep up with the recording. It made a wild sweep across the paper and snapped off its hinges. It hurtled across the room and smacked against the wall with such force that it stuck there, hanging.

Marco quickly turned off all the equipment. He looked from the line recorder to the marker hanging from the wall and back to the machine. He stroked his beard, perplexed.

"I have . . . never in my life . . . seen signals this high before."

He tore off the strip of paper from the line recorder. He smoothed it out on the table and pointed to a spot midway down one of the lines. "Whatever produced this sound . . ." He clicked his tongue. "It's a hundred times higher than anything we've ever recorded."

The physicists and the astronomer shook their heads in unison.

"What about here?" Heller pointed to the top of the line.

"This up here, we can't even classify." Marco nodded toward the recorder arm in the wall. "As you can see."

"But there *is* sound there?"

"Uh-huh. But that's not the crazy thing." Marco was

bewildered. "It's the pattern." He traced the lines on the chart with his finger. "This isn't an electronic signal."

"We haven't been able to identify it at Wilson." Stockwell confirmed Marco's statement. "No one has ever recorded a signal like this."

"What could it be?" Greenwald asked.

"It's a *voice* pattern."

Marco's statement was greeted by a stunned silence.

"Are you sure?"

"I know a voice pattern when I see one."

"It still doesn't do us any good if we can't hear the damned thing." Heller's tone was raw with frustration.

"But you can. I've got an Audio-Frequency Condenser in the van. That will allow us to slow down the tape enough to hear the sound."

"A voice pattern?" Stockwell's long face seemed even longer when he frowned. "Do you have any idea how far away the source is?"

"Your article said a billion light years away," Sinopoli said.

"Our article said *at least* a billion light years away. Gentlemen, the distance is immeasurable. Our technology isn't advanced enough to pinpoint it."

Sinopoli collapsed on the couch. Greenwald whistled shrilly. And Heller lit another cigarette, although one was already burning in an ashtray.

"I'll get that condenser." Marco raced out of the room.

David Kennedy pulled the table under the grilled air vent, which was near the ceiling of the holding room. He knew that his paunchy guard had drifted off to sleep after dinner; he had seen his shadow through the small peephole in the door. The man would sit in a chair, his head leaning to one side. Every now and then he would jerk his head up as David often did when he found himself falling asleep at a concert.

Getting into the hospital hadn't been so difficult. Getting out was another story. There was no way he could slip past the guard—even if he could get the door open. The grill was his only shot. If he worked on it every evening, he might be able to pull it off. At least, it was something to do. In fact, it would definitely become the major event of the endless days in the holding room.

David climbed onto the table and took off his belt. There were six screws in the vent. He tried to use the prong from his belt buckle to loosen a screw. The screw had been painted over and the prong was too bulky to fit into the thickly coated groove. He would have to scratch the paint away before he could make any headway loosening the screw. David couldn't tell if it would be noticeable from the door. Since the agents never came closer than to drop a food tray on the table, which normally stood to the right of the door, he thought not. He'd have to risk it. It was his only hope.

He heard a chair scrape in the hall. He jumped from the table and quickly put it back in place. So much for that evening's break-out attempt.

"I told you he's not to be trusted . . ." Fortner narrowed his eyes at Kellog. "And you wouldn't believe me." His tone was accusing.

"You saw it happen? You saw the hand?" Kellog cracked his knuckles.

"I saw it all. I was standing by the window. Vale and Weston were oblivious—they had no idea I was there."

"Why would he hide it? Why the secret?"

"I keep telling you. Vale is the most ambitious man alive."

"So?"

Fortner huffed with exasperation. "You've seen it yourself. He doesn't want to share Weston with anyone. He wants all the glory. No one can move in on his territory—oh no."

"Why don't you confront him? Have the doctor examine him?"

"What would that accomplish?"

"It would let him know he can't keep secrets. I could put a little heat on him."

"So what? He'd still get what he wants."

"You mean the Laser Projector test?"

"Right."

"Well, that's one of the reasons Weston is here."

Fortner looked at Kellog as if he were a moron. "Look, I have a plan worked out."

"Okay, shoot." Kellog leaned back in his chair as Fortner feverishly outlined his scheme. He waited with eager anticipation when he had finished.

"You're crazy, you know that, Fortner?"

Fortner's face fell. "I thought you'd like it. I thought I could count on you for help."

"How dare you?" Kellog's nostrils flared with rage. "That plan goes against every order I have."

"But . . ."

"No buts, Fortner." Kellog pointed a finger at him. "*You're* the one grasping around here."

"Vale deserves to be put down." Fortner had to keep trying.

"Not by you, he doesn't." Kellog stood up and towered threateningly over Fortner. "I forbid it, you understand?"

Fortner looked down at the floor. Kellog grabbed his shoulders. "Do you hear me?"

"Yes, I hear you." Fortner's voice smoldered with suppressed anger.

"If you try it, Fortner—I warn you—I'll bust your ass."

Jan slammed shut the big novel she had been trying to read. Her mind was spinning with plans. The agent, sitting at the far end of the library, started.

"I'm restless." Jan stood and stretched. "Think I'll get some fresh air."

The agent followed her to the door.

"Must you? I could use a few minutes alone."

The agent didn't bother to respond. He had let her out of his sight once and suffered a severe reprimand from Kellog. That was not going to happen twice.

Jan groaned. "Okay, seven paces behind me then."

When she stepped outside the main building, she surveyed the grounds. She began to walk through the parking lot to the main gate, taking in the cars as she passed.

"Where do you think you're going?" the agent asked.

Jan leaned against a black Volvo. "Don't worry, I won't make a run for it." She glanced into the front seat. Her heart leapt when she saw the keys dangling in the ignition.

"Come on, there's a nice sunset tonight. Why don't you be cooperative and enjoy it?"

"Not a bad idea." Jan smiled at the agent. She strode to the gravel path that bent around the main building and followed it into a Japanese rock garden with a running stream. The sound of the water trickling on the rocks and the perfect symmetry of the understated garden worked like a balm. Jan sat on a stone bench, touched by the serenity of the garden. She looked out over Los Angeles, all burnt orange and umber from the setting sun. From that distance, the city seemed calm and still.

Jan drew a line in the white gravel with her toe. This was the night. She knew it wouldn't work, but she had to try. She couldn't let Jeff be the subject of one more test. She couldn't sit by passively another moment.

She knew Carl would try to dissuade her with all the reasons she already knew. It was obvious she was in this particular maneuver alone. She longed for Carl to help her, but she knew he would never take such a reckless chance. But this was the only chance, and she'd suffer the consequences.

As the sun sank, the sky turned into a palette of mauves and pale yellows. Jan ached for Jeff—for his suffering, but even more for his purity. He was so innocent, and at the same time so strong and gentle, that watching his destruction was utterly unbearable. And confused as her feelings for Jeff were, they were more compelling, and somehow more fundamental than anything she had ever felt.

Jan drew her arms around herself. She had to try to get Jeff away from the Center. Even if she failed, he would know she'd tried. She gazed so intently at the dimming sunset that her surroundings were becoming hazy and dreamlike. When she saw someone approaching her from the edge of the garden, she assumed it was the agent intruding. She turned to ask him to leave her in peace.

Instead of the omnipresent guard, she saw Jeff's figure. He looked as if he was walking toward her, but he was not covering ground. His face was spectral, tormented. She rose to him, but he held up his hand to stop her.

"Your love is very powerful." His voice seemed to float on the still evening air. "But you cannot change the way events are unfolding. My power derives from the inevitable."

Jan did not understand what was happening. What the vision was saying made no sense to her. But she knew that he would help her, that he could help her.

"You will see . . ." His voice faded with the vision. Jan found herself in the garden, her guard leaning on a tree and oblivious to what she had experienced.

Marco pushed a button on the Audio-Frequency Condenser and the reels began to turn. A high-pitched, modulating sound came from the speakers. The sound was a continuous singsong, up-and-down squeal.

"What's the slowest speed you can run?" Heller asked.

"An eighth inch per second."

"Do it."

Marco reached up and pushed the stop button on the tape. He turned a small switch beneath the recording heads, rewound the tape, and pushed the start button. The tape rolled. The room filled with the rich resonance of a baritone voice.

The powerful, thundering voice charged the atmosphere in the lab. Each of the men gathered around the condenser felt it—a weakening in the knees, a falling sensation in the pit of the stomach. They looked at one another—not believing what they were hearing or how it was affecting them.

"I, uh—have to sit down." Greenwald groped for a chair.

"Turn it off," Heller ordered.

Marco pushed the stop button. When the voice died, the silence in the lab was magnified.

Carl Heller was the first to speak. "The phrasing, the intonation, it's a language—no question about that."

"But what language?" Sinopoli was numb. "I've never heard anything like it."

"Me either. And I'm fluent in eight languages," Greenwald said. "Not one word or root was familiar to me."

"What now?" Stockwell asked.

"I'd like to listen to it again," Marco said.

"Hold on a sec." Sinopoli held up his hand. "Give me a chance to pull myself together. I'm still a little shaky."

"I know what you mean, Jim," Greenwald supported his colleague. "It's more than just the shock of hearing those blips we've been listening to for days transformed into a voice. It's . . ." He couldn't find the words to finish his thought.

Everyone nodded in agreement. No one tried to verbalize what he had experienced. They were caught up in their own reflections.

"What we need is a language expert." Heller was anxious to solve the mystery. "Is there one at the Center?"

"I don't think so," Greenwald responded. "Vale mentioned that they bring people in when needed."

"Father Kinney," Marco muttered.

"Who?" Heller asked.

"Peter Kinney. Dr. Peter Kinney—he's a Jesuit. He's the head of the linguistics department at Notre Dame. I worked with him on a project a few months ago."

"What's his field?" Greenwald asked.

"Cryptography—lost languages. He's one of the foremost experts in that area."

"Where is he now?" Heller was excited.

"Last I heard he was off to the Mideast to work on some scrolls."

"Could you find out if he's back?"

"Sure. I'll call his office at Notre Dame. They always have his itinerary." Marco looked around for the phone.

"I'll have to clear the call through the switchboard," Heller said with annoyance. "Hold on."

Heller walked to the phone. After a few moments of conversation, his voice rose. "This is important . . . no I can't wait for you to find Kellog . . . right . . . right." He faced the group and grimaced. "Okay when you get Peter Kinney's office at Notre Dame, put the call through to the Radioactive Materials Lab. If the phone doesn't ring within five minutes, I'm coming over to that switchboard myself—you hear me?"

While Heller crashed down the receiver, Marco asked, "Want to hear the tape again?"

"Count me out," Sinopoli said with a laugh. "I don't have the strength."

"Let's wait for the call." Heller approached the men with a half-empty bottle of vodka in his hand. "Anyone care for a drink? I know I could use one."

"You bet." Greenwald went to get some glasses.

"I don't usually indulge, but tonight . . ." Stockwell smiled.

Marco and Sinopoli nodded enthusiastically.

The phone rang. The agent answered, "Your call."

"Why don't you take it, Marco?" Heller said as he poured the vodka.

The men waited while the audioman spoke. When finished, he turned and said, "We're in luck. Kinney's not only back from the Mideast, he's attending a conference here in L.A."

"Call him. Get him up here—*tonight*." Heller walked to the phone and handed Marco a glass. He held up his own in a toast. "To the mystery voice."

chapter 19

JAN SAT IN her room, her concentration honed to its sharpest. In a few seconds, she was about to do something she would never have believed possible. She had smuggled a full bottle of wine from the supply in the cafeteria in her spacious purse, glad that she had brought the parachute fabric bag with a lot of give. She was fully prepared to do violence, to crash that bottle over her guard's head with all her might. She had several pairs of pantyhose with which to tie and gag him. That should give her all the time she needed. Her room was in a near-empty wing. He wasn't due to be relieved for several hours.

She was willing to go through with it. She had to rescue Jeff.

Although Jan desperately hoped that she would not do the guard any serious harm, in the end, Jeff was all that mattered. She could not allow herself to think of anything else. There was no other way.

She wrung her hands, checked her watch, then headed for the door. She picked up the jug of wine from the table and slung her purse, which was filled with pantyhose, over her shoulder. With her hand on the door, she exhaled deeply.

When she stepped through the door, the guard got up from his chair across the hall. "A little midnight rambling?"

"Can't a lady have a discreet rendezvous?" she asked, praying that she might be able to talk him into letting her slip off quietly.

"Ah." He gave a lecherous grin. "So the little lady has a hot date."

"Yes, the little lady has a hot date and she wants to keep it alone."

"No way," he leered at her. "Do you think I'd miss that?"

Probably not, you jerk, Jan thought as she tightened her grip on the bottle. "I'll just be gone for a half hour or so."

He shook his head. Jan walked toward him. "Oh, please." She felt fear quaking in her stomach.

"What's that behind your back?"

Jan's lips trembled. She forced a grim smile.

"Just a little surprise for you." Jan was next to him now. She took a full swing with her arm. He backed off, arms shielding his head. The bottle arced through the air in what seemed like slow motion. Her arm froze when the bottle was a few inches from his head.

There was a dizzying ringing in Jan's ears. The ringing gradually took the form of Jeff's voice, reverberating in her skull. "Your love is powerful." The words echoed in her mind. "Come to me now. You have done enough."

The guard collapsed on the floor. Not stopping to wonder what had happened, Jan opened the bottle of wine and spilled some in his mouth and on the floor. She left the open bottle near his chair. Charged, she proceeded with her intricate plan.

Minutes later, Jan flattened herself against a recessed

door in the darkened hallway. All was quiet. Her mouth was dry from tension and her heart thudded dully in her chest. The hands of the clock on the opposite wall read 11:45. When she saw a man leave Jeff's room down the long hall, she stopped, holding her breath.

Jan stepped out of the doorway. She crept to the far end of the hall to a door marked EMERGENCY EXIT ONLY. The doorknob was covered with a metal safety guard. A thin wire ran up the wall to an alarm bell.

Jan pulled a small cuticle cutter from the side pocket of her purse. She carefully put the alarm wire between the blades of the cutter. Drawing in an unsure breath, she closed her eyes, clenched her teeth, and snipped the wire. Her shoulders hunched, ready for the blast of the alarm. Nothing happened. Silence was never more beautiful to Jan. She let out a sigh and looked nervously over her shoulder.

After pulling the guard plate away, she opened the door a few inches. The black Volvo was parked close by in the darkness, its motor idling quietly. Jan hoped whoever owned the car wouldn't miss it before she was far gone. Whoever it was, she was grateful he had left his keys in the ignition. She shut the door quietly and hurried to Jeff's room.

She rushed past Jeff's bed to the corner where a folded wheelchair was propped against the wall. She set it up and wheeled it to the bed where Jeff lay in a sound sleep.

She leaned over him and whispered, "Jeff . . . Jeff, wake up."

He didn't respond.

"Come on, Jeff. Quick! Wake up!" She took his shoulder and shook him gently. "Jeffrey, *please*. We don't have much time."

Jan glanced at the wall clock. The red second hand

swept across the face. The minute hand clicked loudly into a new position.

"Wake up, Jeff! The night shift will be here soon." She shook him more forcefully.

Jeff opened his eyes. He smiled lovingly at Jan. "You've come for me."

"Yes . . . I said I would . . . but we have to hurry."

Jeff tried to sit up.

"Wait. We have to take these things out first." Jan removed his I.V. needles, lines, and monitoring wires as quickly as her shaking hands would allow.

At the central operations desk, one light blinked off after another. The two technicians, heads bent over the evening's charts and notes, did not notice.

Jeff sat at the edge of the bed, his legs dangling over the side. He wobbled weakly. Blood flowed from where the needles had been, and Jan hurriedly bandaged them. Her eyes darted to the door when a movement at the window caught her eye. She froze.

There at the window, silhouetted in the dark hallway, was the technician for the night shift. He peered down at his clipboard, unaware of what was happening in Jeff's room.

Jeff started to say something and Jan shot out her hand to cover his mouth. His eyebrows lifted in alarm. A bead of perspiration trickled from Jan's forehead to her cheek. The minute hand on the clock screamed the passing of another minute. The moment stretched like an eternity.

Still staring at the clipboard, the technician shook his head, confused. "Dammit." He turned and walked toward the Operations Desk.

• • •

That stroke of luck gave Jan a few more minutes. Perspiration glistening on her face, Jan wiped a wet strand of hair from her forehead. She removed her hand from Jeff's mouth. The wall clock ticked off another minute.

"Can you stand up?"

Jeff nodded.

"Good. Let's get you into the chair. Quick!"

Jeff concentrated with all his effort. With one surge of power, he pushed his hands down on the bed and slowly, shakily slid his feet off the bed and placed them on the floor. He drew himself up to a precarious upright position, swaying like a child who has just learned to stand. Jan took one of his arms and put it around her shoulders. A strained grunt erupted from her throat as she tried to lift Jeff. The burden of Jeff's full weight burned into her shoulders as she tried to maneuver the chair behind him.

"Take a step, Jeff," she urged him. "Just one step . . . to the chair."

He couldn't lift his foot. The cords of his neck bulged as he strained.

"*Try*, Jeff. Try!"

Desperately, Jeff struggled to move his rubbery legs. He lost his balance and started to fall. Jan staggered under his weight.

Vainly trying to hold him up, she grabbed the side of the bed. She willed her trembling muscles to hold firm, but her small frame lacked the power to sustain the effort. They collapsed to the floor in a tangle of arms and legs.

Jeff was shivering violently, his face was white with exhaustion. Jan crawled to the wheelchair and rolled it in front of Jeff.

"Use your arms, Jeff. Try to get to the chair!"

"I can't," Jeff croaked.

"Yes, you can." Hysteria made her voice shrill. "*Try*, Jeff!"

Jeff heaved against the tile floor and managed to rise a few inches. His lips were drawn back tautly from his teeth from sheer physical exertion. His body shook from the strain. He collapsed again.

"I'll help you." Jan moved behind him. Kneeling, she put her arms under his shoulders and tried to drag him to the chair. She refused to give up. Her hair was dripping, her face pained and determined.

"I got the wrong chart." The technician dropped the clipboard with a clatter on the counter of the Operations Desk.

The man on duty turned in his chair and reached toward the chart file. He stopped when his eyes rested on the wall panel. "Somebody disconnected him! All the lights are out! Hit the alarm!"

Jan pushed, shoved and dragged Jeff, inching toward the wheelchair. The screaming of the alarm ripped through the night. Sobbing, hysterical, Jan doubled her efforts.

"Jeff, please get up! Get up!"

"I can't," Jeff said, defeated.

"Yes you *can*. Try, Jeff! Oh God. Try . . . please try." Jan heaved at Jeff's bulk, one last time. She gave up with a moan. Panting, exhausted, she dropped her head.

"Why don't you save yourself, Jeff?" she whimpered.

The alarm shocked the sleeping Center to life. From

all over, doors sprang open. The halls filled with shouts and confusion as technicians, doctors, and agents raced toward Jeff's room, converging outside his door. Vale pushed through the crowd. "Let me through, let me through! Where the hell is Kellog?"

Kellog appeared with a phalanx of agents, their feet pounding on the floor.

Vale glared at him. "Maybe if your men weren't so busy screening our calls . . . what the hell happened?"

"What about your staff?" Kellog retorted. "You're the one who said the monitors would be sufficient. You're the one who said my men made Weston jumpy. You and Heller have certainly done a job."

"If he dies, Kellog . . ."

They stopped in the doorway, halted by the scene before them.

Sitting on the floor with her legs tucked under her, Jan cradled Jeff in her arms. His head rested in her lap. Tears flowed freely down her lovely face. She looked bedraggled, forlorn. She stroked his silky blond hair and rocked back and forth.

"I'm sorry, Jeff. I'm sorry." She moaned, oblivious to the number of people who were gathered at the door.

"You tried, Dr. Petrie." Jeff's voice was smooth and comforting. "You tried to save me."

"Oh, Jeff." Hopelessness hung around her like a shroud.

Jeff looked deeply into her eyes. He slowly lifted his hand and brushed the tears from her cheek. Her eyes locked into his and she felt a strange energy rising from the base of her spine. As the tingling warmth ascended, it dispelled the sorrow that was flooding her. As it moved upward, the sensation grew more intense.

Each breath became a sigh. When it reached her neck,

Jan knew she had never experienced such excruciating pleasure. Her body vibrated with rapture. She felt as if she were poised on the brink—ready to fly rather than fall off.

Suddenly the blissful force exploded in her skull—like a thousand peonies opening to full bloom in an instant—velvety, lush and fragrant. Jan reeled from an ecstasy that was beyond words, beyond love, and beyond life itself. Her eyes shone with an unearthly fire as she clasped Jeff to her.

"That wasn't too bright, Dr. Petrie." Kellog was ill at ease in Jan's presence. Now he understood what Fortner had described to him—he had seen it with his own eyes. "How far did you think you could get with this?" Jan didn't answer. As they walked down the corridor, she looked at her feet.

"Here we are." Kellog gestured to the agent to unlock the door. "We'll put you in with your friend Kennedy for the night. Sorry for the cramped quarters—we weren't expecting you."

"Jan!" Kennedy cried when he saw her. "Sit down. What have they done to you?"

"Ask her what she did to herself," Kellog said as he slammed the door.

"David, I'm so glad you're here. So much has happened." David patted the bed, indicating that she should sit down.

"Maybe telling you will help me sort it out for myself."

"Shoot."

David listened with growing astonishment as Jan calmly related the events since Jeff was struck by lightning. She spoke with passion, but she was also careful to include every detail. David's eyes widened as she described her own experience with Jeff.

"I was soaring. I felt as if I had exploded into a million pieces and there was no longer the weight of life's cares to hold me down." Jan's eyes glowed and her face was radiant. "It was like achieving nirvana. I've read most of the mystics— written descriptions just don't do it. There's no way to capture the experience, trying to define it just doesn't work."

"This is mind-boggling. This is the most incredible story I've ever heard in my life." David was eager for her to go on.

"You can't imagine what they're doing to Jeff. It's really terrible." Jan's voice grew harsh. "If you could see these people. They're so driven. They're all obsessed by power in one form or another. When they confront real power—perfect, loving power, they conspire to destroy it."

Jan covered her eyes for a moment, then looked up. "If they could, they'd absorb it like parasites. But they can't—they're too small, too corrupt. So instead, they smother it—they obliterate it."

David took her hand without saying a word.

"God, David, I'll never be able to look at people the same way again."

"But you can't forget about Jeff."

Jan nodded. "You're right."

"And when we get out of here . . ."

"You mean *if* we get out of here."

"*When* we get out of here, people are going to hear this story. We'll tell them, Jan."

"What difference will it make?"

"Don't sound so disheartened, we'll make them listen."

"Don't you understand? I don't care about them. Goodness doesn't have a chance. All I care about right now is Jeff." Jan clutched David's hand. "They're going to kill him. Tomorrow. That Laser Projector test—he'll never make it. He was too weak to crawl tonight."

"We've got to get out of here."

"You haven't managed so far."

"This isn't the time for despair—we still have a chance."

Jan looked levelly at the young reporter. "Okay, what do we do?"

"You wouldn't happen to have a nail file in your purse, would you?"

Jan looked at him quizzically. "Sure. I always carry one. What are you planning to do with it? Make a tunnel."

David pointed to the grill. Jan stood under it and peered up. She saw that the paint had been scraped off the screws.

"Where does it lead to?"

"Outside, I think. It's an air vent."

"What are we waiting for?" Jan picked her purse up from the bed and shuffled through it. She pulled out a metal file.

"You stand guard by the door. Turn off the light, they'll think we're sleeping."

"How will you see?"

"I want out of here so badly I don't have to see what I'm doing." David carried the table across the room.

"This will take a while—they're in there pretty tight."

"Wait. I've got some cuticle clippers, too. They may be stronger."

"Great. After I get them started, we can both work up here."

chapter 20

"DR. KINNEY, I'D like you to meet Nathan Stockwell from the Wilson Observatory and my associates, Frank Greenwald and Jim Sinopoli."

"My pleasure." The tall, white-haired, ascetic-looking priest, dressed in the long brown robes of the Jesuits, shook the hands extended to him. "I didn't get any details. My assistant said it was urgent, so I came right over after the breakfast meeting."

A technician entered the lab. "Excuse me." He handed a photograph to Heller. "Here are the Kirlian shots fresh from the photo lab. Dr. Vale thought you might be able to make some sense out of them."

"Thanks." Heller examined the photo. A strange pattern was visible above Jeffrey Weston's chest. "This is remarkable—look at this pattern:

Father Kinney glanced down at it. He pulled out his glasses. An expression of unsure recognition spread on his face.

"May I?" he asked.

"Certainly." Heller handed the photograph to Kinney. He stared at it, eyes widening in confusion.

"Where did you get this?"

"You recognize it?"

Kinney held the photo closer.

"What is it, Father?" Sinopoli asked.

"This is quite impossible. I . . ."

"Do you know what they mean?"

"Well . . . yes, but . . . I don't understand. This is incredible." His attention returned to the vertical rows of symbols. "We deciphered these symbols only seven days ago.

"Only two of us even *know* about the existence of them," Kinney went on.

"What are they?" Stockwell asked.

"Cuneiforms. Ancient Aramaic writing. We haven't submitted our findings to the Church yet. How did you . . .?"

"What findings?" Heller didn't want to answer Father Kinney's questions yet.

"May I have a glass of water, please? This is quite a surprise."

"Would you like some coffee, Father?" Sinopoli asked.

"No thank you. Water will be fine."

Father Kinney folded his hands in front of him and waited in silence for the drink. He took a sip and placed the glass on the table. "Ah, that's better. About the cuneiforms. I've just returned from an archaeological dig in Jerusalem."

He fingered the simple wooden cross that hung from his waist. "We knew that the city had been destroyed in 586 B.C., but certain ancient documents indicated that yet another *older* city had existed there before that time. Archaeologists found the ruins of that city. At a depth of seventy feet, they unearthed a small temple."

He picked up the picture. "*This* picture is an exact duplicate of the cuneiforms they found etched into the walls of the temple . . ."

Vale had been up since dawn working feverishly at his desk. This day was going to bring the culmination of everything he had been working for. Never again would he have to hustle for funds. He didn't care about the celebrity that Weston would bring him. What mattered most to him was what had always come first in his life—his work. To launch his project with a subject like Weston guaranteed success. He would be free of mundane details for the rest of his life. He could spend his time charting the limitless range of the mind.

Vale's excitement was palpable. Putting down his pencil, he gazed out his window. Los Angeles was blanketed by an early morning haze which softened the hard edges of the Center buildings.

The phone rang. He answered, "Vale."

A concerned look crossed his face. "Increase his I.V. and keep a close eye on his monitors. If there's any change, let me know instantly. We might have to move the test up."

"That bad?" Kellog had slipped into the office.

Vale nodded.

"Will he live?"

"I doubt it. He's too weak. But we'll do that test. That's the important thing."

"I don't know about that. The White House wants him alive. I'm going to ask for orders to stop the test."

Vale pounded his fist on his desk. "No, Kellog. That man's going to die. There's nothing we can do for him. If you think . . ."

"If the White House decides there'll be no test, you're out of luck."

"And if he dies—which he will—you're the one who'll be in hot water." Vale realized he had the upper hand, the final say. "You see, if I run the test today, we'll have everything on tape—the total accumulation of Weston's knowledge. And that's better than nothing."

Kellog looked at him with unbridled hatred. "You've got it all worked out, don't you, Doctor? Okay, run the test—it's your big day."

He couldn't leave without taking one more shot at Vale. "By the way, you'll have to proceed without Jan Petrie. She's locked up with Kennedy. I'm sure as hell not going to release her."

Vale tried to mask his worry, but the rapid blinking of his eyes gave him away.

"I can't wait to see what Big Boy will pull when he can't see her. I wouldn't want to mess with him, Doc. You'd better be ready to kiss your equipment goodbye."

"I'll take that chance, Kellog." Vale bluffed. He wouldn't give Kellog the satisfaction of knowing the extent of his apprehension.

Kellog sauntered out of the room with a studied casualness. Before Vale had a chance to reflect on what could go wrong, Dr. Blum rushed in and handed him a chart.

"These are the carbon fourteen results on the wood sample we took out of Weston."

"Well?"

"The particle is between eighteen and twenty-one hundred years old."

Vale received the information with a routine nod of his head.

"A nod? Is that all the response I get for this extraordinary piece of data?"

"Dr. Blum, nothing could surprise me about Weston anymore."

"I don't understand any of this." Blum stroked his beard."

"You will—this afternoon." Vale swiveled his chair around to face the window.

A spasm shook Jeff's body and his face became beaded with perspiration. A nurse hovered over him. She checked an electrode on his temple. When her fingers brushed his skin, her face registered surprise. She placed her hand on his forehead.

"He's burning up!"

The technician who sat across the room to operate the monitoring equipment snapped his head up from the charts. "That's nothing. Look at his body weight."

The nurse turned to read one of the screens. "Wait a minute. Nobody loses twenty-five pounds overnight."

"*He* did. This equipment is functioning perfectly." He surveyed the other screens. "Christ, I'll say he has a fever—look at his temperature."

They both stared at the illuminated numbers on one of the screens. It read: BODY TEMP—107. They watched as the temperature rose steadily in fractions of hundredth degrees.

The nurse slapped her hand over her mouth. "He can't be alive."

"Well, he *is*, dammit! Get Vale in here!"

• • •

"Here's the last one." David held up a screw.

Jan slumped on the bed. David carefully pulled the grill off the wall and placed it on the table.

"Free at last."

Jan walked to the opening and peered in. "Not yet. We still have some climbing to do. That shaft looks awfully narrow. How are we going to do it?"

"This is the only way out—we've got to. I'll get in and reach out to pull you up."

"I don't think I can. It looks so claustrophobic."

"This is no time to get cold feet. Come on up on the table—give me a boost." Jan knelt on the table and locked her fingers together.

"Ready?"

David put his foot in the cup of her hands. With a grunt she lifted him as high as she could. He got a hold on the bottom edge of the opening and hoisted himself up.

As he pulled, he turned, red-faced, to Jan and said, "Okay, here goes. I'll reach down for you. Be ready."

His head and shoulders disappeared into the metal tunnel.

Vale leaned over Jeff, listening to his heartbeat with a stethoscope. "What is it now?" He called to the technician at the monitoring equipment.

"107.9 and rising."

"We're going to lose him." Vale tore the stethoscope from his ears. He jerked his head to Kellog, who was standing at the door. "Notify everyone! The test is to begin immediately. Get everyone to the theater."

"Right."

"We can't do it this soon," a technician from the Medical Theater said hesitantly.

"We have to!" Vale snapped.

"It'll take at least one more hour to reprogram . . . we've been working on it through the night."

"Tell them to move it. I want to run that test in an hour."

"We'll try, Dr. Vale."

"I said an hour—that's it. I'll go with you to talk to the staff." Vale turned to the doctor by Jeff's side. "Get some ice down here. Drop his temperature. But dammit, keep him alive. Get Johnson to supervise."

As he rushed out of the room, he checked the reading. Jeff's temperature had risen to 108.5 "He *has* to last," Vale whispered, "just a couple of hours."

The hallways of the Center surged with activity as the staff prepared for the test. Arnold Fortner purposefully strode down the hall to Jeff's room. At the window, he observed the scene inside. Jeff was submerged in a large, tublike apparatus filled with ice. His face had the pallor and waxy quality of a death mask. His body shuddered repeatedly and so violently that water splashed over the sides of the tub. Dr. Johnson, the senior physician, sat beside Jeff with his eyes glued on the screens.

Fortner pushed through the door.

"You can leave, Bill. I'll take care of everything." Johnson knew about the tension between Fortner and Vale. Everyone at the Center did. Fortner's futile competitiveness was the subject of snickers and a host of jokes.

"But, Richard said . . ."

"I know what he said. He changed his mind. He asked me to take care of it."

Johnson wanted to challenge him, but Fortner's self-important look—like a child who's just been allowed to do something grown up—made him feel sorry for the man. Maybe he finally did badger Vale enough to give him some responsibility at the eleventh hour. Why not? He *was* the assistant director.

"Okay. They're coming down with more ice. Even though it's supposed to stay cold in this device. Weston's temperature is so high it's melting."

"What's his temperature?"

Johnson cocked an eyebrow. "Over there—on the monitor."

"Oh, yes—110 and climbing. Thanks for holding down the fort, Johnson. I'll take over now."

Johnson regarded him evenly and didn't make a move to leave. Fortner busied himself with the charts. Without looking up, he said, "See you at the theater."

Johnson rose from his chair. "If you need me, just call. I can be here in a second."

"I don't think that will be necessary. Thanks anyway." Fortner turned his back on him as he left. When the door swung closed, Fortner put down the charts. He looked over his shoulder and saw Johnson standing at the window watching him. Embarrassed, Johnson waved and bustled off.

Fortner let a few moments pass. He went to the wall behind Jeff and pushed several buttons beneath a small screen. He then took one of the EEG wires attached to Jeff's scalp and yanked it out of the monitor. He plugged it into one of the inputs below the screen, which lit up. He sat by the side of Jeff's tub, eyes glowing with expectancy, and leaned toward Jeff.

chapter 21

IN THE MEDICAL THEATER, Vale stood beneath the screen of the projector. He surveyed the huge room, which was buzzing with activity. Final preparations for the test were in full swing. Suddenly, the light banks of one of the inactive computers came alive with flashes and buzzes. Vale turned to the bank and ordered, "Shut that down." There was no one there.

Puzzled, he checked out the computer. He pushed several buttons, but the computer continued to function. He walked around to the back of the console and studied the complicated web of wires. Something was wrong. Someone had tampered with the wiring. One line led to a little-used input in the wall.

A sense of foreboding gripped him. Someone was trying to sabotage the test. Someone who knew the computers. "Bob." He called the head technician who was working across the room. "Come here." Bob dropped his pencil and came running.

"Someone has been fiddling with the wiring." He pointed to the plug. "See."

"That leads to the main building."

"I know. Who's been working on this section?"

"No one. It's set."

"Did you notice anyone in this area?"

"Dr. Vale, I've been working like a maniac since yesterday afternoon. This place has been chaotic." Bob gestured to the team of technicians milling all through the theater. "Wait a second . . ."

"What?"

"Dr. Fortner . . ."

"Fortner!"

"Yes. He came in very late last night. I was up to my ears in the reprogramming, but I did see him around."

"My God." Vale raced up the center aisle of the theater, leaving Bob staring after him.

His feet flew over the gravel paths. The tails of his white lab coat billowed behind him. He ran panting into the main building, and came to an abrupt halt when he saw Dr. Johnson approaching him.

"Johnson," he said, gulping for air, "why aren't you with Weston?"

"Fortner relieved me." Johnson backed off as Vale drew near him, furious.

"I told you to . . ." Vale bellowed. "Never mind!" He tore down the hall. When he arrived at Jeff's door, he threw it open and charged into the room.

Fortner sat next to Jeff. His hand was clutched tightly around Jeff's forearm and he was staring absently into space, his eyes glazed, wide. His mouth hung open loosely with an odd, vacant grin on his lips.

"What are you doing, you idiot? You'll kill him!"

Fortner continued to stare into nothingness. Vale's rage failed to penetrate his stuporous state.

Vale strode across the room and began to pull plugs and flip switches. "Tell me what you've done, dammit!" he roared.

The humming of the equipment whirred down to silence. As if hearing Vale's voice from far away, Fortner lifted his head and turned toward him. His eyes were ablaze. He smiled at Vale—madness etched into his features.

"He won't die, Richard," he said smugly. "He told me."

"Told you *what*?"

Fortner closed his eyes. He rocked back and forth in his chair, lost in his private vision.

"Fortner!" Vale's voice was threatening as he approached him.

"He won't die, Richard." Fortner broke out into a peal of laughter. "He told me . . . I'm the only one who knows."

"Knows *what*?"

"We're not supposed to know . . . we're not ready yet." Fortner tightened his grip on Jeff's arm. "But I know—I found out—I'm the only one." He giggled shrilly. "This time I'm first, Richard, he told me."

Vale listened as Fortner's babbling grew more frenzied. He had lost his mind—there was no question about it.

"You see, he won't die . . . he's returned . . . and he'll return again and again . . . until we're ready . . . he won't die." Fortner clamped his hand around Jeff's forearm like a vise, unaware in his delirium of what he was doing.

"Let go of him. Take your hands off him." Vale lunged at Fortner and tried to pry his fingers loose from Jeff's arm. But, in his madness, Fortner held on fiercely.

Awakened by the struggle, Jeff strained against the pressure of Fortner's grasp. His face twisting from the effort, he wrenched his arm free.

"God damn you!" Fortner attacked Vale, scratching at his face. Vale easily deflected the smaller man's blows. The more unaffected Vale seemed, the more frenzied Fortner became until he was blindly lashing out at anything. He hurled himself about the room, crashing into the walls and equipment. The violence of his manic movements escalated until, his energy wasted, he collapsed in a heap on the floor.

Vale shuddered when he turned his attention to Jeff. All life had drained out of Jeff's face. His skin had taken on a blue cast. His eyelids fluttered weakly and his breathing was shallow. He had nearly bitten through his bottom lip.

Vale took a step toward the bed. He froze, feeling as if his will had left him, as if every fiber of his being was on hold. The sudden awareness of the crowd at the door reached him. He turned and saw the shocked faces of attendants, nurses, agents and technicians, felt their breathless silence, and their terror.

"Don't just stand there." His voice was hoarse, distant. No one in the crowd moved. Vale straightened his sagging shoulders. This was no time to give in. It was too close—everything he'd ever dreamed of was within his reach. He couldn't let it slip through his fingers. He took a shaky breath.

"You two, get Fortner down to a psychiatric holding room. And you, get Weston to the theater. Right now!"

Two attendants rushed to Fortner and half lifted, half dragged his writhing body from the room.

"Don't do it. You saw what happened to me. Don't touch him," Fortner howled. "If you run that test . . ." His voice faded as he was dragged down the hall.

"Don't listen to him, ignore it." Vale tried to outshout him. "Fortner's mad!"

His eyes swept over the crowd and he knew he had lost them. It was with relief that he picked out Kellog's strong face. At that moment, Vale fully appreciated the man's blind sense of duty.

"Okay, folks, back to work," Kellog boomed with authority. "You heard Dr. Vale. Scofield and Garner . . ." The two agents looked at their boss with dread. "Move Weston to the theater. That's an order."

Reluctantly, the men approached either side of the bed. The air was taut with tension as the crowd waited for the agents to touch Jeff. Jeff opened his eyes and turned his head from one agent to the other. A feeble smile spread on his lips. "Don't be afraid," he said in a soft, resigned voice.

The men moved quickly to transfer Jeff to a gurney. When it was clear that they weren't going to witness another horrifying event, a murmur rose up in the crowd.

"All right, break it up," Kellog said. This time, the crowd dispersed in buzzing clusters.

"Make an announcement," Vale ordered one of the staff. "The test will begin immediately. Have everyone report to the Medical Theater now."

"What about the computer changeover?" one of the technicians asked. "We still haven't . . ."

"To hell with it! We'll take him as far as we can before he dies. Hurry!"

chapter 22

"DR. KINNEY, I can't tell you *why* we need this information, but believe me, it's vital." Heller loomed over Father Kinney, who was seated at the table. Kinney stared stright ahead.

"We can force you to give us the information, Church or no Church. So let's not make things difficult."

Kinney caressed his wooden cross and sighed. He pointed at the picture in Heller's hand. "These cuneiforms were written eight thousand years before the birth of Christ. They accurately prophesy His original appearance on Earth and speak of a return."

"When?"

"Two thousand years later."

"That's all of it?"

"No." Kinney looked at the photograph. "It says: 'For . . . as the lightning . . . cometh out of the East, and shines even unto the West . . . so shall the Coming of the Son of God. . . . Watch, therefore, for ye know not what hour . . . your Lord doth come. . . .' "

"It can't be!" Sinopoli cried.

Greenwald just stared at the photograph. Heller put his hand on the priest's shoulder. "Doctor, I want you to listen to something."

Anticipating Heller's next move, Stockwell had crossed the room to the tape deck. He pushed the start button.

Father Kinney wiped the perspiration from his face with a clean white handkerchief. The resonant voice on the tape echoed in the lab. Awestruck, he stared into space. Heller, Sinopoli and Greenwald encircled him where he sat on the sofa. As the last sounds of the voice were replaced by the thin hiss of empty tape, Kinney swallowed and looked up at the physicists. He nodded, speechless.

"Everyone, please assemble in the Medical Theater. The Laser Projector Test will begin immediately. Please report to the theater now." The message on the P.A. blasted urgently.

Heller wheeled and ran to the phone at the far end of the room.

"What now?" Sinopoli asked.

"We've got to stop the damned thing—before it's too late." He punched out a number on the phone.

"Nobody'll believe it. It's too crazy," Greenwald said.

"But how . . ." Father Kinney stammered, ". . . where did you get that recording?"

"Not *one* recording, Doctor. Two." Heller said from the phone, "I've got to speak to Dr. Vale." He spoke into the receiver. "This is Heller—it's urgent."

"Two?" Kinney's expression was blank.

"Two identical recordings. One, from a retarded man. The second, from a radio telescope," Greenwald explained.

"You don't honestly expect me to believe that, do you?" Kinney said.

"Come on, come on," Heller muttered into the

phone. He spoke to Kinney. "That *is* the truth. That voice came from the lips of a retarded man. It also came from somewhere out there . . . an immeasurable distance away."

Father Kinney shook his head vehemently. "Absurd . . . it's a lie!"

"*If* it suggests that Christ was a space traveler, yes, I'm willing to agree with you, it *is* a lie, provided you have scientific proof."

"This is the most unspeakable blasphemy . . ."

"Heller—at the Radio Lab—it's urgent, I *must* speak to him. No, I can't hold."

Heller turned again to Father Kinney. "Look, I'm not a religious fanatic, Father Kinney. I'm a scientist. Come up with some facts and I'll go down on my knees and pray."

"That man—whoever he is—you have to take me to him. I must see him."

"Wait a second, I think I've got Vale." Heller clamped the phone to his ear. "Dammit I've been cut off." He turned to the omnipresent agent. "Keep trying, will you?"

He walked back to the group. "I'll be damned," he muttered to himself. "It explains everything. *That's* why he spoke the Latin . . . Einstein's voice . . . the equations."

Sinopoli and Greenwald waited eagerly for Heller to continue. Father Kinney was lost in his own thoughts. Heller joined them, but didn't go on. He clenched and unclenched his teeth and nodded.

"What do you mean?" Sinopoli finally asked.

"Don't you see?" Heller looked up at his colleagues. "For some reason, he's become a receiver. A *human* receiver."

"You're losing me," Greenwald said.

"Look. The theory that energy never dies." Heller began to think out loud. "That everything we do and say doesn't cease, doesn't vanish, but remains forever in space as energy."

"So?" Greenwald asked.

"You know the old question: How do you build a machine that can recreate, reform that energy into shapes and sounds?"

"Sure." His associates were following him intently.

"Weston is that device. Something has turned him into a perfect receiver. Something . . . something out there . . . opened a door through which energy beams down to him. A powerful beacon, a stream of some kind. Weston's gymnastics are nothing but the result of that energy."

"Wait a minute," Sinopoli interrupted. "What about the prophesy, the cuneiforms—Christ? How does it all . . ."

"There's got to be an answer." Heller paced nervously. Suddenly, the tape recorder clicked on. All four men jumped, then all of them turned simultaneously to watch the machine. The same voice thundered from the tape, but the recording had changed. Even to an untrained ear, it was obvious that a different language was being spoken.

The voice boomed, *"Hasof Baah. Hasof Baah. Shemoar Otach. Hene Zehn Baah. Ve-ahni eshlach ahpi al otam. Ve-eshpot otah lefi derachechah."*

"What the . . ." Greenwald exclaimed.

"What is it, Father?" Sinopoli asked Father Kinney.

Father Kinney paled. He made the sign of the cross. "Hebrew . . . Old Testament."

"Well, translate," Heller ordered.

Kinney was dumbstruck.

"Let him listen through it," Sinopoli suggested. "Here's some paper and a pen. Why don't you transcribe what you can?"

Kinney waved him away. "No need—I'll never forget those words."

"The Medical Theater is on the line." The agent held out the phone to Heller.

"Vale . . ."

"I'm sorry, Dr. Heller, he's unavailable."

"I've got to talk to him."

"Impossible."

"Tell him that I've deciphered the tape. Tell him that it's *imperative* that he discontinue any further testing."

"Yes, sir. I'll get that message to him as soon as he's finished in the theater."

"It will be too late by then. Tell him *now*, do you hear me?" Heller demanded.

"I can't. The restricted light is on. They've already started the Laser test."

The Hebrew continued to sound, adding to Heller's urgency. *"Ve-achshav ahni eshpoch chamasl al otam. Mashchis Baah veatem shavoo shalom veayn po.*

"Listen to me, you get to Vale immediately. Tell him to STOP THAT TEST!" Heller slammed the phone down just as the voice stopped.

Automatically, as if possessed, Father Kinney began to recite the words on the tape.

"Neither will I have pity. But I will recompense thee according to thy ways, and thine abominations shall be in the midst of thee. And ye shall know that I am the Lord."

Kinney grasped his crucifix in both hands. "An end is come. The end is come. Watcheth for thee. Behold it is come."

His voice broke. His bottom lip quivered. "And I will

send mine anger upon thee and will judge thee according to thy ways."

"We've got to stop that test," Heller cried as he raced to the door. Sinopoli and Greenwald followed.

Father Kinney stayed behind and continued his translation. "Now I will shortly pour out my fury upon thee. Destruction cometh, and ye shall seek peace and there shall be none."

Sinopoli turned back at the door. "Come on, Father. You wanted to see Weston. This might be your last chance."

Father Kinney stumbled to the door.

David dragged himself through the narrow ventilator shaft. Panting, he looked over his shoulder. Jan lay still, her face pressed against the cool metal about five yards behind him.

"Don't give up now, Jan. This is the easy part."

Jan's groan echoed off the walls of the shaft.

"All you have to do is shimmy forward. No more climbing for awhile."

"I can't breathe."

"Just take it slow. Try to inhale deeply and relax, you'll feel better." He heard her take a few jagged breaths.

"It's so dark—it doesn't matter if I close my eyes or not. I feel trapped." She pounded the shaft with her fists. "It makes me want to kick my way out of this . . . this coffin."

"Try not to think about it, just move. Every inch is closer to being out."

"I don't believe it . . ." Desperation constricted her voice. "I don't believe we'll ever get out of here."

"Okay, I'm coming back for you."

David placed his hands under his chest and shoved himself backward. The toes of his shoes resisted the movement and dragged against the metal. He bent his legs up from the knees, lifting his feet the little bit he could and pushed off again. This time he moved a few inches.

"Hold on, I'm on my way."

"Just go ahead, leave me here. I'm just slowing you down." David could tell from her voice that she was about to cry. "What's most important is saving Jeff. Don't waste time on me."

"No, Jan, we're in this together. I can't leave you behind." Their voices echoed dully in the metal shaft.

David's arms trembled from the effort of moving himself backward in the confined space. He couldn't hold his feet up for another instant. They thudded against the thin metal and sent a shock through the shaft.

Jan began to sob. "Please, please go on ahead."

"I'm almost there," he said, breathing heavily. He inched his way backward, collapsing every few inches from the laborious effort. Finally, he felt Jan's hand grasp his ankle.

"Here I am," she sniffled.

"Now pull yourself up over my feet and wrap your arms around my knees."

Jan held both his ankles. She strained to tug herself up to his knees.

"I can't—it's too tight in here." She released his ankles. Her hands fell limply on the metal.

"Okay, I'll flatten out. Try again." David extended his feet and pressed his legs against the shaft. "Keep your head down."

Jan pulled herself up as far as his calves.

"Okay, this will work." He spread his legs as far as he could. "Drop your head between my legs. This is going to be a bumpy ride."

He felt Jan quivering. "We're going to be all right," he reassured her. "Just hold on."

"I'm sorry, David . . . for falling apart on you."

"Don't think about anything but getting out of here. Let's go." David tried to squirm forward, but with Jan hanging to his legs he couldn't budge. "You're going to have to push with your feet. One, two, three, push . . ."

chapter 23

EVERY SEAT IN the Medical Theater was occupied. Center employees filled the auditorium, their faces upturned to the stage. Laser Projector technicians worked frantically in clusters. Others raced from terminal to terminal to orchestrate the final preparations for the test.

The level of excitement was at a fever pitch. Everyone knew that this was the most important moment of the Center's history. They all felt that they were about to witness a major scientific breakthrough. But it was more than that. They knew what was about to happen had a significance beyond their comprehension, beyond the range of their experience.

Richard Vale stood on the stage, dwarfed by the enormous screen. His body was rigid, his movements jerky as he leaned over the edge of the stage to discuss last-minute details with his staff. Beside him, Jeff was strapped into the reclining chair. Since he was too weak to sit, the audience could only see the Medusa-like headpiece with its wires leading to the walls of equipment.

Dr. Vale raised his hands over his head for attention, a needless gesture since all eyes were on him. He squared his shoulders and said, "I've waited twenty years for this moment—so let's get on with it!"

He turned to Jeff and patted his hand. Eyes glistening, he nodded to a technician.

The house lights dimmed.

"Okay, Bob, activate." Vale's voice was strained.

The technician set a dial and flipped a switch.

"Activated."

A shimmering white light enveloped Jeff's entire body, which began to shudder violently. The restraining belts burst in a staccato series of snaps. A collective gasp resounded in the theater as Jeff's body rose from the chair. It floated upward in a fluid movement as if drawn from a force above. The body hovered three feet in the air.

Beams of white light shining from him reached the farthest corner of the theater. The light bathed the crowd with a warmth that drained them of all feeling—even wonder. For a moment, everyone hung suspended, weightless, free of time and space. With a flash, the body vanished, dematerialized before their eyes.

The stunned audience came alive with noisy confusion. Exclamations filled the auditorium—the room was buzzing. On the stage, Vale's hands flew to his face and screamed in anguish, "No-o-o-o . . ." He raced to the chair and began to pat it, as if his eyes had deceived him, as if he expected Jeff's wasted body to be there.

An ear-shattering crash of thunder exploded outside, adding to the clamor inside. A torrent of pounding rain pummeled the theater, and the lights flickered wildly. Then all power blacked out.

Sprinting across the Center's grounds, Heller, Sinopoli, Greenwald and Kinney were blasted by the awesome storm. Raging hurricane winds and whip-stinging needles of rain forced them to huddle together beneath a tree some distance from the theater. The veins of his weathered neck bulged as Heller tried to scream over the storm. But the continuous onslaught of earth-shaking thunder made it impossible for him to be heard.

Pillars of white-hot lightning ripped out of the churning sky and slammed into the ground. Heller grabbed Greenwald's hand and gestured to the others to join hands. Forming a human chain, they snaked their way across the muddy ground. They bent from their waists to offer the least resistance to the ferocious gusts that buffeted them.

Stumbling, Father Kinney let go of Sinopoli's hand to tuck his long robes into his belt. A blast of wind bowled him over and pounded him to the ground. The others struggled to get him up. Once down, they couldn't stand. They all ended up crawling on all fours toward the theater.

Rain poured in through the grille on the side of the main building and slickened the walls of the shaft.

"Can you hear it, Jan? Close. We must be close."

"Thank God," Jan said, her voice low with exhaustion.

At the last bend, David had managed to reverse his position. He was moving backward again. Jan continued to inch her way forward. As long as he stayed near her, she was able to stifle the hysteria that clutched at her.

"You stay here. The water's coming in hard. I'll try to kick the grate off."

"No—no—don't leave me here. I'll come with you."

As they worked their way toward the grate, waves of water swept over them. For every few inches they gained, they slipped back two.

Jan pressed her hands against the sides of the shaft. "Somebody! Help us!" She swallowed water and began to choke. Another wave slapped her. She coughed and gagged. "My God, help!"

Kellog repeatedly clicked the phone disconnect button. "Still dead. What about the sideband radios?" he asked the agent next to him.

"Everything's out. Flashlights, radios—everything. *Nothing's* working."

A panicked nurse grabbed Kellog's arm. "What's going on?"

"How the hell should I know?" he snapped.

One of Vale's maintenance men appeared. "I don't get it. The main fuses are all okay."

"Why haven't you got the emergency generators going?"

"We tried. They won't start."

"Dammit! Something has to work. We need some light in here or we're going to have mass hysteria to control." He drew open the drapes. "With that storm, no one can leave."

He shouted to an agent near the door. "Cooper! You and Jennings take one of the vehicles. Move your tails up to the main power station. Find out what the hell is happening."

"Right." The agent gestured to Jennings, who joined him. He pushed on the door, while telling him what Kellog had ordered. He stopped short. The door wouldn't open. Both agents put their shoulders to the swinging set of doors, but the doors wouldn't budge.

Cooper raced to Kellog. He spoke softly, so no one else could hear. "The doors are jammed. I don't want to make it obvious. That could start a real panic."

Kellog groaned. "Do you at least have some candles?"

"Yeah—they're stored up front," the maintenance man answered.

"Well, get them."

"Where the hell is he?" Vale walked aimlessly around the stage. "We've got to get him back, got to finish the test."

The chief technician regarded Vale with concern. "Sit down, Dr. Vale. We can't do anything until the power's back on."

Vale raced to a console and began to reset the dials. "Maybe . . . maybe if I adjust this . . . we'll be able to finish."

"But, Dr. Vale . . ."

Vale's eye darted to the empty chair. "He's here—can't you feel it? Can't you tell he's watching?"

The technician shook his head. "Face it—you've got to—he's gone. You can't run the test without him."

Vale charged at the unsuspecting scientist. "No!" he screamed. "You're wrong. We'll do the test. He's here I tell you . . ."

He grabbed the technician's shoulders fiercely and shook him. When Vale saw the look of pity in his eyes, he dropped his head on his shoulder and sobbed, "It can't be, it can't be—we were so close."

Heller and his group dragged up the steps of the Medical Theater. They stumbled into the foyer, battered by the storm, and managed to close the doors to the pounding wind. Father Kinney slumped to the ground. Sinopoli bent over with his hands on his knees. Greenwald's chest heaved with wheezing breaths. Heller pushed his dripping hair back and ran to the door to the theater.

"Give me a hand—it won't open."

His colleagues rushed to his side. The three men shoved and pulled with all the strength they had left.

"Can't do it," Heller said.

Kinney weakly pointed to the observation window. The drapes were closed. Heller pounded on the thick pane of glass. Someone peered through a crack in the drapes. Heller gestured wildly and the drapes opened.

Hundreds of candles flickered in the auditorium. They threw off spectral shadows which danced eerily on the walls and ceiling. Kellog's face, illuminated by the candle he held, appeared disembodied in the window. He pointed in the direction of the door and pantomimed opening it.

Heller shook his head, indicating it was impossible. Kellog shrugged. His steely face was uneasy, his eyes troubled.

Heller was distracted by banging on the entrance doors. Greenwald went to unlock them. They burst open from the force of the storm, slamming Greenwald against the wall. David and Jan were swept in the foyer in a torrent of rain.

"Jan, are you all right?" Heller took her bruised face in his hands.

She moaned.

"Don't try to talk." He wrapped her shivering body in his arms.

Sinopoli took off his dripping jacket, which he handed to Heller for Jan. "This is better than nothing. She's in shock—should be covered up."

Kennedy haltingly told them about their escape.

"What's going on?"

"The storm must have blacked everything out."

"Good, that means they can't do the test."

Father Kinney knelt in the corner. His lips moved in prayer. He held the crucifix in his hands and his eyes were turned upward.

A low, vibrating hum sounded from the theater. It grew in volume and intensity until the walls, floors and ceilings began to shake. The group in the foyer felt the vibrations in their bodies—it was like a droning, beckoning call.

Greenwald covered his ears. Father Kinney made the sign of the cross. They all moved as if hypnotized to the observation window.

The ever-increasing humming sound was joined by a chorus of ethereal voices, chanting an atonal fugue. When the voices crescendoed, a blinding white light erupted in the theater.

At the window, the six observers shaded their eyes. Inside, the crews of doctors, technicians, CIA men and nurses stood frozen in the center aisle as the noise and the music blended into a wild cacophony.

A raging wind tore through the theater, throwing chairs and papers everywhere. Equipment ripped out of the walls and smashed to the ground. The wind screamed. Thunder exploded. Thin threads of lightning danced, spiderlike, across the ceiling. The walls cracked with a rumbling sound. The lighting fixtures crashed to the floor.

Screams filled the theater. People held desperately onto seats, onto each other. The floor heaved, swelling and rolling like an enraged sea.

A dull green haze swirled along the ceiling above the projector screen. The giant screen flickered. Every face in the theater gazed up at it. With a flash, the entire screen was filled with the immense figure of Jeffrey Weston, bathed in white light, suspended in eternal space.

He glared down at the people, his eyes harsh. Wails of terror and dread tore through the people below.

"You have crucified me again!" he thundered.

The words cut through the crowd like an arrow, piercing their defenses and shattering their restraint. They were exposed, unmasked before him. People started to weep and others clung to each other. Some fell to their knees as if forced down by unseen hands.

Despair and horror were mixed in equal portions. The room reeked with animal fear; it was a scene of agony and wretchedness. A sense of doom enveloped the room like a fog.

The theater quaked violently and then the noise stopped. The air was electrified, the silence total. Everybody in the auditorium throbbed with an apprehension so profound it was palpable. They felt poised on the verge of the greatest devastation—facing an inexorable finality.

"I have returned." A melodiously soothing voice caressed the breathless crowd.

"And you have crucified me again . . ." Jeff said once more, this time his voice heartbreaking in its grief. His sorrowful eyes bored into everyone in the theater. Each person there felt he had a direct, primal connection to the man on the screen. Their desolation and anguish melded with his. His suffering absorbed and obliterated theirs. The communion was total; the effect calming, consoling and elevating.

He peered down peacefully at the people, his eyes radiant. He slowly raised his arms as if accepting, embracing the entire crowd below him. They basked in his love and wondered at his mercy.

"I will return," he promised. "And then you will be ready. Some of you will tell of what happened here, will prepare future generations for my return."

Beams of light shot from his eyes and illuminated the faces of those who were locked out of the theater, who observed from the window. Everyone in the theater turned to follow the beams of light.

Jan, David, Heller, Sinopoli, Greenwald and Father Kinney felt a shock go through them. A soaring, mighty force shattered their internal structures—all experiences, all feelings, all thoughts ruptured and melted into an overwhelming, consuming love. A passion that lifted them from the mire of human cares, a passion that charged them with an unearthly energy and a certainty beyond any other.

"Go forth and tell the world of my return, for you are my disciples." Jeff's gaunt face was glowing. "Yours is not an easy task, but have faith. I will always be with you and my love will give you strength."

His voice was gentle now, and it drew the crowd toward the screen. They walked, eyes aflame, down the aisles in even columns and climbed the steps to the stage. Jeff still spoke to the six in the foyer.

"Tell them I will return and that their hearts must be ready to receive me. Prepare them for the kingdom of God, for it will be the end."

His eyes rested on his disciples a few moments. They felt his love engulf them. Then, he gazed down at the people who had crowded on the stage.

"Come," was all he said.

He extended both hands from the screen. The ethereal voices rose in exaltation, flooding the theater with an awful power. The people on the stage trembled in a wild confusion of terror and joy. There was a blinding flash, and then it was over. The screen was blank and the stage empty. Only the six at the observation window remained.

And then it all began . . .